THE STABLE MASTER'S SON

D1572491

MINDY BURBIDGE STRUNK

Copyright © 2021 by Mindy Burbidge Strunk

Cover design by Ashtyn Newbold

All rights reserved.

No part of this book may be reproduced in any form or by any electronic or mechanical means, including information storage and retrieval systems, without written permission from the author, except for the use of brief quotations in a book review.

Publisher's note: This is a work of fiction. Most names, places and incidents are a product of the author's imagination. Locales and public names are sometimes used for atmospheric purposes, but any resemblance to actual people-living or dead, to businesses, companies, events, institutions, or locals are coincidental.

CHAPTER ONE

Philip Jenkins was a handsome enough man. He could admit as much. He was no Lord Byron, but there were ladies enough seeking his attention. Not Dorothea, but plenty of others—if he were so inclined to want a lady's attention. Which he was not.

He turned his head from one side to the other, examining his reflection in the mirror as he tied his cravat. Dorothea *had* thought him handsome. She had said he was. But then, that had simply been a ploy of hers. He had learned too late that there was always a motive in what Dorothea did. What her motive in calling him handsome had been, Philip had no idea. But that was years ago. And he thought of her no more.

He frowned and amended the thought. He thought of her *rarely*.

"Sir?" A quiet knock sounded on his door.

Philip stepped away and pulled open the door.

Anne stood in the corridor.

"Yes?" Philip looked down at the girl of no more than twelve.

"Your mother sent me to tell you that breakfast is ready."

Philip nodded. "Thank you, Anne. I will be down shortly."

Philip let out a quiet grunt as he shut the door and turned back toward the mirror, giving himself one last glance. He looked presentable enough for a cricket match, especially when he was playing with the workers. The gentlemen would surely turn up their noses at him, but Philip was used to such reactions.

It was not as if he were after the affections of the likes of Lady Dorothea any longer. Or any other woman, for that fact. Women were troublesome. He had learned that lesson quickly and painfully.

Besides, there was too much work to do. And his horses surely did not care what knot he chose or if he cut his hair in a fashionable style. As long as he had some oats in his hand or an apple in his pocket, they were happy. Which made Philip happy.

He raised a brow. He would surely need to change into something more suitable for his meeting after the match. But he could worry about that later.

Philip turned away from the mirror and headed out of his bedroom. Striding down the corridor, his smile widened. It was bound to be a good day. The sun was shining, and his future awaited him.

He was looking forward to the match this morning at Briarwood. But even more, he looked forward to his meeting with the Duke of Larmont later this afternoon. The man had his eye on Philip's racer, Black Thunder.

A tingle ran up his spine. The duke was surely Philip's means of gaining notoriety as a breeder outside of Somerset. If the duke liked what he saw, he would surely pass along Philip's name to others of the duke's rank and status.

Philip rubbed his hands together. This was how it would all

begin. It was the opportunity he had been waiting for since coming to Somerset almost eight years ago.

He sighed as he paused at the top of the stairs and looked down into the entryway below. His house was not Blenheim or Chatsworth by any stretch of the imagination. It was not even habitable in some areas. But Greystone Manor was home. And it was his. The only good thing to come out of the *incident* with Lady Dorothea.

"Good morning, sir. Are you ready for breakfast?" Mrs. Heaton, their housekeeper, cook, and Anne's mother, stood below, looking up. "Your parents are already in the breakfast room."

Philip smiled. "My sister is still abed?"

Mrs. Heaton shrugged. "I have not checked in on her, so I cannot say. I only know that Miss Jenkins has not come down to eat."

Philip shook his head. "You need not worry. I know Grace well enough to know she is certainly still watching the inside of her eyelids."

"I do not think you know me as well as you think, Brother. For here I am, already dressed for the day." Grace smirked at him.

Philip raised a brow. "Gracie, what raised you out of bed at this early hour?"

She sashayed past him. "I can sleep later. The cricket game only happens once each year. I can think of nothing that should keep me away from it."

Philip raised a knowing brow and nodded. "And just whom are you hoping to see?"

Grace shrugged. "No one in particular."

Philip shook his head at his sister. That was a bouncer if ever he heard one. But he held out his arm to her, anyway. "As you are up, perhaps you would allow me to escort you to the breakfast room?"

She smiled prettily at him. "Why, thank you, Philip."

He sighed. Grace was not long under his roof; of that he was certain. It would be a bittersweet moment when Gracie married. He had grown accustomed to having her around again after her return from Mrs. Bootle's School for Young Ladies last year.

Philip only hoped it was all worth it and that Grace would marry well. Although, all the refinement in the world could not overcome Grace's upbringing. At least in the eyes of the *ton*. But the *ton* is not where he was looking to find Gracie a match. He would be perfectly content if she could secure the affections of a vicar or a well-respected solicitor. Someone not so high in society as to look down on Grace.

She had already turned the eyes of several of the men in town. It could not be much longer before she accepted one of them.

They stepped onto the entry hall floor, and he motioned Grace forward. All he wished was for her to make an advantageous match. But the longer it took to get the horses profitable, the less likely that seemed.

He had made a name for himself in Somerset, but he would never truly feel successful until he was known throughout England. But if he could win the approval of an influential duke, Greystone's reputation would surely gain the notoriety Philip wanted.

He looked at the papered walls and the painted wainscoting. No one walking this corridor would know what lay behind each of the closed doors they passed. Peeling paint and chipped plaster were common in most of the rooms of Greystone—those that were not charred and burned. He had only had funds to repair a few public rooms. The rest had to wait until they were on sturdier financial ground.

He needed to make this house, this land, into a proper estate. But there was little money to do it with. He had thought himself fortunate when Lord Downings had granted the estate to him. But sometimes he thought that perhaps the old Earl had merely wished to be rid of the place.

The fire—which Downings had failed to mention—had done significant damage to the west wing. From the front and south side, it was not so noticeable. But from the north and back, the charred remains were obvious. Many of the bedchambers in that wing were lost, as well as the ballroom and several parlors. The extensive funds needed to repair the rooms the fire had not touched made it hard to imagine rebuilding the fire-damaged section of the house.

A deep breath pushed out Philip's lips.

But his meeting today could change all that. His stomach twisted in knots at the thought of meeting with His Grace. Larmont was a powerful man, and if things went well, Philip's life—his family's life—could change drastically. No more scraping by to pay his few servants or doing without tea and coffee due to the expense of another blood horse.

But the opposite was also true. If it did not go well, it could spell disaster. Philip could not afford to keep this place without a viable income. The paltry amount of land that could be farmed belonged to his tenants.

His small herds of sheep and cattle would not pay the bills, at least not until they grew significantly. If he could just find the money to repair the tenant cottages, the rent might help with revenue until the other sources of money came through. But Philip could not place his whole future on the tenants.

The pressure was on his horses. On him. Black Thunder's inclusion in the General Stud book did not guarantee success.

Philip needed to keep pushing forward and keep expanding the stables with the finest horses in England.

He helped Grace into her seat before sliding into a chair next to his mother.

She smiled at him and patted his hand. "Morning, Son."

He leaned to the side and placed a kiss on her cheek. His mother had had a more troublesome time than the rest of them, embracing the life of an estate owner. Her speech was still coarser than that of Philip and Grace's. Even his father sounded more like the upper classes than did his mother. But she claimed she was too old to change her ways, but at barely nine and forty, Philip thought her trouble had more to do with stubbornness. She *could* change her ways. She just didn't want to. "Good morning, Mother. How did you sleep?"

She spooned her porridge into her mouth and swallowed it quickly. "You know me; I always sleep well. It's in my nature."

Mrs. Heaton brought in a bowl of porridge for Philip and one for Grace. She placed the sugar bowl on the table between the two of them and motioned with her head to the corridor, her eyes wider than normal.

Philip tilted his head to the side. Did she wish to speak to him in the corridor? What could she have to speak with him about privately?

"Oh, it looks as though I forgot my . . ." Philip paused. What did he forget? He could not think of anything that he might need to fetch. "My handkerchief." Yes, that would do.

"Can you not wait until after breakfast to fetch it?" Grace asked.

"But I remember it now." He tilted his head to the side. "Is it not best to retrieve it while I am thinking of it?" He moved toward the door. "You should try it, Grace. Perhaps then you would not forget so much." He winked at his sister playfully. "I will return in a moment."

"Don't take too long or your porridge will be cold." His mother sighed.

Philip moved out into the corridor where he found Mrs. Heaton waiting. "I apologize for pulling you away from the table, sir. But that is the last of the sugar. I do not have enough to make the cakes you requested for this afternoon."

He rubbed his fingers over his brows before withdrawing two coins from his pocket. "Will this be enough? I am afraid it is all I have on me." He need not tell her it was all he had entirely. He thought a little prayer in his mind, asking that money would not be needed for something else. At least nothing urgent. At Greystone, there was always something in need of money.

She took the coins and nodded. "Oh, yes. This is quite enough." She dropped her shoulders, telling Philip she had lost at least a bit of confidence in him. Did she suspect how bad things currently were?

He smiled, hoping she would not see the concern in his eyes.

He moved back into the breakfast room and sat down, not missing the mounded spoonful of sugar Grace poured into her bowl. She pushed the bowl toward him, but he left it alone.

"Philip, might we leave for Briarwood a little early? I had thought to stop in at the milliners on the way. There is a bonnet in the window that I simply must have."

A dull pain traveled up the back of his neck and settled in his head behind his eyes. "No. We do not have the funds for extravagances, Grace. You will simply have to wear a bonnet you already have."

Besides learning to act and speak as a lady while at Mrs. Bootle's, Grace had also come home with a new appreciation for fine things—things Philip could not afford.

"But Philip, I have not had a new bonnet since autumn."

7

She pushed her lip out in a pout. "I told Miss Martindale I would wear that bonnet to the match today. What will she think if I attend wearing the same old bonnet she has seen numerous times?"

Philip shoved his spoon into his mouth, even though his stomach roiled. The sugarless porridge tasted like sawdust. He swallowed hard and pushed the rest of the bowl away. "I have no idea what Miss Martindale will say, Grace. But there is no money for new bonnets. Not just yet. If my meeting this afternoon goes well, then we may discuss the issue further."

Grace let out a huff. "But it will surely be sold before then. And then what shall I do?"

"Why don't we set one of your other bonnets to pieces? Miss Martindale will surely never know it is not new." His mother glanced over at him and the tension in his neck eased.

"Oh, very well." Grace folded her arms across her chest, looking anything but compliant.

His mother pushed his bowl toward him, a concerned look on her face. "Why are you not eating? You need to eat if you are to have the stamina to last the whole of the match."

He pushed the bowl away again. "I am well, Mother. Stop worrying over me."

She raised a brow.

Grudgingly, he pulled the bowl toward him and put several more spoonfuls into his mouth, swallowing before he could taste the plainness.

Pushing out his chair, he stepped to the side as Mrs. Heaton gathered his bowl and moved out into the corridor. Philip jumped up and followed her out of the room.

"Mrs. Heaton?"

The woman pulled up short and looked over her shoulder.

"Will you have time to make it into the village for the sugar?" If not, perhaps he should get the money back. If she would not have time to make the cakes, there was surely something else he could use the money for.

She quirked one side of her lips up. "I will send Anne before the whole of the village shuts down for the cricket match. Everyone is talking of it."

Philip nodded and rubbed his hands together, allowing the excitement of the match to push aside his concerns. "Yes, it should prove an equally matched game." He glanced out the window at the end of the corridor, half expecting the skies to have grayed and rain to be imminent. But was happily surprised to see the sun instead.

"It does look as if the weather might actually cooperate with us." He smiled at her again, but whether to bolster her confidence in him or his own, he was not certain.

Philip moved toward his study but paused and turned back. "And you will have time to make the cakes?"

Mrs. Heaton nodded. "Yes, sir. I will see they are ready for you."

"Thank you." Philip's shoulders sagged.

Before coming to Greystone, he had never assumed it would be so difficult to keep an estate running. Although, he had not expected the house to need extensive repairs either. But maintaining the house was not the only thing proving more difficult than he had anticipated.

Perhaps it would have been better if his family had stayed on at Severdale Hall in the employ of Lord Downings. At least until Philip had secured his reputation and restored the house. The thought of doing this alone—without the help of his father and the support of his mother—made Philip's stomach sink. No, as hard as this was, he was glad his family was here with him.

Philip dipped his head. He knew he should go over the ledgers. Surely there was some money to find somewhere— although, he had yet to discover where. But he could not bring himself to continue on to his study. Instead, he ducked out the front door and headed for the stable yard. He could get in a quick ride if he hurried.

The sunshine forced his hand up to his eyes until they had adjusted. There was still a prick of chill in the morning air, but it would surely give way once the sun was high above.

It was a lovely day for a cricket match. Philip squared his shoulders and sucked in a deep breath. Indeed, it was a grand day to sell a horse and make a reputation for himself.

CHAPTER TWO

Miss Elizabeth Carter tightened her grip on Sophia's hand. Her charge was wont to run off, and in this crowd of people, Elle was certain she would never find Sophia again if she bolted.

Briarwood was a large estate, from what she had seen so far. Although, they had only arrived at the house party yesterday, and most of her time had been in the schoolroom or nursery.

If Elle had her way, the little girl would not even be outside today. She would be in the house with Nurse Jones. But her father was playing in the match, and Lady Kirtley thought it a clever idea for all the children to watch.

Elle let out a heavy sigh and tugged on Sophia's hand, attempting to rein the child in.

Katie stumbled along Elle's other side. "Why must we walk so quickly, Miss Carter? I cannot focus on a single thing surrounding us."

Elle tightened her grip on Katie's hand, too. The last thing she needed was for Katie to trip and fall. "I am sorry, Lady

Katie. But you know how it is with Lady Sophia. When she sets her mind on something, there is no stopping her."

The little girl finally came to a stop in front of a sleek-looking horse. It was smaller than most horses Elle had seen, but it was lithe. Its nearly black coat shone in the sunlight.

"Hosee, hosee." Sophia pointed to the horse and tugged harder on Elle's hand. There were horses standing all over the grounds. Why Sophia was so fixated on this one, Elle could not fathom.

She jerked the little girl back just as Sophia reached forward to touch the horse's hind leg. "No, sweetheart. It is dangerous to touch a strange horse. Especially from behind. What if you scared it? It might kick at you before it knew you wished to be friends."

Sophia looked from the horse to Elle and back again. "It is not a nice hosee?"

The child was finally still for a moment, and Elle lifted Sophia up onto her hip. It would be far easier to control her if she were not on her feet.

"No, I am certain it is a very nice horse, once it knows you. But if you startle it, it will act on instinct."

Sophia scrunched up her nose and her brow furrowed. "What is 'stinct?"

Elle smiled. Sophia really was an adorable child when she was not running headlong into trouble. "*Instinct* is what someone or something does without thinking about it."

Sophia's brow furrowed deeper.

Katie sighed. "It is like when Winston yells and you jerk. Your jerk is instinct."

Elle nodded but bit on her lower lip to keep from smiling. Katie did not like it when she thought someone was laughing at her.

Understanding still did not light Sophia's eyes.

"When you have an itch. You do not usually think about it, but still, you scratch it. That is instinct."

"Hosee kick me out of 'stinct because he fwightened?" Sophia tilted her head and looked at the horse.

Elle nodded. "Precisely. The notion that he does not know you would only make it worse. He may think you are not a friendly little girl."

Sophia's shoulders hunched in disappointment. "But I *am* fwendly."

Elle patted Sophia on the leg. "Of cour—"

"Miss Carter?" A low voice called from behind her, and Elle turned around, regretting it instantly.

His Grace, the Duke of Larmont strode toward her. Gah, she should have pretended not to hear. But it was too late now. They had already made eye contact. Running into old acquaintances, something she rarely desired since her change in status, was a downside to house parties such as this one. They always put her at risk of seeing people she did not wish to see.

In truth, the duke was an old acquaintance of her father's. But she had known him most of her life, even if their contact had been sparse in recent years.

She pasted on a false smile as the duke closed the distance between them. Moving Sophia to her hip, Elle fisted her hands.

"Ouch. Miss Carter, you are hurting me." Katie whimpered next to her.

Elle dropped her gaze to her side. "Oh, Lady Katie, I'm sorry. I did not mean to hurt you. There are just so many people here, and I do not wish to lose you." It was partially the truth.

Katie pulled her hand free and rubbed at her fingers.

"If you are not to hold my hand, please stay close. You may

hold on to my gown if you prefer." Elle glanced around her. Was it too late to disappear into the crowd?

Elle glanced up. The duke was standing not more than three feet away from her. Disappearing, it seemed, was not an option.

She dipped a curtsy as he stopped in front of her. "Your Grace."

"Miss Carter, it has been a long time. Nearly four years, if I remember correctly." His voice was neither kind nor rude, simply factual.

Elle nodded. "I believe you are correct."

The duke shook his head. "I expected to see you and your mother in London these last few years, but we seem to have accepted invitations to different parties." He lifted his chin slightly. Was he testing her to see if she would give him a Banbury tale?

Elle could not believe someone of the duke's status did not know of her family's circumstances. Did not the whole of the *ton* know?

She shook her head. "No, after Papa's death, Mama found it too taxing to make the journey." It was not a complete bouncer. Mama had found most things too taxing. Elle was not certain if they would have gone, even if there had been enough money. But there had not been enough, so there was no way to know for certain.

The duke nodded, his face pulled down in a frown. "Yes, I can imagine. I was sorry to learn of your father's death. He was a good man."

Elle swallowed. Why, after two years, was it still so hard to speak of her father? "Yes, he was." She still missed him exceptionally, even if he had left them in a precarious situation and lost her dowry.

The duke looked over to Sophia, and then Katie, his brow furrowed. "These are not your children, surely."

Elle's face heated with embarrassment. "No, they are my charges." Why must he drag the information out of her when he surely had knowledge of it already? Was it his intent to make her acknowledge her lowly station?

She motioned with her head to Katie. "I am the governess for Lord and Lady Kirtley."

The duke took a step back. "You are their governess?" His eyes flicked away from her, but she did not miss the disdain in his voice. Then he had *not* learned of her fallen state.

Elle blinked several times. "Yes, well . . ." What was she to say? If he had not already heard, she could not be the one to tarnish her father's name. Nor did she wish to besmirch her brother. Not every man had a head for estate management.

Besides, it was not proper to speak of such things. And someone in the duke's position would never understand, would never allow his family—

Elle shrugged, not finishing the sentence.

"Your Grace?" A voice sounded from the side.

Elle glanced over to the man striding toward them. She did not know what he wanted or even who he was, but his was a welcome interruption.

The man stopped at the duke's elbow.

"I know we were to meet after the match, but when I saw you looking at my horse, I thought perhaps to introduce myself before I moved out onto the field."

The man was not yet acquainted with the duke. To approach in such a manner without a proper introduction was brazen, to say the least, but Elle could not have been more grateful. If her mother had not taught her proper behavior, she might have kissed the newcomer.

The Duke of Larmont finally stepped to the side and looked at the man with raised brows.

It gave Elle the chance to do the same. The cut of his coat and trousers were not the finest she had seen, but neither was his clothing rough and plain as those worn by the working men. He must play for the gentlemen's team.

She hiked Sophia higher on her hip.

His clothes were darker than those of his teammates, and the stubble along his jawline seemed to downplay the finery of his clothes.

But it was his gray-blue eyes set beneath dark brown brows that held her attention. Never had she seen any like them. It reminded her of the sky above Kent on a cold winter day. Except, when he caught her gaze, she felt not a hint of cold. Quite the contrary. His appreciative look heated the skin on her neck all the way to the tips of her ears.

The duke cleared his throat, and she flinched. Pulling her eyes away from the stranger, she looked down at Katie instead, casting a sideways glance at the duke from under her lashes.

"And you are?" There was a tone of disapproval in the duke's voice.

"I'm sorry, I thought you knew . . . because of my horse," the man stammered, his face pinking slightly. "I am Philip Jenkins."

The duke's brows rose. "You are the owner of Black Thunder and Greystone stables?" His earlier disapproval dimmed, but only slightly.

Mr. Jenkins's stance stiffened. "Yes, Your Grace. I realize we were to meet this afternoon, but I wondered if you had questions about this horse here?" His voice was less certain— less confident than when he had first approached.

The duke raised his chin. "Perhaps, but I believe this outing is for entertainment, is it not? I would prefer to save our business until later." There was censure in his voice.

Mr. Jenkins swallowed, and his Adam's apple bobbed. "Of course, Your Grace." He dipped his head in a bow. "I beg your pardon."

The duke gave Mr. Jenkins one last long stare, his brow raised high in disapproval.

He turned his gaze on Elle. "It was a pleasure seeing you again, Miss Carter." His tone said it was anything but pleasant. He did not wait for her to curtsy or even offer a reply before he turned on his heel and disappeared into the crowd.

"Hosee kick me?" Sophia leaned forward and tugged on Mr. Jenkins's coat sleeve.

He turned from watching the duke's retreating back, a look of concern on his face. "Did Adonis kick you?" Panic laced his voice.

Elle tightened her arms around Sophia as the girl wriggled and twisted to escape. "No, sir. She was asking a question."

Mr. Jenkins relaxed. "Now, why do you think Adonis would kick you?" His head tilted to the side, and he looked Sophia in the eye.

Sophia frowned. "Because of 'stinct."

Mr. Jenkins's face crinkled in confusion.

"*Instinct*, Sophia." Katie folded her arms in exasperation.

A grin split Mr. Jenkins's face, and Elle realized his eyes were not his only mesmerizing feature. His smile made her insides dance and jig. Which was completely ridiculous.

"Perhaps if you startled him, he might kick out of instinct."

Sophia nodded, her face crestfallen. "And we not friends."

"We *are* not friends," Elle said, correcting the girl in a soft voice.

Mr. Jenkins leaned toward Sophia, and Elle's pulse ticked

17

up. Why was she reacting to him? He was leaning toward Sophia, not her.

"But what if you were to become friends? Then you could approach him from the front and Adonis would be happy to see you, would he not?"

Sophia's eyes widened.

Mr. Jenkins looked over to Elle. "Do you mind if I introduce them, Miss Carter?"

Elle swallowed even as she nodded.

He had paid attention when the duke called her by name. Why did that notion thrill her so?

"I cannot think it a problem so long as I stay close." She lowered Sophia to the ground and grabbed onto her hand. "Please do as Mr. Jenkins tells you, Lady Sophia."

Mr. Jenkins took Sophia's other hand in his and gently ran it down the horse's side. "There, there, Adonis. This is Lady Sophia." He glanced over at Elle, and her breath hitched. Never had she been so affected by the look of a man. Perhaps the heat of the day was causing the reaction? Maybe she should take the children and return to the house.

She motioned to Katie, mostly because she did not know what else to say. "And this is Lady Katie."

He nodded to Katie, then turned back to the horse and ran Sophia's hand down its side again. "Lady Sophia, meet Adonis."

Sophia said nothing, but the utter joy on her face made Elle smile. Sophia had such a simple life. Sometimes, Elle longed for that.

The noise of the crowd grew, and Mr. Jenkins looked over his shoulder toward the pitch. "Ah, it looks as though the match is about to start." He released Sophia's hand, and Elle pulled the little girl closer. He bowed to them. "It was a pleasure to meet you, Lady Sophia and Lady Katie." He flicked his gaze to

Elle. "And you as well, Miss Carter. Perhaps we shall meet again." He moved toward the pitch.

Had there been a note of interest in his voice? Elle was certain she had heard it, but that was silly. They did not even know each other. He must live nearby, if he were meeting the duke later. But even if he lived close, it seemed rather unlikely they would see each other again.

Elle watched Mr. Jenkins's retreating form. He had not treated her differently. Not as everyone else of her acquaintance did. Could it be, after so many years, that she had finally found a gentleman that did not care that she was no longer a part of proper society?

Feelings rose up inside her. Feelings she had suppressed for many years. She looked at Katie and Sophia. As much as she had grown to love these children, this was not where she belonged. She was not destined to care for someone else's children.

She was the daughter of a viscount. She was meant to have her own children and be mistress of an estate. It was what her mother had taught her to be. She looked around her as despair threatened to consume her.

Was Mr. Jenkins the man who could help her realize her destiny? Was he interested, or was she simply wishing for something that was not there?

She looked around the pitch until she found Mr. Jenkins; he stood among the other men, all of them laughing.

She tilted her head and frowned. He must be mistaken. For he was standing with the working men.

CHAPTER THREE

Philip congratulated his team members and swatted the bat against his hand. He paused and rubbed his finger over the *Steele and Sons* brand. Mr. Steele did fine work, there was no debating that.

Philip sighed. If only he had the money to have someone of Mr. Steele's talent carve the missing balusters for his stair railing. But that was for after Philip was successful . . . not now.

Mr. Steele passed in front of Philip, and Phillip reached out, tapping Mr. Steele on the arm with the bat. "A fine job you did on the bats, Steele." He dropped his voice a fraction. "I don't believe a lesser bat could have delivered the ball to Ryecombe's face with such accuracy. I believe you are to be in high demand from this time forth."

Mr. Steele ran a hand down the bat, his lips quirking ever so slightly. "That was not what I intended it for, but I find I cannot regret it in the least."

"I think you would be hard-pressed to find anyone on our team to disagree with you." Philip grinned and flicked his chin toward the man as he walked away.

He moved toward the gentlemen's team to offer polite condolences on their loss. As he neared, he pushed down the smile, assuming a more stoic look. They surely would not appreciate being triumphed over. Even if it had been a glorious defeat.

He waited for several moments for his turn to offer his thanks—because he was expected to be grateful that these men had condescended to play on the same pitch as him—and well wishes to the opposing team.

His father appeared at his side just as he came to face to face with Lord Ryecombe. The earl dipped his head to Philip. "Jenkins. You played well. But do not think to relish it too long. We shall surely take the match next year."

Philip smiled, having a hard time pulling his eyes from the walnut-sized lump gracing the man's right lip. It was surely the reason the earl's lisp was more pronounced. One might even question if he had nipped too much of the brandy.

"Yes, I am certain that is true, my lord." Philip knew it to be a bunch of fustian nonsense. But it did no good to argue or disagree with Ryecombe. He would never concede.

Still, it was in Philip's interest to ignore the man's obstinance and keep the earl's good graces. Ryecombe was interested in buying a matching pair of bay mares to pull his wife's curricle. He had been eyeing them for months, telling Philip he wished to buy them. The last thing Philip wished to do was change the man's mind. "If you wish to come and look at the bays one last time, my lord, I am certain I can find a time amiable to us both."

The earl grumbled. "Now is hardly the time to discuss business, Jenkins."

Philip clutched his fists at his side, and he felt his father stiffen next to him.

"Please send me word when it would be a good time. They

are a splendid pair." Philip did his best to keep the irritation from his voice.

Ryecombe grumbled and turned away from them.

"That man," his father hissed in his ear. "I don't think he will ever come through with the blunt."

Philip shrugged. "You may be right, Father. For now, I need to focus on my meeting with Larmont."

Philip caught sight of Miss Carter. She still held the hands of the two little girls as she made her way through the crowd. Who were the little ladies, and how did Miss Carter fit into their lives? Were they guests of Ryecombe? It was obvious Miss Carter was not the girl's mother. She had referred to them as Lady Katie and Lady Sophia. But what was her connection? A relative, perhaps? Or their governess?

Philip rubbed his thumb over the side of his index finger again and again. Why did he even care? He was not looking for trouble. And in his experience, women were precisely that.

His eyes scanned the crowd until he found the Duke of Larmont. Miss Carter had been speaking to him before the match. Were the two well acquainted? When the duke had left, he had indicated they had some sort of association. Could Miss Carter have any influence on the man?

Philip shook his head. What was he thinking? He had not even met with the duke yet, and he was already coming up with an alternate plan? What had happened to his confidence in himself? In his horse?

"I will meet you at home, Father."

His father nodded and moved off in the opposite direction.

Philip strode toward Adonis. There was no reason to mingle any longer. The loss rankled most of the gentlemen. There was little need to visit with them. They would only come up with more excuses for their loss the more time they had to think on it. Then they would be unbearable.

Besides, if Philip left now, he could brush Black Thunder down once more and then change into more suitable clothing before the duke arrived. Not that he doubted his father had seen to everything before he left for the match.

But Philip liked to be certain. Seeing to Black Thunder now would be better for the sale than any conversation Philip could have with the man. He'd seemed less than impressed when Philip had introduced himself earlier. He would let his horse sell himself. Black Thunder was impressive enough for a duke, or anyone else. Besides, Philip needed the calming influence the brush strokes would bring.

He swung up onto Adonis and replayed the conversation with the duke for the dozenth time. Why had he gone over to talk to the man? Why had he not realized the duke was talking with Miss Carter rather than examining Adonis? Why could he not stop obsessing over this?

He swallowed. Because he *needed* this sale. What would he do if the duke did not buy Black Thunder? A whole new line of questions streamed through Philip's mind. What had happened to his optimism of earlier? They had won the match. Should that not have given him even more confidence?

No. He knew how these gentlemen were. Most were a bunch of insolent pups. It would not surprise Philip to see a few of them exact their revenge by withholding their shillings from the local shopkeepers for a week or two. After all, what did they care if their servants should have to travel several villages over to purchase what was needed?

He flicked the reins, setting Adonis into a canter. The sooner he returned to Greystone, the better. His confidence would return the moment he smelled the hay in his stables. And it would only improve once he was with the horses.

Philip rode into the stable yard and hopped off Adonis before the horse came to a full stop. He strode purposefully toward the first building. He could always lose himself and his worries in the stables.

He shrugged off his tailcoat and draped it over the nearby railing, then set himself to it, losing himself in his work.

The hinge on the stable door creaked and a ray of light appeared, growing wider as the door opened fully. Philip squinted slightly. Had his father returned from the match? He was likely coming to tell Philip it was time to change into clothes more fitting for his meeting.

It was all for the best. He was nearly done here. Philip's hand stilled mid-stroke before he pulled it down to his side. He took a step back, his chest swelling with pride. Black Thunder was impressive. Philip could only hope he would win over the duke.

Movement pulled Philip's eyes from his pride and joy.

The duke moved down the aisle and came to a stop at the side of Black Thunder's stall.

Philip swallowed. Where had the time gone?

Larmont looked at Philip over the rail. "I called for you at the house, but your housekeeper told me you were here." He raised a judgmental brow. "You do not have a groom to perform such tasks?"

Philip's grip tightened around the brush in his hand. *Yes, he did have a groom. Himself.* Philip was master, stable master, and groom. He also managed the cows and the sheep. Although, if he was being honest, he did not do the tasks on his own. His father shared in the duties. And he employed one stable boy. But he was young and still had much to learn.

He bristled at the slight. Why did the arrogance of the aristocracy still chafe? He had been raised in the stables, starting out as a mere stable boy. Never had the upper class shown him any deference. Yet standing here in his own stable, on his own estate, it made him angry to be treated with such disdain.

"I wished for you to see Black Thunder at his best. And what better way to ensure that than to do it myself?" He winced internally at the slight to his father, even though that was not his intention. "I did not want to leave anything undone."

The duke shrugged, noting Philip's appearance. "I suppose I can respect such a decision. Although, I might caution you that not all the *ton* will see it that way. Many will regard you as no better than a servant if you do a servant's work." He stepped into the stall and ran his hand down the side of Black Thunder. "Especially when you choose to play cricket on the workers' team." There was definitely accusation in his voice.

"Your team seemed to be represented well enough." Philip sucked in a long, quiet breath. He had not been asked to play on the gentlemen's team. It showed how he was thought of in his own neighborhood.

"It did not go unnoticed. I can assure you of that." The duke kept his eyes on Black Thunder.

This man was infuriating. Although Philip supposed he should expect as much from a duke. The man had likely not lifted a finger in any kind of work for the whole of his life. He could not appreciate what Philip had accomplished here.

"I shall consider that in the future, Your Grace." There was no point arguing or refuting the duke's words. He likely was not even listening to Philip anymore. "Thank you for your wisdom."

The duke walked around Black Thunder, squinting his eyes and rubbing at his chin. "Does his name have significance?"

Philip moved in front of the horse and pulled a carrot from his coat pocket. Black Thunder lipped it into his mouth and chewed. "Indeed, the night he foaled, there was no moon and storm clouds blanketed the sky, masking even the starlight. It was the blackest night I have ever seen." He pressed his forehead against the horse's. He would miss this horse once he sold him. But it was necessary if he was to make his estate profitable. "As he tumbled onto the straw, a clap of thunder ushered him into the world."

The duke nodded. "And what of his bloodline?"

Philip grinned. He, himself, may not impress the duke, but Black Thunder's bloodline surely would. "His sire is Two Shoes, and he is a direct descendant from the Godolphin Barb."

Larmont looked around the stable. "How did you come to be in possession of such a horse?"

Black Thunder's sire had been offered up as collateral in a game of cards. A game that had not gone the owner's way. It was the only time Philip had considered himself lucky. But he was not about to tell Larmont of the tale. "His sire was given to me as payment for a debt."

Larmont raised his brows but then turned his gaze to the horse. "Impressive, Mr. Jenkins. Very impressive, indeed."

"If you wish to check his bloodline, he is in the General Stud book, Your Grace." Philip's chin instinctively rose along with his shoulders. Indeed, Black Thunder was impressive. "Perhaps we should take the rest of this meeting inside to my study?"

The duke did one more circle around Black Thunder and gave a quick nod. "Yes, of course."

CHAPTER FOUR

E lle placed the slates on the table in front of Katie and Winston. "It is time for your sums, Lady Katie." She tapped Winston's slate. "And for you, Latin. Your tutor will arrive next month, and we do not wish him to think you lacking."

Winston grumbled but pulled his slate closer.

Katie bent her head over her slate and began adding numbers from the paper next to her.

"Lord Culpepper, the word is *amica*."

Winston stared at his slate but made no move to write.

Elle repeated the word. "And do not forget to write its translation." She looked up when she heard no scraping on the slate. "Lord Culpepper, is something the matter?" She had noticed he had been quieter of late. Something was bothering him, but he seemed determined to keep it to himself.

"There is nothing the matter, Miss Carter." The terseness in his voice brought even Katie's gaze up.

Elle raised a brow but placed a soft hand on his shoulder. "Very well, then the word is *amica*." She tapped the slate again.

"And when you are ready to speak of what troubles you, I hope you remember I am here to listen if you wish it."

He looked up at her, and she thought for a moment that he may talk. But then his eyes flicked to the other children in the room—none of whom he knew well—and he clamped his mouth shut, returning his gaze to his slate.

Elle gave his shoulder a light squeeze before moving over to the window and looking out at the grounds where the cricket match had taken place earlier. The sunshine had given way to dark, threatening clouds, but as of yet, no rain had come. "*Navis*," she said over her shoulder.

She sighed when she heard Winston scribble on his slate. Thankfully, the children had settled into their daily routine after the match. It was always difficult to get them to focus after an overly stimulating event.

She tilted her head to the side when her eyes strayed to the tree on the far side of the lane where Mr. Jenkins had tied up his horse.

Mr. Jenkins.

Elle did not know what to think about him. He had seemed every bit the gentleman when they were talking. And the way he had spoken to Sophia was completely unexpected. But then he had played for the workers' team. Why would a gentleman stoop so low?

It baffled her.

As did the flutter in her stomach when she thought on him. Never, even in the two Seasons she'd had before Papa had died, had she ever had such a reaction to a man.

"*Equus*," she called out.

The schoolroom door flew open, and Elle turned from the window. Nurse Jones came hurrying in—at least as much as Nurse Jones could hurry. She was aged and did not move so quickly anymore.

"What is it, Nurse Jones?" Elle moved over to the woman when she saw her distressed expression.

"It is Lady Sophia. She ran off after a butterfly and before I could catch her, she disappeared." Nurse Jones wrung her fingers, her lip quivering slightly.

Elle placed her hand on the woman's arm and gave it a soft squeeze. "Stay here with the children and see they continue their studies. I will go find Lady Sophia." She lay the paper beside Winston's slate. "Practice writing the words and continue to translate them, please."

Turning toward the door, she looked back over her shoulder. "Which direction did she go?"

Nurse Jones pointed out the window toward the far side of the cricket pitch. "That way. I lost sight of her at the copse of trees."

"I will be back shortly." Elle put an extra lilt in her voice, hoping to ease Nurse Jones's anxiety.

She hurriedly pulled on her spencer and bonnet, tying the strings as she left out the servants' door. Her chest tightened, and her stomach twisted. What if she could not find Sophia and they had to ask Lord Ryecombe for help? What would happen to Nurse Jones? What would happen to Elle?

She did not think they would reprimand *her* for not finding the child, but she could not say the same for Nurse Jones. Elle had overheard Lord and Lady Kirtley discussing whether the nurse was too old to look after Sophia—a notion that had become clearer since Miss Babineaux's marriage.

Miss Babineaux. Elle's hands fisted at her side. She knew she should call her Lady Brinton now, but she found herself hard-pressed to do so, and she bit back the irritation that always accompanied those thoughts.

Miss Babineaux had spent a significant amount of time with the children, allowing Nurse Jones to play less of a role, especially with those activities out of doors. But since her marriage that was no longer the case, and Nurse Jones simply did not have the stamina to keep up with such a lively child.

Elle frowned. She liked Nurse Jones. They worked well together and got on tolerably well. Indeed, Elle would miss her if she left.

Hiking up her skirts, Elle quickened her pace. She must do everything in her power to see that Nurse Jones did not go anywhere.

Elle reached a stone wall that obviously marked the end of the Lord Ryecombe's land. She placed her hand to her eyes and looked at the surrounding landscape. In the distance, she could see the stables and the manor house of the neighboring estate. Could that be where Sophia had gone?

It looked as if a groom was in the paddock, but his attention was on the horse he was tending.

She looked at the wall and frowned. Did she dare cross it? It was not very high. She could cross over it with little trouble. It would be very unladylike, and she would surely be trespassing. But Sophia's safety justified it, surely.

She lifted her skirt up higher and placed her slippered foot on the rock wall, using one hand to brace herself while she hopped up on top. After straightening and readjusting herself, she jumped onto the ground on the other side.

She dropped her skirts and glanced around to see if anyone had seen her. The groom still seemed intent on the horse, though, from this distance, she could not be certain where he looked. But why should a groom take an interest in her? And more importantly, why should she care?

She glanced back at Briarwood. Being seen from that house seemed more troublesome than a groom she was unacquainted with. But fortunately, no one was within sight.

Running her hands down her front, she straightened her gown and then her shoulders. All was well.

Elle hurried through the field, her pulse picking up when she noticed the crushed ankle-high grass in front of her. The tracks were small and barely discernable, but Elle felt certain Sophia had made them. She glanced back up at the dark skies. If it rained, these tracks would surely be lost. Even so, Elle breathed a little easier. She was certain she was on the right course. She needed only to make haste and she would find Sophia.

Following the crushed grass, Elle moved toward the paddock she had seen from the wall. Only as she drew near did she see the tiny body perched atop the fence rail.

Elle's breath hitched. What was Sophia doing up so high?

She rushed over and put her hands around the little girl's waist. "Lady Sophia, what are you doing up there? You could fall and hurt yourself."

Sophia let out a yelp and squirmed to watch the horse. What was it about these horses that had her so captivated? Their stables at Dovehaven had plenty of fine horses. What drew her to these?

The man in the paddock looked over. It was Mr. Jenkins? What was he doing out in the paddock with the horse? Did he not have a stable master or groom for such things? And why was he allowing a little girl to sit up so high on the fence? What if she fell, and the horse trod over her?

Elle's heart pounded at the thought.

"Good day, Miss Carter." Mr. Jenkins smiled. He strode slowly over to them, releasing the lead rope and giving the horse the chance to wander about.

Sophia wiggled and squirmed in Elle's arms. "I watch the hosee!" she hollered, tears springing to her eyes.

Elle sucked in a breath to calm herself before speaking to

the flailing child. "I did not say you could not watch the horse, Lady Sophia. I only want you to do so safely."

Mr. Jenkins reached the fence and placed his folded arms on top. Seeing her battling with Sophia, he smiled.

Hot anger flared up inside her.

He was the cause of this tantrum, and all he could do was find humor in it? "Just what do you find so humorous, sir? What were you thinking, allowing her to sit so high? What if she had fallen?" The words came out haltingly and much sharper than she had planned.

He leaned back as if her words had physically assaulted him. "She climbed up herself. I thought little about it."

"Yes, I figured that much out on my own," Elle snapped at him.

He dropped his arms from the rail and took a step back. "I beg your pardon, Miss Carter. Perhaps it would have been better for me to shoo her away so no one knew her whereabouts. I was trying to be helpful, but I see now, I was not."

Elle's cheeks burned. She had allowed her fear for Sophia to make her behave poorly. Her mother had taught her better. She licked her lips. "No, it is I who should be apologizing. I am sorry for snapping at you. You did nothing wrong."

Mr. Jenkins's body relaxed slightly. "Perhaps we should start again?" He bowed to her. "Miss Carter, it is a pleasure to see you again."

Elle smiled and dipped into an awkward curtsy with Sophia still on her hip. "The pleasure is all mine, Mr. Jenkins."

He leaned against the railing and draped an arm over the top, staring out at the paddock.

Elle carefully placed Sophia on the top rung, but placed an arm on either side of her, just in case. "Congratulations on your team's victory this morning."

Mr. Jenkins grinned. "Thank you. It was a fine day for a

cricket match." His voice trailed off and his smile dropped away. He turned toward her. "How do you know the Duke of Larmont?"

Elle's head tilted. That was not a turn she had expected the conversation to take. Why was the man interested in the duke? Or rather, her association with him? "He was a friend of my father's."

"You are not close, then?" He turned his face away from her.

Elle shrugged. "There was a time when I thought we were. We used to visit his estate in Cheshire when I was a girl, and his family would visit ours in Oxfordshire. But it has been many years since that has happened."

He did not look at her, keeping his gaze on the horse. "I see."

What did he see? Because Elle did *not* see. She did not know what had caused the riff in her family's relationship with the duke. How had her few words given Mr. Jenkins an understanding Elle, herself, did not have? Was it merely their current situation? She had thought the duke kinder than that. She had thought many people kinder than they actually were.

Her mind turned to memories of her youth as she watched the horse prance around the paddock. Those had been good times. They were the memories she thought on often when drifting to sleep in her small chambers just off the schoolroom. Not necessarily the memories of the duke, but of the times when her family had had status. Had influence. *Had money.*

Elle pushed the thoughts away. Such memories were intended for the quiet moments before sleep when she could allow herself a few tears over what she had lost. But now was not such a time.

She cleared her throat. "And how are you acquainted with the duke, Mr. Jenkins?"

He finally looked over at her. "Oh, I had never met him until today. He wrote and expressed an interested in one of my horses—a racer—and wished to see it while he was visiting Briarwood. He mentioned possibly purchasing him." His brow furrowed, and he looked back out at the field. "He came and saw Black Thunder after the match."

For someone who was about to sell a horse for what Elle assumed would be a large profit, Mr. Jenkins did not seem overjoyed. Had the meeting not gone well? Or was he just lamenting over losing his horse?

Elle studied his profile.

Mr. Jenkins was very handsome if one liked the disheveled look of the working class. He had obviously changed from the clothes he had worn at the match as those he wore now were of a courser nature and much more worn.

He was different from any man of her acquaintance. And she reacted to him differently than she had other men. It was quite disconcerting to be acting like a ninny over a...groom? For that seemed to be precisely what he was. But had he not said he owned Greystone to the duke?

She looked back at the manor house. It was certainly a lesser estate. The house was respectable, but it was not Briarwood or Dovehaven.

Elle tilted her head to one side. What was the story of Mr. Jenkins?

She would likely never know. It was not as if she and Mr. Jenkins were to become friends. They were barely even acquaintances. And Elle would return to Kent with Lord and Lady Kirtley once the house party was over. Her duties with the children kept her occupied, making it unlikely she would see Mr. Jenkins again after today.

Her stomach sank and she chided it.

She patted Sophia on the leg. "Lady Sophia, we should

return to Briarwood. I am certain your brother and sister are taking full advantage of Nurse Jones. And you look as if you are ready for a nap."

Sophia jutted out her bottom lip. "I not tired."

"Yes, I am certain you are not. But I think Nurse Jones is. So perhaps you may pretend to sleep just long enough to allow Nurse Jones a rest." She winked at the little girl. "It will be our secret."

Sophia giggled. "I like secrets."

Elle grinned down at her. She may be vivacious and rather headstrong, but she was also adorable.

Elle pushed off the railing and lifted Sophia to the ground, taking hold of her plump little hand.

Mr. Jenkins tipped his cap to her.

Her breath hitched. *Why* did she react so strongly to him? It must stop. Truly, it must. "Thank you for your help with Lady Sophia, Mr. Jenkins."

He smiled at Sophia. "She is welcome to visit anytime." He turned his gaze on Elle. "And you are welcome to accompany her."

Elle swallowed. Did he want her to come back? Why did that thought thrill her to the tips of her toes? And just what excuse could she use to see that they did return?

CHAPTER FIVE

E lle walked slower on the journey back to Briarwood than she had in leaving it. She told herself it was for Sophia's sake, but in truth, she wished to take some time to compose herself before returning to the schoolroom.

Mr. Jenkins and his stormy blue eyes had left her quite unraveled.

Then there were the memories. Memories of before her father had died, before she had lost everything. As much as she'd tried to push them away, they still hovered in her mind, leaving her full of remorse and regret. It had been years now. Why could she not move past it? Why did she still let it affect her after all this time?

Because it was unfair, that was why. Her life had been stripped away from her. And by no fault of her own. She had not made the ill investments. She had not been the one to gamble away the family's money. She had not even demanded expensive gowns, as many of her friends had when going to London for the Season.

Elle had been content to have her wardrobe made by the

village seamstress. Perhaps that had been her mistake. Maybe if she'd had those fine gowns for her first two Seasons, she would have made a match before her father and brother had ruined all her chances.

She let out a heavy breath, feeling disloyal to think of her father in such a poor way. Sophia looked up at her.

"Miss Carter, you sad?"

Elle shook her head. "I was before I discovered where you were. But I am well, now." She tilted her head and gave Sophia a stern look. "You must not run away from Nurse Jones anymore, my lady."

"But I not run away. I saw a flutterby and followed it. Why did Nurse Jones not follow it too?"

It was not the worst logic Elle had ever heard. "I believe you move too fast for Nurse Jones. You need to slow down and give her a chance to catch up with you."

"I sowy." Sophia looked contritely at the ground.

Elle gave her hand a slight squeeze. "I know you are, my lady. I am not mad. I only hope your parents are not either."

Sophia pressed her lips together, her little brow scrunched up.

Elle lifted Sophia up onto the stone wall, just as a crack of thunder split the air. She hefted her skirt to follow, but Sophia scampered along the top before Elle could even place her foot.

She dropped her skirt and hurried to catch up. "Lady Sophia, you must stop running ahead. There may be something dangerous that you do not readily see. How am I to protect you if you never wait for me?"

Sophia stopped and Elle caught up to her, breathing heavily.

She looked over at Elle and giggled. "I as big as you."

Elle grinned. It was hard not to give in to Sophia's happy-go-lucky ways. "Yes, you are very tall now. But please, hold my hand."

Sophia reached out and placed her small hand into Elle's, and they followed the wall for the length of the field. A little gate broke up the stones, allowing Elle to move through onto the earl's land.

She lifted Sophia off the wall and pointed to the house in the opposite direction. "You must come off the wall now. If we continue to follow it, we will move farther from the house." She retook Sophia's hand as soon as the girl's feet touched the ground. "Come along. I wager tea will be ready by the time we return." She noticed Sophia's steps had slowed. Had her endless stores of energy finally depleted? One could only hope.

"Will there be tea cakes?" Sophia gave Elle a side-eyed stare.

Elle shook her head. "I should not know. Your mother did request at least biscuits with tea to ward off your hunger until dinner."

Sophia did not look thrilled by the idea. "I hope they betto than yestoday's biscuits." She pushed her lip into a pout.

Elle shrugged. Sophia was not wrong. Yesterday's biscuits had been dry and tasteless. Elle suspected it was because they were several days old. But in truth, even the day-old biscuits that Lord and Lady Kirtley's cook made tasted better than yesterday's fare, so Elle had concluded that the Briarwood cook was simply inferior to theirs at Dovehaven.

"I suppose the longer we take to get there, the drier they will become. And we both know those biscuits cannot afford to become any drier. Let us hurry a little faster."

Sophia picked up her pace, though she did not seem overly excited. "Why do we not miss them altogether?"

"If you do not eat them, you will be hungry long before dinner is served, my lady." They were almost to the house, and then Elle could turn Sophia over to Nurse Jones. "Besides, it is not safe to be out of doors when there is lightning nearby. Make haste."

They finally stepped onto the drive just as Elle felt the first raindrop on her cheek. She let out a squeak and ducked her head, tugging Sophia toward the front stairs, where she met with something solid.

Elle stopped and looked up.

"Elizabeth? Er . . . Miss Carter?"

Elle looked up and dropped Sophia's hand. Henry Wallingford stood on the first step of the staircase, looking down at her.

"Henry?"

His was a face she had not seen in years. Not since he'd left for the continent four years earlier. "What are you doing here?"

Elle grabbed for Sophia as she jumped up the first two steps.

Henry smiled and Elle felt as if no time at all had passed since their last meeting.

"Ryecombe invited me. He is an old friend of my father's." He stepped down onto the pebbled ground and stood in front of her. "I did not think to see you here."

Elle's smile faded. They were not attending the same house party. She was here as a servant. Some might object to classifying a governess as such, but Elle was not one of them. *She* knew what she was. "Yes, I should not think you would."

He lifted his arm to her. "But I find I am exceedingly happy to find you here. It has been far too long since last we spoke."

Elle looked at his arm and then at the front door. What was she to do? Walking through the front entrance on his arm, with Sophia's hand in hers, felt too . . . she did not know what the word was. Familiar? Perhaps hopeful? As if she were trying to create a scene which she would never have.

Still, if she rejected his offering, it would send an entirely different message. Henry was a dear friend, and one she did not wish to offend.

Swallowing her pride—it was her pride that stung her—she placed her hand on his arm, and they made their way up the staircase. It felt odd, yet familiar—like an old blanket she'd not had need of for years.

They waited for the door to open under the overhang of the balcony above, as the rain came down. Henry looked down at her. "The years have been good to you, Miss Carter."

"You are too kind, Mr. Wallingford." Elle found it hard to look at him. There were so many memories tied up with those eyes. "I hope your family is well. I have not seen your mother and Lenora in years. Although, I did see Robert my last Season . . ." She did not wish to move the conversation to her last Season.

She glanced up into his gaze but saw no joy or excitement there. Only sadness and resignation. What had happened to her childhood friend?

"Not Mr. Wallingford, anymore." He cleared his throat. "You obviously have not heard."

Elle frowned. "Heard what?"

"Robert died just over a year ago. It is why I returned from the continent." He looked past her.

"Oh, Henry, I am sorry." She released Sophia's hand, and the girl ran inside the house, leaving the door wide open. "Lady Sophia . . ." Elle sighed when her charge disappeared up the staircase. She hoped Sophia found her way back to the nursery. She knew she should follow behind, but to excuse herself now seemed rather cold and heartless.

Elle placed her now-empty hand atop his, giving him a light squeeze. While Henry and Robert had never been overly close, she could see the pain in Henry's eyes.

"I suppose I should call you Lord Amesbury, then."

He smiled, a shadow of a grin on his face. "From you, Elle, I think Henry will do."

She returned his sad smile, barely noting the increasing number of raindrops falling around them. There had been a time when her use of his Christian name might have passed as acceptable, considering the closeness of their families and their childhood familiarity. But that was no longer the case. Servants did not use Christian names with their superiors. "I wish it could be so, my lord. But you and I both know that cannot be."

Henry opened his mouth but then shut it as the butler approached and looked out at them through the open doorway.

Elle dipped her head and dropped her hand from Henry's arm. "I should make certain Lady Sophia made it back to the nursery." She looked down at the front of her damp gown. "And change my gown. Good day, Lord Amesbury." Gracious, that felt odd on her tongue.

Elle hurried to the stairs and lifted her skirt, taking only a moment to look over her shoulder for one last look at Henry. *Oh, Henry.*

There had been a time when Elle had thought she might have a tendré for him. But that seemed a lifetime ago. Now there was not even the slightest flutter in her middle when she looked on him. But maybe that was because she knew nothing would ever come of it.

She frowned. Did that mean she thought something might come from the flutter caused by Mr. Jenkins?

Elle shook the thought from her head. That could not possibly be the case.

CHAPTER SIX

Philip paced from one end of his study to another, scrubbing his hand through his hair and over his face. *I'll need to think on it.* The duke's words repeated in his mind.

Thunder and turf! What was there to think on? Either Black Thunder impressed the man, or he did not. But how that could be possible, Philip did not know.

A full day had passed since his meeting with the duke, and still, Philip had heard nothing from the man.

It sounded more like an excuse than anything. He let out a grunt. But why did Larmont need an excuse? Was it something to do with Philip or was the problem with Black Thunder?

Certainly, it was *not* Black Thunder. Which meant Philip was to blame. He muttered a curse.

It was not as if Larmont did not have the funds. Of that, Philip was certain. The man was one of the richest men in England. It was one reason Philip had been so pleased when the duke had written to him and expressed an interest in purchasing Black Thunder. Money equaled status, and status was just what Philip needed. If the duke rode one of Philip's horses, then others would want one, as well.

But by the end of their meeting, Philip was uncertain that the sale would ever happen.

He shook his hand at his side, bouncing his thumb off his thigh. Was it the price? Two hundred and twenty pounds was well within reason, especially based on Black Thunder's bloodline. And the duke had not seemed to flinch when he heard it.

It must have been me. I am the deficient one. It seemed to always come back to that. It had been the case with Lady Dorothea, and it seemed likely it was the case now.

Philip turned on his heel and made another pass in front of the firebox. Could it have more to do with Philip's negotiating skills or with Philip himself?

After the look of disdain the duke had given him at the match yesterday, it was obvious the duke did not respect Philip. And the looks the duke had given him while in the stable had only confirmed that notion in Philip's mind.

Seeing Philip in the stables, working with the horses, had obviously offended the man's sensibilities. But perhaps it was more than that. Was Philip's language too coarse? He had spent years refining his language and taking the stables out of it. But there were still times—usually when he was nervous or overly excited—when it still slipped in. Had that happened, and it had offended the duke? But was something so small enough for Larmont to back out on the sale?

Philip released a heavy breath, running his hand through his hair again. He had hoped to have the money in hand today or tomorrow, at the latest. But that was looking less and less certain.

He stopped at the mantel and swallowed hard. What was he going to do?

"Son, are you well?" His mother poked her head in the doorway.

Philip smiled. "Yes, of course. I was merely thinking, and you know I think better when I move about."

"It was not the pacing which concerned me."

He raised his brows. "Oh? Then what is causing you concern?"

She pierced him with a look that made him feel seven years old again. "It is the cursing and the grunting."

The corners of his lips curved upward. Ah, she had heard the curses. He sighed. "I am sorry you had to hear it, Mama. I am merely perplexed, is all."

She continued to look at him. "Perplexity rarely requires curses, Son." She moved into the room and sat down on the couch, facing the fire. Patting the seat next to her, she looked up at him. "Come. Tell me what has you so *perplexed*."

Even though he didn't want to, Philip moved to the couch and settled in next to his mother. "I was only trying to figure out why the duke did not buy Black Thunder yesterday." He sighed. "I have concluded it must be because of something I did or said, but I cannot say precisely what."

She patted his hand. "Why must there be a reason? Perhaps the timing just wasn't right."

Philip balled his fists. "But I need the timing to be right. We need the sale, Mama."

She placed her hand atop his, sending a calm radiating up his arm. "Perhaps that is the problem. I've learned that the rich can smell desperation."

He ran his hand through his hair. He *was* desperate. His family and business needed the money. And the notoriety. But was that the problem?

Perhaps he would not feel so desperate if Lord Ryecombe would come through and purchase the matching bays. They would not bring in as much money as Black Thunder. But it would be enough to keep them holding on until Philip could find another buyer for Black Thunder.

"Last week I was so certain I would have sold both the carriage horses and Black Thunder by now. What happened?"

There was a knock at the door, and Anne pushed in, a tray in her hands. "The tea you requested, madam."

Philip raised a brow.

His mother's eyes focused in on his hair, and she smiled. "I thought you might need some refreshment."

He frowned. "Mama, we don't have enough tea for such niceties. I used most of what we had left for my meeting yesterday."

She shrugged. "I know. I told Cook to reuse the leaves for the time. It might not be as strong as you have grown accustomed, but it will serve its purpose." She placed the tray on the low table. "Surely you can remember the days when we could not even afford genuine tea, let alone full-strength. This will surely taste better than the bark tea we used to drink before."

Philip nodded, her words only adding to the weight already pushing down on him. They could not go back to those days. He would not allow it.

"I know you do not want my interference, Son. But things will turn around. You need only have faith."

Philip pushed out a breath. Ah, his mother and her sermons on faith. Mr. Applebaum, the vicar, could take a note or two from her.

"You are the eternal optimist, Mama." He moved over to the table and poured out the tea. She was right. The color alone told Philip it was weak in flavor. He sighed as he noticed the absence of the sugar bowl.

"You used to share that trait with me." She raised her brows. "What happened?"

Philip sighed. "I may just be running out of optimism. It is hard to remain so when you have not a grain of sugar or a tea leaf to your name."

A slight weight lifted at the admission. It was refreshing to share some of the burden with someone else. It did nothing to *relieve* the burden, of course, but knowing he did not carry it alone was something.

His mother tsked. "Philip, we'll survive a few days without sugar and tea. We have done it before. Why should you think we can't do it again?"

Philip shook his head. "But I had thought those times behind us, Mama. I expected it in the beginning when we were just starting out. But we have been at this for over seven years. The breeding should turn a profit by now."

"It has been profitable." She looked around the room before folding her hands in her lap. "And perhaps it should be more so. But no one could have planned for the bad luck we've had the last few years. Two colts breaking a leg only weeks into their training? And who would have predicted that Addie Mae would lose her foal just after delivery." She stared at him. "But things are turning around. You will see."

He sighed. "That was my hope, too. But I have one of the finest horses in England in my stables, and what good is it doing me?" He ran his hand back through his hair. "I have a stable full of fine horses and it is all for naught if nobody knows of them."

"Patience, my boy. Your time will come." She stood and moved toward the door. "You need only figure out a way to make the duke see he needs your horses." She turned and left him to his weak tea and day-old cakes.

Philip picked up his cup and placed it to his lips.

His mother meant well, but she had no head for business. Philip could not simply wait until fate decided it was his turn.

He needed to make his own fate. But currently, he was too frustrated to see how that was possible.

He needed a distraction to help clear his mind. Miss Carter's handsome face appeared, and he replayed their brief discussion at the paddock.

She had been a pleasant distraction, he would give her that. Not that he would allow himself to think of her as anything more.

He smiled into his cup as he sipped. As far as distractions went, she was a lovely one.

He paused and set his cup back on the tray as a new thought settled in his mind.

Miss Carter.

She might be the key to all this. She had mentioned the duke was friends with her father. And anyone with eyes could see they had chatted amiably before the cricket match. She may not believe them close friends, but Philip had the impression the duke still considered her with some regard.

Could she possibly be the help Philip was looking for? Could she make the duke see what he would miss if he did not buy Black Thunder?

He bit absently at his cake. But how could he see her again? It was not as if the earl would invite Philip over to play a round of battledore.

No, Philip would need to concoct another reason for a trip to Briarwood. But even then, would Miss Carter be about, or would she be in the schoolroom with the children?

A knock sounded at the door, and Philip grunted.

Barnaby, the stable boy, poked his head in the door. His eyes were wide. "Athena is in labor, sir. Your father sent me to fetch you."

Philip nodded. "Very good. I will change my clothes and

come immediately. Please make sure there is fresh hay in the stall."

"Yes, sir." Barnaby ducked out of the door.

Philip grunted as he pushed himself to standing. It looked like his plans would have to be put off. At least for now. Athena needed him.

He strode from his study and up to his chamber, choosing breeches and a coat he had kept from his days as a groom in his father's stable.

He retied his cravat in a simple knot as he hurried from the house, a new excitement pushing his worries away for the moment. If everything went according to plan, this was the first of four racers to be born at Greystone this year. It would be several years before he could train and sell the horses, but when he did? His pulse ticked up at the thought. Perhaps fate would not have to wait so very long.

CHAPTER SEVEN

Philip sat at the kitchen table, breaking off a piece of biscuit and chewing it thoughtfully. Athena had foaled a filly last evening. It was an event that brought hope, but also more worry. There was much that could still go wrong with the young horse, as he could attest.

Add that to the fact he still had not received a note from Larmont, and Philip was nearly bursting.

The duke had not outright declined buying the horse at their meeting, which meant Philip did not feel he could actively pursue finding another buyer. If he sold the horse and the duke came back to purchase Black Thunder, it would surely ruin any chance Philip had of becoming known outside of Somerset. Besides, one did not disappoint a duke and come out of the encounter unscathed.

He sighed and took a sip of his ale. It was only the first day without tea and already he was missing it.

But what was he to do? As the hours ticked on, he felt more and more desperate.

He had decided Miss Carter was to play a role in his plans with Larmont, he just had not figured out how.

Could it be he was focusing too much on Black Thunder when he should come up with a plan to sell the bays to Lord Ryecombe?

He could hitch up the pair and take a ride over to the Earl's estate. Perhaps then he could at least complete that sale.

From everything Philip had seen of Ryecombe, the man was proud. He might buy the horses on the spot, just so his guests might see the exchange. It was manipulative, and under normal circumstances, such actions would be beneath Philip. But these were not normal circumstances.

Philip smiled and plopped the rest of the biscuit into his mouth. It was the best plan he had come up with so far. It was not great, but it would have to do.

And besides, maybe he would glimpse Miss Carter while he was there. If he did, perhaps she would come speak with him, and Philip could discover if she knew any information about the duke that could help Philip with that sale.

He took another sip. Now he need only think of a reason to visit Briarwood. One did not simply show up for no reason at all.

Brushing off his hands, Philip wiped the crumbs off the table and into his palm, dropping them into the waste bin. "Thank you for breakfast, Mrs. Heaton."

She shook her head. "It was not much, sir."

Philip waved her words away. "It was enough to give me the start of an idea. Do not sell your food short. It is very inspiring."

He pushed the stool under the table. Now, what reason did he have to visit Briarwood? He tapped his thumb against his leg as he thought.

If there was someone else interested in the bays, would it

not be polite to inform the earl? But it would be a lie and Philip did not conduct business based on lies. Unless . . . he could *find* someone to show an interest.

He tilted his head to the side. "Mrs. Heaton, do you have any interest in horses?"

She stared at him as if trying to understand where the shift in their conversation had occurred. "I suppose I am as interested as anybody."

Philip smiled. "Oh? And what of the bays? Are you interested in them?"

She shrugged. "I can't say as I have seen much of them."

Philip led her over to the window and pointed to the south paddock. "There they are. Are they not two of the most beautiful creatures?"

Mrs. Heaton leaned forward and squinted. "They seem to be, sir."

"Now that you have seen them, would you say you are more interested?"

She shrugged but eyed him as if he might be one step away from Bedlam. "I suppose so."

He patted her on the arm. "That is all I needed to hear. Thank you." He strode out of the kitchen, intent on currying the bays before he set off for Briarwood. He would see that they looked their finest.

If everything worked out as he hoped, he might just have to walk home and fetch another pair of horses to bring home his curricle. But he would not mind in the least. Not if it meant he had made the sale.

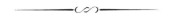

The bays' coats gleamed in the sunlight as Philip secured them to the curricle. The conveyance itself was not much to look at, something Philip regretted. The bays would surely look better attached to a finer carriage, but that was beyond Philip's control. If he could not afford tea leaves, he certainly could not afford a newer carriage. But it was not the carriage he was trying to sell, and he would do well to keep that in mind.

He led the horses out of the carriage house and climbed into the driver's seat. His stomach hitched up into his throat. It was not the best-formed plan, but it was all he had.

The wealthy did not understand the plight of the working man. He did not have the luxury of waiting around for the elite to make up their minds. If the earl did not wish to buy these horses, perhaps Philip would at least have leave to sell them to someone else.

It did not solve his problem with the duke, but it would move him in the right direction financially. Then he might at least be able to afford some tea and supplies to mend a few of the tenant cottages.

He flicked the reins, and the horses set out.

If nothing else, this recent downturn in funds had made Philip see the importance of diversifying the estate more. He had spent too much time and money focused solely on the horses, when he should have been doing more to bring the estate up to a higher standard. That included fixing the tenant cottages and finding renters for them. He could see now that rent needed to become a priority.

He guided the horses down the lane. It would be faster to walk to Briarwood along the back path. Indeed, Philip could have done that and still had a conversation with the earl. But would the conversation not have more impact and meaning if the horses in question were there for Ryecombe to see and touch?

Philip knew he was using the bays—and the house party— to push the man into a decision. He should feel guilty about such actions, but Ryecombe had said he was interested in the horses months ago. When was he to make good on his word?

Philip obviously had to force the man's hand. And if that meant appealing to his vanity and sense of superiority, then so be it.

Philip turned onto the lane leading to Briarwood as a brisk wind gusted, nearly taking his cap with it. He had taken his time in currying the animals, thus ensuring he did not arrive too early for propriety.

As Philip approached the house, he saw a group of people on the lawn where the cricket pitch had been the day before. They had set up several lawn games. Some people were playing battledore on teams of three or four, the gusts blowing the shuttlecock way off course, while others played pall-mall on the other side of the lawn.

Philip breathed in deeply. This was better than he could have hoped. How could the earl *not* buy the horses with everyone outside watching? But he had better make haste before the weather drove everyone back inside.

He guided the curricle around and stopped it at the side of the lawn. He looked out over the people, hoping to spot the earl among the players. Sure enough, he was there playing battledore. It looked as though Larmont was playing as well. Perhaps this was a better plan than Philip had realized.

He hopped down and tied the reins to a nearby post. Striding over, he stood on the side, waiting until there was a break in the action.

Philip's brows rose. The earl was skilled at Battledore, something Philip would not have guessed. The man was rather portly and had not moved with such ease in the cricket match. Although, Philip noted, the earl did keep the shuttlecock longer than was proper. It should not surprise him the man seemed hesitant to share.

After bouncing the bird into the air nearly a dozen times, the earl finally tossed it high in another direction and several ladies ran after it, their heads tilted back and their eyes following the shuttlecock. The wind picked it up and carried it far behind them. It was an accident waiting to happen. But that was none of Philip's concern.

Ryecombe looked over and saw Philip watching the game. The earl gave one last look at the shuttlecock and then strode over. "Jenkins. To what do I owe the pleasure of your visit?" His voice held no pleasure and Philip was confident it had nothing to do with the discolored split of his lip.

Philip motioned with his head to his curricle. "Someone is interested in the bays, my lord. But you expressed an interest in them first. I thought it only proper to offer them to you before selling them to another." Philip's collar felt tight, and he had the urge to pull it away from his skin. It was not an outright lie, so why did he feel so uncomfortable? Manipulation was not the way he liked to do business.

The earl scrunched up his face and flicked his gaze to the mares on the lane. "They are a fine-looking pair." He pushed his lips out and grunted before putting a finger to his injury. "They would be for my wife. Perhaps I should leave the decision up to her. I will bring her around to look at them soon."

Philip sucked in a quiet, albeit deep breath. He was now using his wife as an excuse not to buy the horses? Why could the man not make a simple decision? Was the price the problem? Perhaps if Philip asked for less, the earl would make a decision.

He opened his mouth just as the front door opened with a whoop, and Philip looked over his shoulder at the house. A child streaked down the stairs, running toward the horses.

Miss Carter was not far behind, her skirts held up as she

scampered down the stairs, calling after the child. "Lady Sophia. Please, stop. They do not know you, dearest."

Philip grinned, deciding that if, for no other reason, seeing Miss Carter run after the child made his plan worth it.

And he loved seeing how much Lady Sophia loved his horses. Normally he would jog over and intercede, but those two mares were the most docile animals he had ever encountered—which is what made them perfect for a lady's curricle. Lady Sophia would be perfectly safe with them, regardless of the ruckus she was making. There would be no surprising them with her approach.

A man Philip did not know but recognized from the cricket match stepped up behind Ryecombe. "I could not help overhearing your conversation. You are looking for a matched pair? I should wonder at your delay in deciding, Ryecombe. They are some of the finest horses I've seen. Even better than Tattersalls, of late."

Philip puffed up slightly. He may not know the man, but he was inclined to like him if he could see the worth of the bays.

"And my daughter seems quite taken with the animals. Perhaps if you don't purchase them, I shall."

The girl was this man's daughter? That would make him Lord Kirtley, and likely the one who employed Miss Carter as nurse to his children. She may prove influential with more than just the duke.

The earl blustered.

Could it be there was truly another interested party? Someone besides Mrs. Heaton? He licked his lips and looked between the two men. Both of them turned their gazes to the horses.

Philip followed suit, not at all disappointed that he had an excuse to watch Miss Carter and Lady Sophia.

Miss Carter held Lady Sophia on her hip as she held the child's hand and ran it down one of the horse's noses.

"Do you not have horses, my lord?" Philip asked. It was curious that a child who had horses at home should be so interested in Philip's.

"Indeed, we do. She loves them, but I have never seen her act in such a way." The stranger turned his eyes on Philip. "There must be something special about your horses, sir."

Philip smiled. He thought that whenever a new addition was foaled. It was time someone else realized it. "Yes, my lord. I have always thought as much."

The earl cleared his throat. "If you are through trying to buy my horses out from under me, Kirtley . . ." The older man narrowed his eyes at Philip. "I dislike discussing business in front of my guests. I shall come along and we can meet when the house party is over."

Philip clutched his hands at his side. This is what he had been doing for the last two months. Why could the man not commit? "I understand, my lord. And I hate to put you in this position. But I am afraid I need an answer. If you do not wish to purchase them, I should like to sell them to the other interested party."

Lord Kirtley took a step forward. "I should like a chance at them before you sell to someone else."

The action was enough to spur the earl into action. "You said it would be one hundred pounds for the pair?"

Philip bit back the terse reply. The earl knew very well that was not the cost. They had discussed it on at least two other occasions. Philip cleared his throat. "No, sir. It was one hundred and seventy-five pounds for the pair, but—"

The earl blustered. "I am certain that is higher than when last we spoke. Are you trying to cheat me, Jenkins?"

Philip's face burned as he glanced around at the faces of

those pretending to still play the lawn games but were intently listening to the conversation. Would everyone think Philip a cheat? Such accusations could not be good for his reputation. "Of course not, my lord."

He looked over at Miss Carter. Had she heard? For reasons he could not understand nor think on at present, that notion bothered Philip more than any other.

Lord Kirtley placed a hand on the earl's shoulder. "Surely you can see those horses are worth at least two hundred. Look how docile they are. My daughter is handling them with no problems. It is difficult to find a horse like that, let alone a pair. They would be perfect for *my* wife's curricle." Lord Kirtley put a finger to his lips. "I will give you two hundred pounds for the pair."

Philip jerked his gaze away from Miss Carter and Lady Sophia. What? What was happening? This had not been part of Philip's plan. Although, he could not be unhappy about the turn it was taking.

In truth, Philip had thought he would have to let the horses go for one hundred and fifty pounds because he was feeling desperate. But he knew if that had been the first number he gave the earl, the man would have talked him down to one twenty-five or perhaps even less.

The increase in price was certainly a welcome surprise.

"What are you doing, Kirtley?" The earl turned a shade of puce as a vein pulsed on his brow. He scowled at his friend and then at Philip as if this was his fault. If the earl had not procrastinated the sale for so long, none of this would be happening.

The earl growled. "Very well, two hundred pounds. But not a ha' penny more."

Philip dipped his head. "You have been more than fair, my lord. I would not think of asking for more."

The earl glared at him. Not the face of one who had just

agreed to buy such majestic animals. Philip might be worried after their welfare if he did not know the stable master and head coachman at Briarwood. Both men would take good care of the horses.

He felt a slight tightening in his chest. He would miss them at Greystone, but this was for the best—it was their purpose.

"I'll send Winslow over with the blunt this afternoon."

Philip nodded, but the earl did not see. He had already turned and stomped back to the game of battledore.

Lord Kirtley moved closer. "If he does not make good on the purchase, I am in earnest. Just send me word, and I will buy the pair." Lord Kirtley raised one brow. "Do you have others for sale?"

Philip nodded. "Yes, my lord. Several, including a racer. Although, the Duke of Larmont has expressed an interest in that horse."

Lord Kirtley looked over his shoulder toward the duke. "Then he should make good on his word. What is the name of your stables? I should like to come look while I am here. Tattersalls has been rather disappointing of late."

"Mine is the next estate over." Philip jerked his head toward his home. "Greystone Manor."

Lord Kirtley grinned. "Very good. Are you available tomorrow afternoon? Say around two?"

Philip nodded. "Of course. The horses will all be ready for your inspection."

"I shall see you then, Mr. Jenkins." Lord Kirtley nodded and turned away.

Philip felt like shouting or perhaps jumping out of pure relief. This plan, while it had gone completely off course, had been far more successful than Philip had ever imagined.

CHAPTER EIGHT

E lle stood next to the horses, holding Sophia tightly in her arms as the little girl ran her hands down the nose of the horse.

"Nice hosee," she whispered with each pass.

"You have good taste in horses, Lady Sophia." The deep voice of Mr. Jenkins set Elle's stomach fluttering. "These two are some of my favorites."

Sophia paused mid-way down the horse's nose. "May I wide it?"

Elle cringed slightly at the omission of the *r* sound. She had been working with Sophia to correct the speech issue. But she would never think to correct her in front of Mr. Jenkins.

Mr. Jenkins put his hand to his chin, looking most pensive.

"Normally, I should not mind in the least, but I just sold these two horses to Lord Ryecombe. They are not mine anymore."

Sophia's bottom lip pushed out and quivered. "You sold them? Do you not love them anymore?"

Elle's eyes widened. "Lady Sophia, it is none of our

concern what Mr. Jenkins does with his horses." She cautioned a glance at Mr. Jenkins to see if he was angry.

A soft smile barely turned the corners of his lips. "On the contrary. I love them very much. But I raised the horses so one day another family could love them like I do."

Sophia scrunched up her brow. "Lord Wyecombe will love them like you do?"

Mr. Jenkins shrugged. "Perhaps he won't. But the earl has a very kind stable master and head coachman. They will take excellent care of these two horses."

"You see, my lady? They will be fine. You need not worry over them." Elle helped her run her hand down the horse's neck one last time.

"I have many other horses in my stables if you ever wish to come visit them." Mr. Jenkins's eyes flicked up to Elle, and he smiled at her before returning his gaze to Sophia. Was he including her in the invitation? Elle grimaced. Of course he was. It was not as if he expected Sophia to visit on her own.

Sophia's head nodded furiously. "Oh, yes. May we come after tea?"

Elle gasped. "Lady Sophia. I am certain Mr. Jenkins did not mean we should come today. I expect he was speaking in general terms."

Mr. Jenkins's grin widened. "I would be honored to have you come after tea."

Sophia looked back at Elle, a satisfied smirk on her face. "You see? He wishes us to come today."

Elle dropped Sophia to the ground and took a firm hold on her hand, lest she try to run off again. She looked to Mr. Jenkins apologetically. "You need not go to any trouble. I am certain you are very busy and have no time to entertain a three-year-old."

Mr. Jenkins shook his head, his gaze holding hers. "I can

honestly say I would like nothing more than to entertain a three-year-old. Especially if her nurse would care to accompany her." His face pinked instantly all the way to the tips of his ears.

But Elle hardly noticed.

Her chin instinctively rose at the slight. "I will ask *Nurse Jones* if she is available." She raised a superior brow but dropped it slightly when she noted the confusion furrowing his brow.

Why had she felt it necessary to point such a thing out? He was obviously meaning her, yet she had gone and complicated the situation by pointing out his mistake. Yet she felt compelled to inform him of her position. She was a governess. She had an education. She knew how to act as a proper young lady, and Lord and Lady Kirtley paid her to teach such things to the children.

She let out a huff. Anyone could be a nurse, but such was not the case for a governess. "I am not the nurse." She looked at the ground, resentment welling up inside her. She should not even be a governess. This was all Robert's fault. She pulled in a calming breath through her nose. It did no good to cast blame.

"I am sorry. I did not realize . . ." His voice dropped off and he took a step back. A step away from Elle. That was not what she had intended.

She had volunteered rather quickly to follow Sophia out to see Mr. Jenkins's horses. While she was hesitant to admit it was because she wished to see Mr. Jenkins, she knew it was true. But now her pride had gone and ruined everything. There was something about Mr. Jenkins that made her feel . . . she was not sure what she felt. Friendship? Belonging? It was an absurd thought, but it wouldn't leave her mind. It was only that Mr. Jenkins made her feel . . . *seen.* All she knew for certain was she wished to feel it more. And that required more time with him.

"I am the governess to the older children, Lord Culpepper and Lady Katie. But Nurse Jones is not as quick on her feet as she once was. At times, I am called on to chase after Lady Sophia."

Mr. Jenkins nodded but did not retake his steps. Why would he not retake his steps? Would he retreat more if she took the step instead?

"Ah, I see. I am sorry if I offended you."

Elle shook her head. "You need not apologize. I likely would have had a similar thought had I been in your situation." It was not completely the truth. Elle would have seen that she was too refined and well-spoken to be a simple nurse. But then, she did not know if Mr. Jenkins was familiar with such differences. Had he been raised with a nurse or governess? Something in her mind told her he had not.

She smiled and let out a little laugh that sounded far too forced. But she needed to do something to alleviate the awkwardness that now filled the space between them. Awkwardness that was entirely of her making. Had she just ruined Sophia's chance to visit the stables? Mr. Jenkins would not withdraw the offer, would he?

"We do not wish to be a bother, sir. But I believe Lady Sophia would enjoy meeting your other horses." Elle bit on the inside of her cheek. Did she sound as desperate to his ears as she did to her own? And just why did she feel so desperate?

Mr. Jenkins's face relaxed into a grin. "Very good. I shall expect you later this afternoon." He dropped to his haunches and looked at Sophia. "I will see to it they are looking their best for you, my lady." He leaned in as if he were telling her a secret. "And as a special surprise, we even have a foal that was born just yesterday."

Sophia's eyes widened. She giggled, pulling on Elle's arm as she jumped up and down.

Elle looked between the two and wondered for a moment if Sophia's fascination was with Mr. Jenkins's horses, or with Mr. Jenkins himself. It was hard not to agree with the little girl.

Mr. Jenkins put his hands on his thighs and pushed himself up. He turned to Elle, his smile still full on his lips. "You may bring the other children along also."

Had he always had that dimple in his chin? Elle did not think she had noticed it before now. But how was that possible? His face would not be nearly so handsome without it. She tilted her head to the side. And how had she not realized his lips were perfectly symmetrical?

Her eyes widened. Had she just thought on the nature of a man's lips? What was happening to her?

"Miss Carter? Did you hear me?"

Elle snapped to attention, heat traveling up her neck. It was bad enough to be caught woolgathering, but to be caught thinking about his lips? She swallowed. "I'm sorry?" Gads, he must think her incredibly rude.

"I said you may bring the other children along if you wish."

Elle nodded like a simpleton. "Oh, yes. Thank you. I am certain they would enjoy the outing."

Mr. Jenkins joined in her nodding. From a distance, they must both look like idiots. Two people standing on the lane nodding at each other. *Stop it,* she mentally shouted at herself.

"Yes, well . . ." Mr. Jenkins shifted from one foot to the other. "If I am to have the horses ready for Lady Sophia's arrival, I must be on my way." He dipped his head to them and moved away.

Elle stood, watching him as he checked the harnesses and whispered something to each horse. He had such a gentle nature to him. She could understand Sophia's interest. At least to a point. He was an interesting man. An interesting man who turned her insides into a raging tide and made her warm just looking on him. *Confound it, take ahold of yourself, Elizabeth Carter!* She nearly stomped her foot for emphasis. She was not acting as the lady her mother had trained her to be. A lady certainly did not become giddy over the likes of a man. At least not a man of Mr. Jenkins's status.

She and Sophia stood on the edge of the grass, watching as Mr. Jenkins's curricle and matching bays traveled around the circular lane and headed away from the estate.

But just what was Mr. Jenkins's status? She did not rightly know. He had mentioned he owned Greystone to the duke. And his manner of speech spoke to him being educated. But in no other ways did Mr. Jenkins appear to be a gentleman. Indeed, he seemed more suited to the stables. But in observing the earl, the small amount Elle had, she did not think he would condescend to speak to another man's groom. And Mr. Jenkins mention that he had just sold the horses. Would not a gentleman sell his own horses?

She shook her head. She had so many questions, but it seemed unlikely she would ever receive answers to many of them. Unless she managed to ask them all this afternoon.

This afternoon. The tingle returned to her stomach.

Sophia tugged on Elle's arm. Slowly they walked back into the house and up to the nursery where Elle turned Sophia over to Nurse Jones. At least until it was time to take her over to see Mr. Jenkins's stables.

A small smile curved Elle's lips. She could not think of a better outing for the children. At least from her point of view.

CHAPTER NINE

Philip pulled the brush one last time down the side of Bonnie Mae. The horse gleamed from the effort.

Philip looked down his front. Straw and horsehair hung from his waistcoat and breeches. His horses looked well, now it was time to get himself looking as he should for visitors.

He brushed a streak of dirt from his waistcoat and turned from the stall, leaning against the railing separating it from the next. His father was hunched over, digging dirt out from Adonis's hooves.

"I believe we are to have visitors today."

His father looked up briefly but kept his attention on his task. "Oh? Someone interested in buying?"

Philip shook his head. Yesterday, it would have disappointed him it was not a potential sale. But today, he was content that it was to be a social call. Especially knowing it was Miss Carter he expected. He had used the little girl as an excuse—which might have been wrong—but his true intention was to have Miss Carter come to Greystone.

He could not rightly say why for it seemed an unwise decision. He had no interest in forming an attachment; he had learned his lesson with Lady Dorothea. But there was something about Miss Carter that drew him in—made him want to speak with her.

It was a friendly sort of thing. Nothing more. Besides, it would be good for Gracie to speak with someone other than Miss Martindale.

"A child of a guest attending the house party at Briarwood is quite fond of our horses. I invited her to visit the stables."

His father stopped what he was doing. "You invited a girl to visit? What do you know about children? And more particularly, little girls?"

Philip grunted. "I need not know anything. Her governess will accompany her."

"Ah, her governess." His father raised his brows.

Philip shifted to his other foot. He did not like the look on his father's face. It was far too knowing, especially considering there was nothing to know. Philip pushed off the railing. "My point in mentioning it is only to prepare you. I did not want you to be surprised by their presence."

"A wise decision. Thank you, Son." His father nodded, but Philip did not miss the slight twitch of his lips.

Philip turned and headed toward the stable doors. He should never have mentioned it. All it had done was serve as an amusement for his father.

"And where are you off to? I should think if you are expecting company here at the stables you would wish to be here when they arrived."

Philip stopped. "I thought to change into something less . . . horsey. I am certain ladies do not wish to have horsehair clinging to their gowns."

His father did not even attempt to hide his smile this time. "Surely they should not expect such a thing when they are visiting a stable." He waved Philip away. "Go and make your-self presentable. If they should come before you return, I will see to them."

Philip narrowed his eyes at his father for a moment before shrugging and moving out of the stables toward the house. He squinted against the sunlight and paused at the sound of horse hooves on the lane.

Placing a hand above his eyes, he squinted toward the sound. A man in livery—the Earl of Ryecombe's livery—slowed as he neared Philip.

He came to a stop in front of Philip and dismounted. The man extended the satchel in his hand. "I am here to collect the bays. Here is the payment. I am to escort the horses back to Briarwood." He tossed the bulging satchel to Philip.

Philip looked down at the bag of jingling coins. The earl had not sent bank notes or a draft to pay for the horses? That was odd. But perhaps it was simply the earl's way of showing Philip he was displeased with the way the deal had concluded. Although, what the earl had to be angry at Philip about, he did not know. The man was buying extraordinary horses.

Philip raised a brow at the footman. "You are to escort them? I had thought to curry them before I delivered them to the earl."

"I'm only doing as his lordship instructed me. I am not at liberty to change the instructions, sir."

Philip stared at the footman a moment, then shrugged. He wanted to be irritated, but it was not this man's fault. Besides, it was difficult to be angry when he held two hundred pounds in his hands. He tossed the bag lightly. Funny, but he expected two hundred pounds to have more weight to it.

"Come with me." He waved the footman behind him as he moved back into the stable. It was likely considered bad form to count the money in front of the buyer, but this footman was not technically the buyer, so Philip continued.

He pulled the string securing the satchel and dumped the coins onto a nearby table. There were a lot of coins. Indeed, Philip did not think he had ever seen so many at one time. He counted out the quid and guineas, squinting down at them when the number came up short.

He counted again. When the second counting came up the same as the first, he fisted his hand and slammed it down on the table, causing the coins to bounce. Zeus! The earl had only sent one hundred and twenty-five pounds. Did the man not think Philip could count? Was that the purpose in sending the payment in coins?

Philip glared up at the wide-eyed footman before he gathered the coins back into the satchel and tied it shut. He tightened his fist around it.

"I am setting out for Briarwood. I will not be away long," Philip called to his father. "See that no one takes the bays."

His father looked up. He surely saw the anger in Philip's features, but he made no comment, only dipped his head in acknowledgment.

Quickly saddling a horse, Philip led the horse out of the stables and mounted. He nodded to the footman. "You said you wished to accompany me to Briarwood. Well, make haste about it, man."

The footman looked back at the stables and then at Philip. "Are you not bringing the horses? The earl said I was to bring back two horses."

Philip raised a brow. "Evidently, the earl says many things that do not come to pass. The horses will stay here for now. The earl and I have things to discuss."

The footman did not mount, only looked back and forth

between Philip and the stables. He seemed at a loss to know what to do.

"You may stay here with the horses if you wish, but they are to remain in my stable until Lord Ryecombe and I have resolved our differences." Philip pulled the reins to the left and led his horse down the lane.

Once he was away from the footman and the stables, Philip let his frustrations out. "Of all the underhanded—" he muttered to himself, his hands clutching the reins with whitened knuckles. And the earl had called Philip a cheat?

Philip rounded the bend onto the main road leading to Bath just as the footman came even with him.

They spoke not a word to each other, which was perfectly acceptable to Philip. He would likely only have snapped at the man, anyway. His brain knew the footman was not to blame, but that did not mean his mouth would not say its piece. And that piece was that the earl was a pinchpenny and a cheat.

How dare the man agree to a price publicly and then try to pay an insulting amount in private. Did he truly not know the value of the bays? Was he so ignorant? Or did he simply think Philip so uneducated as to not know the difference between two hundred and one hundred and twenty-five? Whatever the man's reasoning, it was indisputably dishonest.

Philip had a mind to throw the satchel at Ryecombe's face and then sell the bays to Lord Kirtley.

As Philip's temper flared, his horse trotted faster until they were nearly at a canter when they turned onto the drive leading to Briarwood. He reined in the horse, knowing if he did not gain control of his anger, he would do something he would surely regret later—like give the earl a matching split on the right side of his lip. Philip closed his eyes and took in several deep breaths.

When they finally arrived at the stable yard, Philip swung

down, tossing his reins to a groom. "I will not be long. You need not attend to my horse. Please, just tie him up." He strode purposefully toward the front entrance. Halfway there, he stopped and waited for the footman.

"Come along. You are now a part of this."

The footman looked at the servants' door. "But sir, why should you need me? This is between you and his lordship."

"Not anymore, it isn't." Philip had no confidence that his neighbor would not try to claim that the money had all been there when he sent it along. He would likely claim that Philip had taken the money and was now trying to squeeze him for more.

Philip marched up the front steps with the footman trailing along behind. Rapping three times on the door, Philip turned and folded his arms across his chest. He took in several deep, long breaths, trying to calm his pounding heart.

He had never been so disrespected. And the fact that it was from his own neighbor was telling. Did all of the village hold him in such disregard?

Philip had known it would not be easy to join the ranks of Society. And in truth, he did not particularly wish to. He simply wished to make a name for himself and his stables and provide his sister with a dowry so she might marry well. But the likes of Ryecombe and several other gentlemen in the area refused to allow Philip even that small wish. They were intent on thinking of him as a servant, no matter that he owned his own estate. He shook his head.

The door opened, and the butler looked out. He raised a brow when he spotted the footman standing off to the side. "Good afternoon, Mr. Jenkins."

Philip nodded. "I need to speak with Lord Ryecombe immediately. It is of great import."

The butler shook his head. "I am sorry, but his lordship is not at home."

"I said it was important. Please ask again." Philip clenched his teeth together until his head ached at the temples.

"I am sorry, sir. I shall tell him you stopped by."

Philip reached into his pocket and tossed the satchel at the butler. "Tell him I would like to speak with him about that." He turned on his heel and jogged down the steps two at a time but turned back before he reached the bottom. "He has until noon tomorrow and then I shall sell the bays to someone else for an honest price."

Philip strode to the stables, muttering the whole way, his mind jumping between indignation and regret. He had just given the Earl of Ryecombe an ultimatum. That could not be advisable. Yet, what choice did he have?

The man was toying with Philip's livelihood as if it was no matter. Two hundred pounds may be nothing to a man like Ryecombe, but it was something to Philip. Something of great import.

Whether or not it was the right decision, he had done it, and Philip could not take the words back. If he did, the earl would surely lose the miniscule amount of respect he had for Philip, if he had any at all.

Lord Kirtley had said he would buy the pair, but was he in earnest, or was it a joke he was playing on the earl? Philip did not know the man well enough to know the answer. He would just have to wait and see.

He had issued the ultimatum. Now all he could do was wait until noon tomorrow and see what the earl intended to do. If he did not come through, Philip would speak to Lord Kirtley when he came to see Greystone's stables.

He rubbed at the spot between his brows. What would this incident do to his relationship with the earl? They were already on tenuous ground. Was this what would tip them to being outright enemies?

Philip ran a hand through his hair. He could not care for the earl's approval or censure. Philip had a business to run, and he could not do that effectively if he was overly concerned about pleasing men who would never be pleased. But when Philip's reputation was so closely tied to his income, he did not have the luxury of disregarding anyone's ill opinion. Especially not an earl's.

He mounted Bonnie Mae and headed down the lane. Closing his eyes, he allowed himself to breathe slowly. Miss Carter and the children would be at the stables soon, and it would do no good for them to see him in this state.

He allowed his lips to lift. Miss Carter would be at the stables soon. That thought alone drained away the last of his anger and frustration. He opened his eyes and rotated his shoulders a few times. There was nothing more he could do until tomorrow where the earl was concerned. He might as well enjoy the afternoon with Miss Carter and her charges.

Digging his heels into Bonnie Mae's side, he set off at a canter. He did not want Miss Carter to arrive before he did, and he would prefer to change his clothing. For reasons he chose not to examine, he wished for Miss Carter to see him at his best.

CHAPTER TEN

E lle held firmly to Sophia's hand. Katie and Winston strode alongside them. Mr. Jenkins had said the other children could come along and they needed a rest from their studies. It seemed a perfect way for them to receive fresh air.

They walked along the back path, moving through the gate in the rock wall onto Mr. Jenkins's property. Elle probably should have taken them around and come up the drive properly, but she assumed it would be a much longer trip and one not suited to the children, at least not Sophia.

"Why are we visiting this Mr. Jenkins?" Winston grumbled. What was wrong with the boy? He grumbled about being inside and he grumbled about being outside. What, precisely, would make him happy? This Winston was not the boy Elle was used to teaching.

Was it something she should mention to Lady Kirtley? She glanced at him from the corner of her eye. Perhaps it was simply that he missed home. If it continued once they returned to Dovehaven, then she would address it with the lady. But for now, Elle would try to wheedle the information out of him herself.

"Because he invited Lady Sophia to visit his horses. You like horses, do you not, Lord Culpepper?" She looked over at him, and his brow furrowed.

"Of course. Who does not like horses? But I am certain Briarwood has horses we could have visited. Why go all the way to another estate just to see horses?" He scowled.

"You would prefer to be in the schoolroom?" Elle frowned at the boy. He really was in the doldrums. "I had thought you might enjoy the fresh air and exercise. Next time, I shall only include the ladies in our outdoor excursion."

Winston kicked at a rock protruding from the ground and grunted. "No. I would not rather be in the schoolroom. Although, it is where I belong if I am to be ready for the tutor."

Elle slowed her step and studied Winston. Was the tutor causing his melancholy? But why? She would have thought he would be happy to be out from under her charge. "Do you not want a tutor, Lord Culpepper?"

He shrugged. "A tutor means I will soon leave for Eton."

Elle's lips parted as the answers fell into place. He was uneasy about leaving home and living at school. How had she not figured that out earlier?

"But that is not for at least another year. And I am certain when the time comes, you will be ready for the adventure." Elle was not at all certain of such things. But she could hardly say otherwise. She remembered how uneasy she had been when she was first hired to be a governess. That carriage ride to Dovehaven had been anxious and tense. She knew as well as anyone that leaving what was comfortable and familiar was frightening.

Winston swallowed. "Yes, I am certain you are right."

Elle put a hand out and stopped him. "My lord, all

throughout our lives, we are presented with paths to take. Some will go left, and some will go right, even while others forge straight ahead. We do not know what is at the end of those paths, and yet we must choose one all the same." He looked at her. "The only wrong choice is the path that leads us backward."

Winston dug his toe into the ground. "But what if I do not want to pick a path?"

"And then what would you do? Sit on the ground where you are? Then you will stay the same."

His face fell. "But what is wrong with who I am now?"

Elle's heart pinched for him. She had often wondered that same thing. "There is nothing wrong with the person you are now, my lord. Paths are not about the here and now. They are about the future. Do you really wish to be this same person in five years, or ten? Each path we take gives us new challenges—new opportunities for growth. It shapes us into who we will become."

Winston sighed and continued to look at the ground.

She had done nothing to ease his concerns. This was the part of being a governess that Elle did not know if she would ever get right. She could school them in Latin and French. She could teach them mathematics and geography. But could she instill in them what was most important? That they were important and had worth? That they were destined for great things? It was that notion which kept her up at night because she did not think she was up to the task.

"It will be a change when you leave for school. But we still have some time. Put it from your mind and let us enjoy ourselves to the fullest until it is here. Then you will have many memories to recall while you adjust to Eton."

Winston looked up at her. "Do you think it will help? I thought it only to make me sadder I was away."

"May I tell you a secret?" Elle quirked up a brow.

Winston nodded earnestly, and they picked up their pace to catch up with Sophia and Katie. "When I first came to Dovehaven, it was very difficult. I missed much about my former life. But when I remembered the good things from my childhood, it was easier to be of good cheer." She shrugged. "Perhaps the same will be for you. Some memories may make you wish to be home. But I think most oft, it will help you through the hard times. And it will give you something to look forward to when you return home for holidays."

He nodded. "That is why we are going to Mr. Jenkins's stables? To enjoy ourselves to the fullest?" A hint of a smile appeared on his face.

Elle nodded. "At least in Lady Sophia's estimation. And according to Mr. Jenkins, his horses are some of the finest in England."

"Is that not what every gentleman says about his horse?" Winston looked skeptical.

Elle relaxed. This was the Winston she was accustomed to speaking with. "I suppose they do. But I believe Mr. Jenkins might be truthful. His horses looked very fine to me."

Winston jumped over a boulder. "And you are a good judge of horseflesh, are you, Miss Carter?"

Elle raised her chin in mock indignation. "Indeed, I am, Lord Culpepper."

Winston smiled, and Elle knew the melancholy of moments before had passed. At least for the time.

They came to the stable, and Elle looked around. She had thought Mr. Jenkins might come out to meet them. Should she enter the stables to look for him? Is that where he would be? It seemed possible. He had been in the paddock working with a horse the last time she had been here. But then, this time was not an unannounced visit as the last was.

She glanced over at the house. Perhaps she should inquire within.

Sophia pulled on Elle's hand, her eyes focused on the stable doors. "Lady Sophia, please be patient. We will see the horses, dearest. But you must wait until we find Mr. Jenkins."

A groan sounded, and Elle looked up to see the door of the stable opening. Mr. Jenkins *had* been in the stables. Only, it was not Mr. Jenkins who appeared. It was an older man.

He pulled the door closed behind him and latched it shut. As he turned back, his eyes widened. "Begging your pardon. I did not see you there." His smile was kind and reminded Elle of Mr. Jenkins. Who was this man?

Elle stepped forward. "I am sorry if we startled you. We are looking for Mr. Jenkins. He invited Lady Sophia to come and meet his horses."

The smile on the older man's face widened, taking in the whole of his face. The skin around his eyes crinkled, and his eyes became mere slits. "Ah, yes. He told me you would be coming." He dipped his head and touched his hat. "Mr. Jenkins was unexpectedly called away. I don't believe he will be long. If you would like, I can start the introductions."

Elle twisted the loose hairs on the back of her neck. "If he is too busy, we can return another time."

The man waved her words away. "Nonsense. You came all this way. I should not like it to be for nothing."

"Please, can we stay? I want to see the hosees." Sophia's bottom lip pushed out.

The man smiled down at Sophia. "How about I start the introductions until Mr. Jenkins returns?" He pulled open the stable door and motioned them inside.

Was this man the stable master or simply a groom? If he were the stable master, why did Mr. Jenkins do so much of the labor with the horses himself? She let out a breath. The more she learned of him, the more questions she had.

Sophia pulled out of Elle's grasp and ran toward the man.

"Lady Sophia," Elle called out. But the girl was already inside.

Elle sighed and looked at the man. "I'm sorry. She is quite headstrong." She hurried in after Sophia, hoping to catch her before she startled any horses. She would have a talk with the child when they returned to Briarwood. Elle could not allow Sophia on such expeditions if she would not show some restraint.

The older man chuckled and followed in behind Elle. "No need to apologize, miss. I remember having such enthusiasm once."

Elle paused when she heard him chuckle and after checking to make sure Sophia was not in danger, looked more closely at the man.

He had many similarities to Mr. Jenkins. Their eyes were the same shade of blue, and they even had the same cadence in their voices. Then there was the crease in his chin. Was this man related to Mr. Jenkins?

"Are you the stable master here?" The words were out of her mouth before she could call them back. Not that it was a wholly improper question. It was only her thoughts that should not be voiced aloud.

"Indeed, I am." He dipped his head. "My name is Richard."

Elle smiled, liking Richard immediately. He had an easy way about him that set her at ease. "It is a pleasure to meet you, Richard."

The door to the stable slid back, and all of them turned to look. Mr. Jenkins stepped inside, his face puckered and angry. He stomped in, nearly knocking Winston to the ground.

"Excuse me, Father." He looked up and his face registered

immediate surprise. He reached out to steady Winston. "I beg your pardon. I did not realize we had guests, already." His eyes scanned the group, first seeking out the stable master and then landing on Elle.

The creases smoothed out, and his face relaxed. "Miss Carter. I am sorry I was not here when you arrived. Especially after I am the one who extended the invitation."

Elle smiled without thinking. "You need not apologize. Your stable master was very amiable and offered to begin the introductions."

She looked between the two men. Now that they were together, it was more than just a few similarities she saw. The younger was almost an exact copy, the older only having a few more wrinkles and a slight stoop to his back. It was no wonder she liked him almost instantly.

"Yes, I thought he might." Mr. Jenkins nodded to his father. "I do not suppose proper introductions have been made. Miss Carter, this is my father, Richard Jenkins."

Elle nodded to him. The father was the stable master at the son's estate? Elle had never heard of such a thing. "We have already been introduced. Although, not as your father." She motioned with her hand to the children. "This is Lord Culpepper and Lady Katie." She frowned slightly and motioned to the stall nearest them, where Sophia held out a handful of hay to the occupant. "And I believe you have already met Lady Sophia."

The older Mr. Jenkins moved over next to Sophia. "I do not believe Hestia can smell the hay from down here. Shall I lift you up, so she might know you have something for her?"

Sophia nodded slowly. "Yes, please."

The stable master grinned and placed his booted foot in the crack between the boards, forming a separation between the two stalls. "Climb up here on my knee, little lady. That should place you high enough."

Elle clasped her hands in front of her and watched. The older Mr. Jenkins was just as kind to Sophia as his son.

"Miss Carter, might I look around?" Winston looked at the horses with an interest she had not seen in many weeks.

Elle shrugged. "This is not my stable, my lord. You will need to ask that question of Mr. Jenkins."

Winston looked at the older Mr. Jenkins first, and then the younger. "Which one do I ask, miss?" he asked quietly.

The younger Mr. Jenkins grinned. "Why do I not simplify things? You may call my father Richard."

Winston looked at his feet and scooted a little closer to Elle. "That did not answer my question. Who do I ask, Miss Carter?" he whispered.

"Mr. Jenkins, I believe," she whispered back.

Winston looked up. "Mr. Jenkins, may I look around? I promise not to touch anything."

Mr. Jenkins nodded. "Of course, my lord. If you have questions, just call them out. Either myself or my father will be happy to answer."

Katie moved in closer, worming her hand into Elle's.

"I hope we are not inconveniencing you. Your father said you had an urgent matter of business arise. Do you need to attend to it now?" Elle tilted her head to the side, only now noticing the state of his clothes. His cuffs were worn through, and horsehair clung to his coat and breeches. Even so, she hoped he did not say yes. She was—rather, the children—were enjoying themselves, and she did not wish to cut their time short.

He waved her words away. "I have done all I can for now. Now I must wait and see what comes of it. Lady Sophia, I have something I believe will interest you." Mr. Jenkins waved her over. "Come along and see."

Sophia hopped off Richard's knee and scurried over, placing her hand into Mr. Jenkins's. Elle raised a brow, questioning again whom Sophia liked more, Mr. Jenkins or his horses. But she kept her mouth shut and walked beside them.

After passing several empty stalls, they came to the last one. A brown horse with black legs stood over a much smaller horse with similar markings. "A foal!" Sophia lurched forward, but Mr. Jenkins was quick to pull her back. "Easy there, my lady. That foal was born yesterday. She is still unsteady on her legs. And her mother is very protective of her. We must make slow and quiet movements so as not to spook them."

Mr. Jenkins stepped forward and led the mother into the next stall.

Richard moved over next to Sophia and guided her forward. "Nice and slow, my lady. You are doing very well."

Mr. Jenkins stood in the walkway and folded his arms across his chest, a smile curving his lips.

"You are very kind to let us come. Especially with a new foal." Elle looked down at Katie. "Do you wish to see the foal, my lady?"

Katie shook her head and tightened her hold on Elle's hand.

"It is my pleasure. I enjoy showing my horses to people who appreciate them." His face darkened slightly. "Some do not see their full worth."

Elle chuckled. "I do not believe Sophia falls in that category. She has a full appreciation."

His smile returned. "She is welcome to visit anytime." He cleared his throat and glanced quickly at her, then away. "Did you not say on our first meeting that you are acquainted with the Duke of Larmont?" He stared straight ahead.

Elle's brow furrowed. "Yes, I am acquainted with him.

Although, it was my father that was friends with him." Had she not already told him this?

"But when the two of you were speaking, it seemed, as if you were more than mere acquaintances."

She bristled. "Perhaps, until he learned I am now a governess."

His brows furrowed. "Surely you are mistaken. From where I stood, I saw only joy at seeing a friend."

Elle looked at him sidelong. Why was he asking about the duke? Why was he so insistent that Elle was closer to the duke than she was? It was a strange topic of conversation.

She felt him turn his gaze on her.

"Perhaps next time we can schedule a visit at teatime." There was a slight hesitation in his voice.

She turned toward him, but he had his gaze trained on Sophia and the foal. Was he asking because he wanted Sophia to spend more time with the horses, or because he wanted to spend more time with Elle? Her stomach jumped.

She turned back toward the stall. Could this man be inviting them all over for tea just so he could spend time with her? She shook the thought away. Lawks, what a notion. It seemed she still had a few grand thoughts of herself left in the recesses of her mind. But they did her no good, and she would do well to rid herself of them.

"That would be lovely. Sophia would certainly enjoy seeing your horses again." She kept her eyes moving between Sophia and Winston, hoping she would not catch Mr. Jenkins's gaze and allow him to see her true thoughts.

CHAPTER ELEVEN

Elle sat at the table with Winston and Katie. They were not the best dinner company she had ever had. But they were also not the worst. She took comfort in that.

The door to the nursery opened and Lady Kirtley walked in. She smiled at her children and then at Elle. "Miss Carter, your presence is requested at dinner."

Elle's brow wrinkled. Her presence was requested at dinner? But why? Who would do such a thing? It was highly inappropriate.

Her shoulders dropped. *Henry. Lord Amesbury*, she reminded herself. It was just something he would do. He would not, however, realize how uncomfortable it would make her. There were so many reasons this was not desirable. By singling her out, people would suppose there an agreement between them—or that there was one forthcoming. She did not wish to be the subject of gossip, nor endure the superior looks that would surely come her way. Why would Henry do this to her?

"Hurry along now and change. You are holding up dinner."

Lady Kirtley shooed Elle toward the door and they moved down the corridor to the small bedchamber she was sharing with Nurse Jones. "But I do not have a gown appropriate for such an occasion."

Lady Kirtley let out a breath. "It will be even more improper for you to decline the invitation. Come, I will help you pick something."

A knot formed in Elle's stomach. Henry surely thought he was doing her a favor, returning her to where she belonged. But he could not understand the utter humiliation this was causing. It was not as if Elle had dinner gowns any longer. She still had a few from her London Seasons, but they were long since out of fashion. And in her wardrobe back at Dovehaven.

A dull throb started behind her eyes and forehead. Why must Henry have been invited to come to Briarwood? Why could he not have attended another house party? She had thought it pleasant to see him at first, but now she could not think it so.

Lady Kirtley opened the small wardrobe and sifted through the gowns inside. She grunted occasionally, pulling out a gown and then replacing it. She bit on her lip. "Hmm. You have some gowns that are not too worn, but I am afraid their style is quite outdated."

Elle nodded. Would she make Elle's excuses to Henry and allow her to stay with the children?

"Come, let us see what there is in my wardrobe. They may not fit perfectly, but I think them better than the alternatives."

"I could not impose in such a way, my lady." Elle shook her head. "Perhaps you could just convey my regrets?"

Lady Kirtley sucked in a breath. "Nonsense. It is no imposition. Come along now. We do not wish to detain dinner any longer than we already have." She walked quickly down the corridor and to the staircase.

"Can I not just plead a headache, my lady?" Elle called after Lady Kirtley, but the woman's silence was reply enough.

In mere moments, they were standing in front of Lady Kirtley's wardrobe. Lady Kirtley pulled out gown after gown and held them up to Elle's front. "I think this is the one. It will look lovely with your coloring." She thrust the gold-colored gown toward the maid standing in the corner. "Heath, please hurry and see to Miss Carter. The entire party is waiting for her in the parlor.

Elle opened her mouth to object again, but Lady Kirtley patted Elle on the arm. "I think he wishes to be of service to you, Miss Carter. But sometimes men do not understand the waywardness of their good intentions."

Elle nodded. "Yes. He is a childhood friend. I am certain he is only trying to be kind."

She shrugged. "He is a formidable man and one I should not wish to disappoint. Do make haste."

Elle nearly snorted at the description. Formidable was hardly a word she would have used to describe Henry. He was too kind and caring to be truly formidable. But then, she had never known him as a baron. Perhaps the title had changed him or maybe it had been the war.

Elle automatically lifted her arms as Lady Kirtley's maid lifted her dress over her head and replaced it with the borrowed gown.

Elle closed her eyes. It had been a long time since someone had taken care of her needs. Oh, how she had missed it!

The maid fastened the few buttons in the back and then led her over to the dressing table. She removed the pins from the knot low on Elle's head. The brush moved in long, quick strokes until Elle could hear the low crackle of her hair. She closed her eyes, relishing in the moment, but knowing it would be over all too soon. And then she would be back in the school-room in her serviceable gowns.

"There you are, miss." The maid stepped back and allowed Elle a moment to examine herself in the mirror. Small braids formed a coronet around a knot at the crown of her head. A golden ribbon, perfectly matching the satin of her gown, was woven among the plaits encircling her head.

Elle swallowed as tears pricked at her eyes. Why did Henry have to do this? Why did he have to make her remember? This one moment would surely torture her for months to come. And all so Henry could think himself her hero. She clenched her fists. With friends like him, she was not in want of enemies.

Lady Kirtley nodded. "You look lovely, Miss Carter. Now, come along."

Elle followed along behind Lady Kirtley until they came to the parlor. As they stepped over the threshold, Elle scanned the room for Henry. Was he watching for her? Did he anticipate seeing appreciation and gratitude upon her face? He would be mistaken if he did.

She spotted him at the far side of the room speaking with a man Elle did not know. She squared her shoulders and moved quickly in his direction, hoping not to catch the eye of anyone else in attendance. She did not need to see the looks she knew were being cast in her direction.

When she reached Henry's side, she offered the stranger a brief smile and curtsy. "Pardon me, but I must speak with Lord Amesbury. It is quite urgent."

The man sketched a bow and stepped away, starting a conversation with someone else.

"How could you do this to me, my lord? I thought you were my friend?" Elle hissed through clenched teeth.

Henry's brows furrowed. "How could I do what?"

Elle scowled up at him. She opened her mouth but was

stopped by the booming voice of Lord Ryecombe. "It seems we are *finally* all here." Annoyance fell from his lips, and he raised a brow at her. "It has been requested that precedence not be observed tonight. Please, find your partner and proceed into the dining room. Hopefully, all the food has not gone cold." Again, his gaze shot her way.

Elle's face burned with humiliation. Why had he singled her out? While he had not called her by name, it was certain everyone in the room knew to whom he had been referring.

She turned to Henry, but he was no longer at her side. Instead, he was speaking with another lady, his arm already lifted for her to take.

Elle's face burned deeper. Why had Henry insisted she come down if he intended to abandon her for another? She thought back over the years of their acquaintance, trying to recall some time when she had wronged him. Only revenge could explain what he was doing to her now.

"Miss Carter." The Duke of Larmont dipped his head to her. "You look lovely tonight. I hope I did not cause you too much trouble by asking for you to join me."

Elle swallowed. It was Larmont who had requested she dress for dinner? Her eyes flicked from Henry to Larmont and back again. Her brain could not seem to let go of her earlier assumptions. They seemed far more likely than the reality she was facing just now.

"It was you?" The formidable comment from Lady Kirtley suddenly made much more sense.

He offered her a smirk, but she supposed it was meant to be a smile. "Yes. Who else would it have been? I am the only one with enough influence to make your presence here possible."

Elle's brow creased. "But why?" After the words were out, she questioned whether she should have said them. But she could not think of a single reason the duke would do such a thing.

He shrugged. "I suppose I feel I owe something to your father." He looked her up and down. "And once you are out of those servants' clothes, you are a very handsome woman. In that gown, I should not be completely opposed to being seen with you."

Elle swallowed. That had to have been the worst compliment she had ever received. Larmont, however, likely thought he was paying her rather high praise. How was one to reply to such a comment? Thank you seemed ill-fitting because she was not thankful and especially not to him. How could he think he had done her a service?

He reached out and grasped her elbow. "Come, we shall not have a decent seat if we do not hurry. It is the risk I took by requesting we not sit by rank."

"You did that as well?" Again, she wanted to ask why. Why would he do such a thing?

He let out a chuckle. "Of course. What good would it do me to request your presence if they forced you to eat in the kitchens because you no longer hold any rank?"

Elle nodded, her body numb. He had dressed her up in finery only to set her down verbally? But to what end? Were there not others of a more respectable nature whom he would prefer to berate and belittle? Must it be her? Could he see she was already in a fragile state and wished to capitalize on it?

He moved his hand to the small of her back and propelled her toward the door.

Elle stumbled along, hardly seeing anything. The food she ate held little flavor and she could not remember a single conversation from the table. Only the words of Larmont echoed through her brain. *What good would it do me to request your presence if they forced you to eat in the kitchens because you no longer hold any rank.*

She sat in the drawing room with the ladies, waiting for the men to return. Elle's head pounded until she thought what little she ate may come back up. But she dared not excuse herself. It would surely only prove Larmont's point that she was no longer worth the notice of society.

Once the men finally joined them, Larmont came and stood in front of her. "Miss Carter?"

Elle looked up.

His face creased. "Are you well? You look quite ill?" If she did not know better, she might think him concerned.

She shrugged. "I have a headache is all."

"I suppose this was rather a lot for one night. I think it best if you return to your rooms. We can speak more tomorrow." He bowed to her and moved off in the direction of the card table at the far side of the room.

We can speak more? That implied they had spoken much at dinner. But other than their brief conversation in the parlor, Elle could not remember him saying a single thing to her. Although she remembered little from the dining room. If he had spoken to her, what had he said? And what had she said in return?

Lady Kirtley stood and came over to her. "Miss Carter, the duke is correct. You do not look well. Shall I help you to your room?"

"No, thank you, my lady. I can manage on my own." She stood and made her way out of the room. Away from the drawing room, she paused and closed her eyes, breathing in the cooler air that hung in the corridor. She did not know what to think of the evening she'd endured. Perhaps it was best not to think on it.

She snuck into the children's rooms, dropping a kiss on

93

each of their brows before sneaking out again. In her own room, she carefully slid Lady Kirtley's dress up over her head and draped it carefully over the wardrobe door. She would see that it was returned tomorrow, along with the ribbon.

Elle knew she should be grateful to Larmont for his intentions—even if she did not understand them—but she could not make herself feel it. Perhaps when he found her tomorrow, she could express her gratitude but insist he stop at once.

She picked up the book that sat on her night table and sighed. She had missed story time with the children. The book fell open to where the silk ribbon rested on the story of the Frog King. She had promised Winston they could read it tonight. Perhaps tomorrow night she could fulfill the promise.

For now, she would try to forget about tonight. Forget about the feeling and longing that had resurfaced. Forget about the hurtful things Larmont had said to her. Forget that she was no longer welcome in the drawing rooms of Society. She closed her eyes, a tear slipping free and running down her cheek.

Unfortunately, such thoughts were not so easily forgotten.

CHAPTER TWELVE

Philip passed his mother the pot of potato soup, grimacing slightly at the poor fare. He had not anticipated this. He had believed he would have at least one of the horses sold, possibly even three of them by today. Perhaps he should have accepted Ryecombe's one hundred and twenty-five pounds. At least it would have been something.

Philip shoved his spoon into his mouth, questioning his rash behavior of this afternoon for at least the hundredth time. But every time, he came to the same conclusion. If he had accepted the earl's money, the man would never respect Philip as a businessman and would continue to underpay for his services.

"Soup, again? Can we not at least have some fish with it?" Grace dribbled the soup from her spoon. "Philip, you need to speak with Mrs. Heaton and let her know we will not tolerate this."

Philip looked up at his sister from beneath his lashes, but she did not see him as she continued to spoon up the soup and pour it back into the bowl again.

"He will do no such thing, Gracie. We are not above eating

a simple soup for dinner." His mother raised a brow at Grace and flicked a glance at Philip. "I find it a good reminder of where we came from and where we are now. If you must speak with Mrs. Heaton, Philip, tell her thank you."

Grace let out a huff. "If we wished to eat like we used to, then why did we leave Severdale and endeavor to become a part of the *bourgeoisie?*"

Philip looked at the ceiling. There were times he regretted sending Grace to Mrs. Bootle's School for Young Ladies. Not only had his sister misinterpreted it as a sign of wealth and become rather insufferable, but it had required him to trade a horse to the school as payment. He could have made more money on the horse if he had sold it outright. But educating his sister was important. Especially considering that she'd had more to learn than most of the other girls there.

Philip ran a hand along the back of his neck. Had they had these kinds of worries when his father had been the stable master at Severdale? Food was simpler—as his mother called it —but they had never feared they would starve.

He stared at his parents sitting on the other side of the table. At least he did not *believe* they had ever feared starvation. But he did not rightly know. It was not something they would have discussed with him.

He dipped his head down and sighed. Had he been foolish to think this would ever work? If the stables were not succeeding after nearly eight years, would they ever be successful? He had thought his stables would be widely known by now, yet he still felt as if every sale was only staving off the inevitable. The last year had been harder than those before it, but still, they had made it. What if this was it? What if his business never became more successful?

Grace let out an irritated sigh.

Philip opened his mouth, intent on telling his sister to stop her whining, but his mother spoke first.

"Who was the lady with the children in the stables, Son?" His mother smiled at him. From the look in her eyes, Philip was certain she already knew the answer to the question. His father had surely provided her with plenty of particulars.

Philip tilted his head slightly and smiled at her. This was her way of trying to change the subject. And he would be grateful were this not an even less desirable subject than the last. He knew, inevitably, his mother would steer the discussion toward marriage. She always did, and he could not see how tonight should be any different.

"Her name is Miss Carter." He thought about slurring the miss, hoping his mother would not catch on that she was unmarried, but as his father had surely already told her, it seemed fruitless to even try. "She is staying at Briarwood for the earl's house party." Philip tried for a look of disinterest but was certain he failed completely, so he looked at his soup instead.

"She is a guest at the earl's house party?" There was a look of defeat on his mother's face, but her voice had far too much merriment. She was trying to wheedle the information out of him. "She looks young to have so many children. Especially the boy. He looked to be at least seven or eight."

"She is not their mother. She is their governess." He glanced at his father and raised a brow. "As I am certain you already know."

His mother's eyes lightened. "Is she now? A governess?" She leaned forward on the table and stared at Philip with hawkish eyes. "Perhaps I should invite her over for tea."

Philip sat back and folded his arms across his chest. "And what would she do with the children, Mama? She is not at Briarwood to socialize. She is there to educate and take care of the children. I doubt she will accept such an invitation." He felt a slight niggle of guilt in his stomach. Perhaps he should tell his mother he had already invited them all over for tea, but that would surely only make her believe her plans were viable.

"Just because she is a governess does not mean she is content with her life. And you are not so handsome for nothing, I am certain." His mother looked at him with the eyes of an adoring mother. "I only wish to see you happily situated."

"I am happily situated, Mother."

She huffed and gave him a bland expression. "I mean I wish to see you married."

"I know what you meant." He sighed, as he usually did whenever they had this conversation. It was like a theatrical performance that was repeatedly the same. "I must first make the horses a success so I have something to offer a lady."

His mother raised her chin. "You have very much to offer, even without considering your horses."

"Leave the boy be, Harriet." Philip's father finally jumped —or rather dipped his toe—into the conversation.

He glanced over at his father to see a look of both guilt and contrition. He should feel bad for putting Philip in this position.

Philip sat back in his chair and fiddled with the utensils next to his plate. He could not place all the blame on his father. After all, Philip was the one who had extended Miss Carter the invitation to come. It was likely this conversation would have happened with or without his father's involvement.

"But she is such a handsome woman. And she carries herself so gracefully."

His father cleared his throat.

"Oh, very well. I shall not say another word on the matter . . . for now." His mother lifted a brow and pinched her mouth shut.

THE STABLE MASTER'S SON

"Son, perhaps we can retire to your study after dinner," his Father said. "There is a matter I wish to discuss with you."

Philip nodded. Most of the time he enjoyed talking about the business and, more particularly, the horses. But today? He was blasted sick of it. He wished they could retire to the parlor and sit quietly before the fire, thinking of nothing at all.

"Then we shall retire to the parlor and leave you two to discuss business." His mother waited until his father stood and pulled out her chair. He held out a hand to assist her and placed a kiss on her cheek as he guided her toward the doorway.

She smiled up at him with such love, even after all their years of marriage.

Philip's chest tightened with a familiar pang, and he looked away. The annoying pang seemed to grow a little with each passing year. While he tried to seem as if he did not care or even wished to avoid such entanglements, in truth, he longed for what his parents shared. But there did not seem to be the time or money for such things. Nor had he found a woman he deemed...worthy of his attentions.

Philip stood and helped Grace from her seat. "I can speak to Mrs. Heaton if you do not wish to do so, Philip." She looked at him as if he disappointed her.

"You will do no such thing. I am the master of this house, and you would do well to remember it."

She smirked. "What will you do if I forget? Turn me out?"

Philip smirked back. "No, but I may finally concede and give Mr. Yardley my blessing."

Grace's eyes widened. "You would not dare!"

Philip grinned and raised a brow. "Would I not?"

"You are the cruelest brother there ever was." She stomped around the table.

"I have not given my consent . . . yet. Do not make me change my mind."

Grace tucked her hand into her mother's arm and the two left the room, his mother's soothing voice fading as they moved down the corridor. It seemed he had made neither of the ladies in his home happy tonight.

"That was unkind, Son," Father said. "You know Mr. Yardley is not a suitable match for Grace."

Philip shrugged. "I know no such thing. It is not so mismatched as you think. Mr. Yardley is a respectable barrister and for some reason, he is enamored with Gracie. She could do much worse, Father." He scratched at his earlobe. "Indeed, I cannot think she will do any better. Not considering our circumstances."

His father sighed. "Perhaps on paper and in here"—he tapped his head—"the match is acceptable. But it is not acceptable here." He touched his chest.

Philip touched his own head. "Many matches are formed here, Father. Not everyone can have what you and Mama do." He shrugged. "I was only putting her in her place. But I wish she would consider Mr. Yardley." He shook his head as he stepped into the corridor. "It should thrill her to have secured the affections of such a man. He would take good care of her."

"I believe your mother would be content if *you* would choose someone. Even if it was only with your head." His father gave him a bland look.

"I need not hear the lecture from you also, Father. Mama has made her wishes perfectly clear."

They moved into his study, and his father sat in the chair across from Philip's desk.

"Must we be so formal? Can we not sit in front of the fire where it is more comfortable?" Philip pulled at his cravat.

"But I am coming to you as your stable master. Not as your father."

Philip let out a sigh. "In my eyes, they are the same." He relented and moved around his desk, dropping heavily into the chair. "What did you need to discuss with me?"

"Mr. Larkin came by yesterday. He is interested in purchasing Lucy Mae."

Philip pushed his lips out on a sigh. "But she is not yet trained. It will be six months before we may even begin."

His father nodded. "Yes, he understands. He wishes to take on the task himself."

The hairs on the back of Philip's neck lifted. Many men *thought* they could train a horse. But it was not so simple a task. "He wishes to train her himself? Has he any experience in such things?"

Philip's father shrugged. "He claims to know what he is about—said he has broken and trained several horses."

Philip guffawed. "I find that difficult to believe. I saw the man last week in town. He nearly beat his horse to make the poor creature do his bidding."

His father licked his lips. "Be that as it may, I believe we need to consider it."

Philip shook his head firmly. "No, I will not."

"What choice do we have? We need the sale." His father leaned slightly forward.

"We can only sell her for a fraction of her worth if we sell now. Not to mention it cannot be good for our reputation if he muddles the breaking and then tells someone he purchased her from us." Philip raked a hand through his hair. "And that is nothing to what her life will be with someone like him." He stood up, placing his palms on the desktop, and leaned forward. "I do not care if we are starving. I will not allow that man to ruin one of my horses."

"Do you have another plan?" His father looked at him. There was resignation in his eyes, but also a hint of . . . disappointment? How could his father be disappointed that Philip would not sell a horse into abuse?

"I have several, actually. Do not believe me sitting on my hands waiting for something to come about." He settled back into his seat. "I have given the earl until tomorrow to either purchase the bays for the price we agreed on, or I will sell them to someone else."

"Is there someone else?" His father leaned forward, a suspicious look in his eyes. "Or is that just something you are saying to spur the earl into action?"

Philip lifted his chin. "Yes, there is another interested party. A Lord Kirtley will visit the stable tomorrow, and if the earl has not put up the money by then, Kirtley has offered to purchase the bays. He said he may be interested in some of the other horses as well." Philip cleared his suddenly parched throat. "And I have not lost complete hope in Larmont. I believe I have someone who might be of assistance on that front."

He just had to discover the best way to ask her. He had tried to broach the subject when she had been at the stables today, but it had not felt natural. And they were not well enough acquainted to ask such favors outright.

Was it too much to hope that the children would come with their father? If they did, would Miss Carter come also? Perhaps Philip should do as his mother suggested and send her a formal invitation to tea.

The only problem with that notion was that he had no tea. Which was why he needed Miss Carter's help. It was a rather vicious circle, was it not?

CHAPTER THIRTEEN

Elle sat next to Katie. They both stared at the canvas in front of them. "What do you wish to paint today?"

Katie looked disinterested. "Nothing. We have been at this for days, and it looks no different. I have no talent for painting, Miss Carter."

Elle sighed. Winston was out on a ride with his father, and Sophia was playing with blocks in the nursery with a few of the other children whose parents were attending the house party. No one would miss them if she and Katie went out for a walk.

"Put aside your oils, my lady. There is a break in the clouds. If we hurry, we may take a turn before the next storm begins."

Katie let out a whoop and Elle tilted her head to the side, her mouth pursed slightly. "A lady does not make such sounds." She motioned Katie toward the door. "Besides, we do not wish to disrupt the others and have them want to go outside as well. That would not do in the least."

Katie covered up the paints they had already placed on the mixing board.

"Do not think yourself so clever. When we return, you will

set to work on this painting." Elle looked outside. "But perhaps something on our turn about the grounds will help to inspire you."

Katie nodded. "I should think it will, Miss Carter." She was at the door before Elle could push their stools closer to the easel.

They collected their bonnets and spencers, tying their ribbons as they walked down the staircase and into the entryway. Katie rarely moved with such efficiency. She must truly hate painting.

Elle frowned. How did someone hate painting? It seemed a most unlikely notion.

They pushed outside and made their way down the stone stairs. Elle paused on the lane. "Where do you wish to go, my lady?"

Katie looked in both directions and pointed, "I think we should walk that way."

Elle nodded, not completely surprised they were walking toward the rock wall that separated Briarwood from Greystone. She moved in next to her charge. Katie was young still; at only six, she still had many years of teaching ahead of her. But she was a thoughtful girl, more prone to read in a quiet corner than play with other children. Elle had often thought she would have liked such traits in a younger sister. Although, she would not wish for anyone else to go through what Elle had.

"Why did you not want to go down to dinner last night?" Katie glanced over at Elle quickly, then returned her gaze to the path.

"It was not proper."

"Why was it not proper? Was not your father a viscount?"

The questions were innocent enough, but they still felt like pin pricks to Elle's heart. "Yes, my father was a viscount, and my brother now holds the title." And lives on the estate and rides all the horses. Although, he had likely had to sell all the horses just to pay the few remaining servants.

Elle had not heard from her brother in over a year, but she could not think his situation had changed so very much. If it had, would he not have sent word that she could return home? Not that it would change anything for her. Her reputation was irreparable.

Elle shook her head. What would her parents think of their children's situations? "But I have taken employment. Many believe that of more import than who my father was."

Katie kicked at a stone. "That does not seem right. I think your manners much better than many of the ladies here, and you are prettier as well."

Elle smiled. Sometimes she wished she could embrace Katie as she would a little sister. Usually, it was for the girl's benefit, but sometimes, like then, it was for Elle's. It had been a long time since she had felt a closeness with someone. But it would not be proper to show such affection toward one of her charges. She was the paid governess, after all. "Thank you, my lady. I believe you will be quite the loveliest of ladies when you make your come-out." Elle hurried to add, "But not for some time yet. Do not grow up too soon."

Katie pointed off in the distance. "Is that not Mr. Jenkins?"

Elle's pulse ticked up, and she squinted. "It could be. That is his land. But it seems more likely it is an undergardener." There was no need to feel anticipation over an undergardener. She mentally shook herself. As there should not be anticipation over Mr. Jenkins.

The man crouched down on his haunches, doing something with an animal. "Perhaps it is the gamekeeper," Elle amended.

They continued in his direction, the low wall and ha-ha the only things separating them.

As they came closer, Elle searched for any clues that it may, indeed, be Mr. Jenkins. He was an odd man. One who seemed perfectly content to do chores more suited for a servant. Yet, he was the landowner. She had never met anyone like him before.

They came to the rock wall and paused. "Will you not call out to him?" Katie looked up at Elle.

Elle shook her head. "If it is Mr. Jenkins, he is obviously busy. We need not disturb him." Besides, it was likely *not* Mr. Jenkins. And what would a gamekeeper think of her calling out to him, a stranger?

The man reached up to run the back of his hand across his brow, turning his face slightly in their direction. Elle's breath caught in her throat.

It *was* Mr. Jenkins.

Her knees felt wobbly, which was completely ridiculous. She chided herself for being such a ninny. Why must she be so . . . so giddy at just the sight of him? It was unheard of and completely unacceptable.

"Mr. Jenkins," Katie called out and raised her hand in a wave. What was she doing?

Mr. Jenkins looked over and Elle could see his smile. Her stomach warmed. Good gracious, she was an idiot.

He stood up and walked over to them. "Good day, ladies." He smiled down at Katie. "Lady Katie, it is a pleasure to see you again."

Katie beamed up at him.

"Mr. Jenkins looks to be busy. We will not disturb you any longer." Elle took Katie's hand.

"Do not go," he nearly shouted at them. "I am finished now." He hooked his finger over his shoulder toward the cow, his smile growing larger. "She was my last cow to deliver. Nearly doubled the herd this year." His chest puffed out as he clasped his hands behind him and bounced on the balls of his feet.

Elle tilted her head and looked at the filth covering the front of his clothing. Large muddy patches colored the knees of his breeches. He was here seeing to the animal's delivery? She frowned. Was not that a job for the gamekeeper? This man continued to perplex her.

"What brings you out this morning?"

Katie smiled shyly. "We are hoping to receive inspiration for our paintings."

"Ah, you are painters, are you?" His smile widened.

Katie shrugged. "Miss Carter is quite proficient, but I cannot boast as much."

Mr. Jenkins looked to Elle. "You paint?"

"Lady Katie is being kind. I enjoy painting, but I am not a proficient." Elle felt her face heat.

Katie nodded furiously beside her. "Oh, but you are. Your paintings are lovely."

Mr. Jenkins's brows rose. "My sister enjoys painting. I could introduce you to her. Perhaps you could join us for tea as we discussed yesterday?"

Elle's head dropped to the side, and she studied him. She had not thought him in earnest yesterday. Why would he invite her for tea? He was not attending the house party, nor was his sister. And Elle was not attending as a guest but as a governess. It was not as if she could excuse herself from her duties so she might take tea with this man's sister. It would be a sure way to find herself in need of a new position.

"While I am certain that would be lovely, I do not believe it possible. I am here to teach and watch over the children. Not socialize with the local . . . gentry." She drew out the last word, uncertain if he really qualified.

He tilted his head to the side. "I see no reason why you could not bring the children. My father and I can help to entertain Lord Culpepper while Lady Katie enjoys the company of you and my sister. Indeed, I am certain my mother would love to join you as well." His ears pinked. "She was asking about you at dinner last evening."

"She asked after me?" Elle did not how she felt about being discussed by Mr. Jenkins family, even if she was slightly flattered that his mother had taken an interest in her. But just what kind of interest was it? She knew many among the *ton* had talked about her situation—about her family's situation—but to know that this man who was practically a stranger was speaking of her to his mother left her uneasy. "How does she even know about me?"

Mr. Jenkins shrugged. "I believe she saw you leaving the stable yard yesterday. She asked after your name."

Elle's shoulders dropped a fraction. Then they had not been discussing her family's fall from society.

"Will you consent? May I tell my mother and sister you will join them tomorrow?" He looked so hopeful, it was hard not to accept on the spot. But Elle refrained.

"I will need to look at the children's study schedules. Especially that of Lord Culpepper. He is to have a tutor at the end of the month, and I do not wish for him to be behind in his studies."

Mr. Jenkins's smile faltered slightly, but he nodded. "Ah, yes, that *is* important. I will have my sister send around a card with a more official invitation, but if you are unable to arrange it, we will understand."

Elle nodded, and they both stood firmly in place, smiling and nodding to each other again. Why was this how they always ended up—nodding at each other like a pair of nodcocks? Finally, Elle pulled her gaze away and cleared her throat. "We should return to the house before the storms comes." She glanced at the dark clouds in the distance.

Placing a hand to her face, she could feel the warmth radiating even through her gloves. What was the matter with her? Why did she react in such a way when she was around this man? She could not explain it. He was someone who would have been decidedly beneath her before her fallen state. Though now it seemed he was likely above her.

She looked around the estate, with the sizable house and the land surrounding it. Her throat tightened. This man may not be as respectable as others of her acquaintance, but he was a gentleman nonetheless, and that put him out of her reach. An alliance between them would only tarnish his reputation. She would be nothing but a burden to him.

She clasped her hands together and stepped to the side on the pretense of returning to the house. But in truth, she could not bear staring at him a moment longer.

It was strange how the simple actions of others had changed her life so completely. The path she had chosen—not that she had many others to choose from—ensured that she would never again be welcomed into the ranks of society. And she would bring anyone she tied herself to down with her.

Elle bit her bottom lip and squeezed her eyes shut tightly. She would not cry in such a public manner. She had learned over the years to keep her emotions in check. But there were times such as this when the completeness of her loss was so overwhelming, it nearly took her breath away.

She swallowed hard, tightening her hand around Katie's. "Come, my lady. Let us return to the house."

"Ouch." Katie pulled her hand from Elle's and looked up, a frown turning down her lips. "But I do not yet feel inspired."

"Perhaps we will see something on the way back to satisfy you." Elle dipped her head. "Good day, Mr. Jenkins."

As Elle tugged Katie away from the rock wall and Mr. Jenkins's property, Katie looked back over her shoulder. Elle knew she was looking at Mr. Jenkins and she had an overwhelming urge to do the same. But how would that look?

Instead, she lifted her chin and refused to give in to her desires. Now was not the time to harbor tendrés—to pretend that her life could be any different than it was. No, she had given up on that notion years ago.

The more distance she put between them, the easier it was to relax and take a more sedate pace on their walk. She pointed out trees silhouetted against the horizon and talked to Katie about the best way to paint them.

Katie nodded along as Elle spoke, but Elle did not miss the girl's sly glances over her shoulder. Was Mr. Jenkins still watching them?

"Miss Carter?" The sound of her name ended any fantasies she had about Mr. Jenkins's watchful eyes.

Elle turned and smiled falsely at the duke.

He lifted a hand to block the sun from his eyes. "Who is that man? Was he bothering you? I shall speak to Ryecombe about it if you wish."

Elle shook her head. "Not at all. Indeed, the opposite is likely true. It was we who were bothering him." She took the chance to glance back to the place she had been speaking with Mr. Jenkins. He had moved away from the wall and kneeled in the field beside his cow and new calf. Even from this distance, she could see him look up at them from time to time. "You need not speak to Lord Ryecombe about him."

Larmont squinted into the distance. "Are you certain? It is not wholly proper for a gamekeeper to be socializing with you and your charges."

Elle tilted her head. "He is not the gamekeeper. Mr. Jenkins is the owner of that estate."

"Ah, I should have known. Mr. Jenkins is rather odd." He grunted. "I understood when he insisted he groomed his horses himself to make sure they looked their best, but to be out in the fields with his livestock?"

A defensiveness on the man's behalf reared up inside Elle. "He takes an interest in his herd, that is all. I think it a sign of an attentive master."

Larmont grunted. "It's highly improper, and he will never receive any respect from society if he does not stop." He shrugged and clasped his hands behind him. "But let us not speak any longer of Mr. Jenkins. May I join you on your walk?"

Elle nodded but not before looking one last time over her shoulder. Mr. Jenkins no longer seemed interested in them, his head lowered over the calf.

Elle turned back and smiled a smile she did not feel in the least. At least not toward the Duke of Larmont.

CHAPTER FOURTEEN

Philip tried not to watch Miss Carter as she walked alongside the duke, but he could not stop himself from the occasional glance. *Occasional* might have been a bit of an understatement, for several times, Miss Carter had nearly caught him staring at her.

Which would not do.

He bent low over the calf and pretended to be examining it. He had already made the examination after the cow had birthed the calf, so the action was completely unnecessary. But what else could he pretend to do? He could not seem to leave, not until Miss Carter was out of view.

As if she knew his thoughts, Miss Carter, Lady Katie, and the duke moved around the corner of the house and out of sight. Philip placed a hand to the burning pit in his stomach.

Philip sighed and pushing himself to standing while glancing one last time toward Briarwood. Had she not said she and Lady Katie were returning to the house? Why, then, had they moved around to the back gardens? He shook his head. It was none of his concern what Miss Carter did or with whom.

He rubbed his hands together, dusting off the dirt and other grime. He was acting like a nodcock pining after some chit. He was not interested in a match at present. He could not even think on it until the stables were providing a consistent income. He only needed Miss Carter for her influence over Larmont. That was all.

Philip turned back toward the stables. Another buyer was to come and look at Philip's horses today. Philip would do better to curry the horses and ensure a sale than linger his thoughts on Miss Carter.

He pulled out his pocket watch and checked the time. The earl only had an hour before Philip offered the bays to Lord Kirtley.

Philip rolled his shoulders and twisted his head from side to side. Why had the earl made this such a difficult situation? Selling the bays to someone else would surely incur the man's displeasure—more than his usual amount. But what was Philip to do? He could not sell his horses for what the earl had sent along as payment. Not only would Philip lose money on the deal, but what would it say to Philip's business sense? Word would surely spread that he was a weak negotiator. Every gentleman who came to Greystone Stables in the future would think they could set their own price, no matter how offensively low it was.

No. This was Philip's business, and he could not allow neighborly considerations to take precedence. It was not as if the earl cared his offer might make Philip displeased. So then, why was Philip so worried that he had displeased Ryecombe?

Philip sucked in a deep breath and ran a hand through his hair. Because he did not have the power to destroy the earl's good name, as the earl could Philip's. It would not be beyond the pale for the earl to make it known to his friends that they should not purchase a horse from Philip.

He pushed through the doors of the stable. If the duke purchased Black Thunder, his word would far outweigh the earl's. Perhaps this Lord Kirtley would prove to be an ally as well.

Philip leaned against the railing of the nearest stall and slumped forward. Why did he feel as if it were him against the earl? So much for neighborly kindness.

He picked up a brush and went to work on the bays. He would see that they were shining and hitched up to the curricle so Lord Kirtley might handle the bays and see how well-suited they really were.

"What are you shining up the bays for, Son? Did the earl finally come through on the price?" His father stood off to the side.

Philip shook his head. "No. Although he still has an hour before I offer them up to someone else."

"Then why the special attention?" His father put his elbows up on the rail and crossed his arms. "Seems a waste of time."

Philip did not glance up from his brushing. "I told you last night that a lord attending Ryecombe's house party asked if he could come and see the horses this afternoon. He said if the earl did not buy the bays, he would. I wish to have them ready and hitched so the man might see them at their best." He paused and looked at his father over the back of the horse. "I am determined to sell a horse today, Father. Even if it is only a carriage horse."

His father nodded and pushed off the rail. "Then I shall see to the other bay. Are you to offer up Black Thunder as well?"

Philip swiped the brush across the horse's side. "Not yet. I still have hopes that the duke will purchase him. I have just over a week until the house party ends, and I intend to convince him before he leaves." He did not know how he planned to do such a thing, but he knew he had to try. He just had to figure out a way. Miss Carter still seemed a likely solution, especially since he'd just seen her walk to the gardens with the man.

His father was just fastening the buckle on the second bay when Philip heard the clip-clop of horse hooves on the lane. He stepped out of the stables just as Lord Kirtley dismounted.

Kirtley looked around for someone to hand his horse off to, but no one appeared. Philip bit his lip. Where was Jim?

Philip jogged over. "Let me take your horse for you, my lord." He looked around. It was not like his stable boy to be absent. And why, of all the times for him to disappear, was it happening now?

Lord Kirtley nodded. He said nothing, but Philip noticed a slight uptick in his brows.

"I, uh, I do not know where the stable boy is. But I should not like to keep you waiting." Philip cleared his throat. "He is quite young and still in training." Why was he continuing to ramble on? Philip's servants were not any of this man's business.

"Yes, young boys can be rather unreliable." Lord Kirtley smiled.

"It's not that he is unreliable, my lord. He is still learning which tasks take precedence. I am certain he is busy doing another task somewhere around the yard." He was defending his stable boy? How would that look to someone of Lord Kirtley's status? "I am certain once he learns, he will be a fine stable boy."

Lord Kirtley continued to smile. Was the man always a pleasant sort of fellow? Or was he simply smiling to hide the awkwardness of the situation—an awkwardness which was completely Philip's doing?

"You came to see my horses, did you not? Why do we not set to it, shall we?"

Lord Kirtley rubbed his hands together. "I can hardly wait. I confess, I nearly came yesterday. After listening to Winston speak so highly of what he saw when he visited with Miss Carter, it was difficult to wait until our appointed time."

Philip grinned. He knew he liked Lord Culpepper. Motioning Kirtley inside, Philip led him over to the bays. "Your son is a good judge of horseflesh?" If he found Philip's horses exceptional, then Philip was inclined to say he was.

He looked over at the man. The boy could not be much over nine or ten. It surprised Philip that Kirtley would place such value on the boy's opinion.

"I wouldn't send him to Tattersall's unattended, but yes, I believe he is a good judge."

Interesting.

"These are the bays you saw the other day. I thought you may wish to try them out for yourself."

Lord Kirtley shook his head. "I wish I could, but you already sold this pair."

Philip shook his head. "You are misinformed, my lord. We did not complete the sale."

Lord Kirtley reached into his coat pocket and withdrew a letter. "Lord Ryecombe wished me to give this to you. And he asked me to convey his regrets for its delay." Kirtley eyed Philip. "I do not know what you said to the man, but it was effective."

Philip smiled and took the offered paper. He fingered the seal and made to put it in his pocket. But what if the earl was tricking him? Philip could not afford to let Lord Kirtley leave without the bays if Ryecombe still had not come through.

He nodded to his father, who stood back in the shadows of the stables.

117

"Please put this in my study." He handed over the letter as he eyed his father, hoping he understood what Philip was asking him to do.

"Yes, sir." His father moved away but not out of sight.

Philip ran a hand down the bays. "I am sorry to have misled you about these two being available."

He glanced over even as his father cracked the seal on Ryecombe's letter. His father glanced over the contents then nodded to Philip, a smile spreading across his face.

Ryecombe had come through.

Philip's shoulders relaxed, and he took in a deep breath.

It would not place them close to the upper stations of society—not even the lower ones, really—but it would allow them to live. And hopefully, it would be the first of many sales that month.

Philip schooled his features, hoping the man in front of him did not notice the change.

Lord Kirtley smiled wider. "While I wish I were the one to take them off your hands, I am glad you and Lord Ryecombe came to an *agreement*." The way he said agreement made Philip wonder if Lord Kirtley knew something he was not sharing.

"I do not suppose they are your only horses?"

Philip shook his head and chuckled. "No, no. There are many more in the stables. Come and have a look."

The two men moved through the doorway, squinting while their eyes adjusted to the dim light. Kirtley let out a low whistle, and Philip looked back at him. His eyes had widened slightly, and a smile slid across his face. "This is quite the stable you have here, Mr. Jenkins."

Philip's shoulders lifted, and his chest expanded. "Thank you, my lord. I have worked hard to make it such." He pulled his gaze away from his horses. "Now, where would you like to start?"

Lord Kirtley pointed to a blue roan. "That is a fine horse there."

Philip nodded. "Perhaps if I knew what you needed the horse for, I could point you in the right direction."

Lord Kirtley clasped his hands behind his back and walked toward the rear of the stable. "My wife recently lost her horse. It was an old mare, one her father gave her as a girl. It has been difficult for her." He stopped at several of the stalls, staring at each horse before moving on to the next. "I should like to buy her a replacement."

Philip nodded. "I should think there will never be a replacement for such an animal. But perhaps you may find her a new friend." Philip stopped in front of a dapple-gray horse. "This one here is very gentle. Indeed, I would feel comfortable allowing your daughter, Lady Katie, to ride her. And as you can see, she is just the right height."

"What is her height?" Kirtley asked.

"Fifteen-one." Philip ran a hand down the horse's flanks. "And you will not find a kinder soul." He reached into a nearby box and pulled out a handful of oats. The horse nibbled at the offered treat.

Kirtley stepped next to the horse. "Yes, she seems to be the gentle sort. Is she a decent jumper? While my wife does not like to race, thank the heavens, she does like to jump occasionally."

Philip grinned. "I believe your wife will find Rainy Day more than adequate. But if she is unsatisfied, you may bring her back, and I will return your money."

Usually, Philip felt apprehension when he offered such terms to people. Not because he did not have confidence in his horses—

he knew they were quality creatures—but because he did not have confidence in the buyers. People often had the strangest reasons for being dissatisfied. *He lifts his tail when he canters. His front legs are darker than his back.* The rich were an eccentric bunch.

He had not mentioned the policy to the earl because he figured the man would simply use it to pay less. But he felt no such hesitation with Lord Kirtley. The man seemed honest, and Philip felt confident he would only return the horse if his wife truly were unhappy, though how anyone could be unhappy with Rainy Day, Philip could not fathom.

Kirtley nodded. "I like a man who stands behind his horse." He furrowed his brow. "How much is she?"

Philip licked his lips. "She is ninety pounds, my lord. Although, with the help you have provided with the earl and the bays, I believe I can let you have her for eighty."

Kirtley shook his head. "Nonsense. I will pay what she is worth. I did not drive the price up with Ryecombe merely to earn myself a cheaper price on my purchase. I did it because that is what the animals are worth." He ran his hand down the horse's legs and lifted each hoof to inspect. He looked in her eyes and mouth, then rubbed her on the nose. "I believe you have yourself a deal, Mr. Jenkins." He stuck out his hand, and Philip grasped it. Two sales today. It was a grand day, indeed. Now if only Larmont would come through, Philip could breathe easily for a month or two.

CHAPTER FIFTEEN

Philip entered the parlor and sat down next to the writing desk.

Grace scribbled at a paper, then lifted the feather and swished it about her chin.

"What are you doing, Gracie?"

She looked over at him with a slight pout—an expression she undoubtedly learned from Miss Martindale. The girl was a year younger than Gracie but was already more than proficient in the ways of flirting. Philip was not sure if that came with her station in society, or if it was a trait all her own. Regardless, he was certain she would return from her first London Season with a husband. Philip shook his head. The poor nodcock.

"I thought we should have a dinner party. I was making a list of those we must invite."

Philip sucked in a deep breath. "And was I to have a say in this?"

Grace smirked. "Of course. But I cannot imagine why you would object."

Philip closed his eyes. His sister vexed him more and more

of late. She had taken to this role of young lady far too readily, forgetting that she was not a lady of means nor an heiress with unlimited funds. This was also surely the influence of Miss Martindale or perhaps Mrs. Bootle.

Philip took the quill from her hand and pulled the paper toward him.

"What are you doing?" She peered over at him.

"I am making a list of reasons this dinner party is not to be."

She huffed and snatched the quill back. "How am I to find a match if you will never allow us to take part in social events?"

Philip gestured to the room around them. "Look around you, Gracie. Where do you suggest we host this dinner party? We have no dining room. At least not one without cracked paint and peeling paper."

Grace dropped the quill to the table. "And why do we not? We have lived here for nearly eight years. Why have you not made the improvements so we might entertain our neighbors?"

Philip ran a hand through his hair. "Gracie, we have been over this. The horses must come first because they provide the living. And until they can provide enough for us to live on *and* make improvements, the improvements must wait."

She pushed out her lips in a pout. "I will be on the shelf before you make the improvements."

He sighed. "You are not prohibited from all social events. Did you not attend the assembly just last week?"

She shrugged. "That could hardly be considered a social event, Philip. Hardly any of the desirable society was in attendance. Miss Martindale was not even there." She frowned. "The only tolerable gentleman was Mr. Yardley." She tilted her head in exasperation. "And you know how I feel about him."

Philip smiled. "He seems an amiable man. And he seems to have taken an interest in you. Why must you frown when you speak of him?"

She huffed. "He is only a barrister, Philip. Miss Martindale says I am handsome enough to secure the affections of a much better match. She said she believes I might even marry a baron." She clasped her hands in front of her chest, her eyes taking on a dreamy sort of look.

"I believe you should stop listening to Miss Martindale. I find the notion highly improbable that a baron would offer for someone with no dowry and very little breeding."

Her mouth dropped open, and tears pooled in the bottom of her eyes. "How can you be so cruel? I have breeding. Did I not attend Mrs. Bootle's?"

Philip shook his head and clenched his fists under the table. "I am not trying to be cruel, Gracie. I am trying to set realistic expectations for you. Mr. Yardley would be an excellent match for you. I believe he could make you very happy."

Gracie pushed out from the table. "I shall never be happy with the likes of Mr. Yardley. Why can you not see that I am destined for greater things? Miss Martindale can see it, but my own brother cannot."

She turned to leave, but Philip caught her arm. "Gracie, I did not mean to insinuate you were not desirable. You are worthy of a duke just as you are. But life is not always fair. Those in society do not always see what is beneath the surface. They only see the money attached to the lady. I simply do not wish to see you disillusioned."

She sniffed.

Philip stifled a groan. She had taken to such theatrics these past few years. Aside from having no money, what kind of man would wish to yoke himself to one so prone to dramatics? "Perhaps we may put aside the dinner invitations for now."

She opened her mouth to object, but he lifted a finger.

"And instead focus on a small gathering for tea? I had

thought perhaps to make it *al fresco* if the weather holds. What do you think of that?"

Grace tilted her head to the side and pulled her bottom lip between her teeth. "May I invite Miss Martindale?"

Philip's nostrils flared slightly. "If it would make you happy." The bothersome, meddling girl would likely make Philip quite mad, but what was that to Gracie's happiness?

Grace smiled. "An *al fresco* tea sounds diverting. Who else are we to invite?"

Philip's shoulders relaxed. "There is a governess visiting Briarwood. I had thought to invite her and her charges to join us. I think mother would do well to have some fresh air also. Do you think you might send a note over and ask Miss Carter if tomorrow is acceptable?"

Grace studied Philip, and he saw a hint of the intelligent girl his sister used to be instead of the insipid girl she had become of late. "Why are you inviting a governess and her charges?"

Philip's cheeks heated. He blustered. "Do not look at me in such a way. She is friends with the Duke of Larmont. I am hoping I can gain some information that will help me convince the duke to buy Black Thunder."

Grace continued to stare. "That is all?"

Philip nodded furiously. "Of course that is all. What other reason could there be?"

Grace raised a brow, looking very much like their mother when she did. "I can think of several. None of which involve a horse or a duke." Perhaps he *did* prefer the insipid girl.

He shrugged. "They are not correct, whatever your reasons. The horses are involved with every decision I make." He pushed himself to standing and slapped several coins down on the desk in front of her. "Now I believe I promised you a new bonnet."

Grace let out a squeal of excitement. "Oh, Philip! You are in earnest?"

He nodded his head. "I said when I sold Black Thunder I would allow you to purchase a new bonnet. While I did not sell the horse I had intended, I believe I can spare enough money for you to have your bonnet." He nodded to the quill in her hand. "Please inform me when you receive their acceptance." He turned but stopped before the door. "And inform Mrs. Heaton when you have an answer also. I should like her to make some cakes or scones for the event."

He caught the quirk of Grace's lips as he turned back toward the door. She thought she was clever and had discovered a secret. But the joke was on her because there was no secret to uncover. Philip only wished to elicit Miss Carter's help.

CHAPTER SIXTEEN

M iss Carter held on to Katie and Sophia's hands. Why had she not sent their regrets to Mr. Jenkins and taken tea in the schoolroom with all the other children and governesses? Black clouds covered the sky, and it was sure to begin raining again at any moment. She pulled her shoulders together to ward off the cold.

She was only making the journey so the children could see the horses. Besides, it was rare for the children to be invited to tea at someone else's home. It was a chance to teach them the proper way of it. Those were the only reasons she had agreed.

Their outings to visit the stables at Greystone had made an impression on all the children. Winston seemed less anxious. Katie had started to paint a lovely field with a calf lying next to its mother. And Sophia took better naps after their visits. It seemed a productive use of their time.

And besides, the invitation was from *Miss* Jenkins.

Elle was not certain Mr. Jenkins would even be in attendance. Had he not said he and his father would take Winston out to the stables so the ladies could take tea together?

She was not calling on him and he had not asked her to come alone. She was here with the children. She must not assume something that was not there. Elle frowned. And she must not allow herself to form any partiality.

They crossed through the break in the stone wall and onto Greystone's property. All the rain they had received left the fields smelling of earth and grass. It was lovely, even if it was chilly, to be outside. It almost made Elle sad to be returning indoors for tea.

There was a call from somewhere in the distance, and Elle lifted her hand to shade her eyes from the sun. Under a large chestnut tree stood a lady, waving her hand back and forth.

Elle smiled at the informal greeting. Her mother would have been mortified by such a greeting, but then her mother would be mortified by most of Elle's life these days.

Elle picked up her pace and hurried toward the tree. Once they reached the shade, she dropped the hands of both girls and offered a shallow curtsy.

"Good afternoon. I am Elizabeth Carter, and you must be Miss Jenkins?"

Miss Jenkins grinned back. "Indeed, I am."

Elle returned the girl's smile, liking her immediately. While her manner of speech was proper, there was a slight apprehension in the way she fidgeted with the neckline on her gown and shifted from one foot to the other. "It is a pleasure to meet you." She introduced Katie and Sophia and then Winston, who keep his gaze trained on his feet.

"Philip should join us shortly. It will disappoint him you arrived before he returned."

As if saying his name conjured him, Mr. Jenkins jogged through the field and came to a stop just short of Elle.

"Miss Carter. I had thought to make the introductions. But

I assume from the amiable way you are speaking to each other that I missed my opportunity."

Miss Jenkins tsked him quietly. "We are capable of doing such things on our own, Philip."

He looked at his sister for a moment, then turned his gaze on Elle. "We are very pleased you agreed to join us." He looked at the sky. "And that the weather is to cooperate with us. Though, I do not know how much time we have."

"Will we see any of the horses or just drink tea?" Winston looked suspiciously toward the stable yard beyond.

Elle looked at him with a brow slightly raised.

"I beg your pardon. Thank you for inviting us to tea." His voice sounded anything but appreciative.

Elle noted a slight twitch in Mr. Jenkins's lips.

"Perhaps after tea, we could find my father at the stables."

That seemed to satisfy Winston enough for him to sit down and cross his legs in front of him.

"Hello? Miss Jenkins, I have arrived." A shrill voice sounded from the distance. "Mr. Jenkins, will you not come and walk with me over this uneven terrain? What if I should twist my ankle?" A lady—perhaps girl would be the better word —wobbled exaggeratedly toward them with a parasol in one hand.

Miss Jenkins paused with her hands in the hamper.

"Mr. Jenkins," she said, her tone sharp. "What are you waiting for?"

Mr. Jenkins stared at his sister, his eyes narrowed and lips pinched tightly. He pushed himself to standing, then sauntered over to the girl. Steering her over toward the rug, he moved around her as soon as they reached it.

Elle glanced at Mr. Jenkins from the corner of her eye. His jaw worked furiously.

Miss Jenkins looked from Elle to the new arrival. "Miss

Carter, this is my dear friend, Miss Martindale from Clovergrove."

"It is a pleasure, Miss Martindale." Elle dipped her head. "Is Clovergrove a nearby village?"

"*Of* Clovergrove, Miss Jenkins." The girl's lips pursed, and she turned to Elle. "Clovergrove is my father's estate. I am surprised you do not know of it. It is quite well known." She raised her nose in disapproval.

"Miss Carter is not from around here. She is visiting Briarwood as the gov—"

"Her father was the Viscount Crammer," Katie said hastily, one brow raised high in challenge. Where had she ever learned such a look?

Miss Martindale's chin dropped, her haughtiness wavering.

Elle bit her lip. She should correct Katie's assertion. While the information was correct, it was giving the wrong impression —that Elle was at Briarwood as a guest, not a servant.

She opened her mouth but caught Mr. Jenkins's gaze. He looked both confused and impressed. Or maybe he was only simply amused.

"And this is Lord Culpepper, Lady Katie, and Lady Sophia." Elle motioned to each of the children. Miss Martindale's chin dropped a little more with each introduction.

Miss Jenkins returned to the hamper. "I must apologize in advance for the state of the teacups. With this being *al fresco*, I had not thought it wise to bring the good china. There may be a nick or two."

Miss Martindale tsked and shook her head. "What is it I always say, Miss Jenkins?"

Miss Jenkins paused and looked up. "Best foot forward at all times?"

Miss Martindale nodded. "Precisely. And is this your best

foot?" she asked in a condescending tone. "It should not matter if you are dining with savages. Always use your best."

Miss Jenkins's face tinted crimson. "Yes, but I thought—"

"You thought incorrectly." Miss Martindale cut her off. "Next time, you are welcome to send me a note if you have questions. I shall try to answer you in a timely manner." Miss Martindale looked around the group, but her eyes rested on Elle. It felt as if the girl was staking her claim on Miss Jenkins's friendship. "Unless I have more pressing matters. Papa has many important things to attend to. With Mama gone, he looks to me for help now."

"Did your mother die recently?" Elle felt herself thawing toward Miss Martindale. Losing a mother could not be easy on a girl of any rank, high or low.

"It has been two years now."

Elle tilted her head to the side. "I am sorry for you. I lost my own mother about the same time."

Miss Martindale, however, did not appear to soften toward Elle. She looked just over Elle's shoulder. It was no matter. Elle did not see a friendship developing between them. Her status would come out eventually. And from their brief time together, Miss Martindale had proven she had a high opinion of herself, too high to form a friendship with a governess.

Miss Jenkins pulled out the teacups, and her brow puckered. She looked at Miss Martindale from beneath her lashes as she placed a napkin bundle on the rug and untied it, revealing a stack of small cakes.

Miss Martindale leaned forward to take one, but Katie cleared her throat. "I beg your pardon, Miss Martindale, but I believe my brother Lord Culpepper, my sister, and I outrank you. It is only proper for us to be served first. Followed by Miss Carter."

Elle looked over at Katie, her mouth slightly agape. What

had happened to the girl? Where was the shy Katie who hovered at Elle's arm and barely looked people in the eye? This superior child next to her was a stranger.

Mr. Jenkins cleared his throat and covered his mouth with his hand, but not before Elle saw his grin. Was he happy Katie had put Miss Martindale in her place? He did not seem in the least bit pleased with the way she treated his sister. While Elle did not blame him, he should not encourage Katie's unacceptable behavior either. Elle would discuss this with Katie once they returned to Briarwood.

Katie picked up a cake and placed one on a plate for Sophia. She then took the tea Miss Jenkins offered her.

"Thank you, Miss Jenkins." She said the words to their hostess, but her eyes stayed trained on Miss Martindale. "This looks delicious."

Miss Jenkins smiled, and her body relaxed slightly. Perhaps Katie did not deserve as much of a reprimand as Elle had thought.

"It sounds as if Clovergrove is a grand estate, Miss Martindale." Elle smiled politely.

"Yes, it is. My father purchased it several years ago and many of the townspeople have said it has never looked so well."

"It has not been in your family for long then?"

Miss Martindale fanned out her skirt. "No."

Elle bit back a smile. It appeared the girl's father had likely made his money in trade. Many would not consider Miss Martindale worthy of Society. Indeed, there had been a time when Elle would have looked down her nose at such presumption. But she now realized money was money, no matter where it came from. All money had power.

"Your father is a viscount, is he?" Mr. Jenkins grinned. Did he think Katie had been telling a Banbury story? Why should he believe it the truth? Elle was working as a governess.

Elle nodded. "He was, but my brother now holds the title."

Mr. Jenkins's smile faded, and he stared at her. "It must have been a difficult adjustment when your father died." His voice quieted.

Elle nodded. He had no notion how difficult.

Miss Martindale took a small nibble at her cake and then placed it on the plate, pushing her teacup away without even tasting its contents. She let out a long sigh. "I am sorry, Miss Jenkins but I have another engagement I am to attend. I had not realized you would have other guests. Had I known you would not be alone, I should have declined the invitation. Now that I know you are to be entertained, I must beg your pardon and leave. Please say you forgive me." She pushed out her bottom lip in a pout.

Elle glanced over when she heard Mr. Jenkins sigh.

Miss Jenkins smiled kindly, even though Elle could see the disappointment in her eyes. "Of course, Miss Martindale. I am sorry to have kept you for so long." Miss Jenkins looked at her brother and motioned to Miss Martindale with her head.

Mr. Jenkins looked heavenward before pushing himself up and offering Miss Martindale a hand.

"Please, do say you will visit soon." Miss Jenkins looked up at her friend.

"I should enjoy that." Miss Martindale flicked a gaze at Elle. "But perhaps when you are occupied with fewer guests."

Elle stood up. "It was a pleasure to meet you, Miss Martindale. I hope to see you again soon."

Miss Martindale nodded and smiled as false a smile as Elle had ever seen. "Indeed." She disregarded Mr. Jenkins's offered arm and stomped off—rather sure-footed— across the field and disappeared around the side of the house.

Mr. Jenkins retook his seat on the rug. Everyone sat in

silence for a moment, drinking their tea and looking at their cakes with apparent fascination.

Mr. Jenkins's eyes closed each time he took a sip of his tea, savoring it as one might if they had not tasted it in a while. It was an odd reaction, but who was Elle to judge?

"May we see the stables now?" Winston finally broke the silence as he dusted off his hands.

Mr. Jenkins pushed himself up. "I believe now is a good time, if you are finished." He looked down at Sophia. "Would you like to come also?"

Sophia shot to her feet. "Yes, please." She immediately tucked her hand in Mr. Jenkins's, and Elle's chest squeezed. Both happiness and regret warred within her. Happiness that she could be a governess for children she had learned to love more than she ought. And sadness that such a picture would only ever be of her charges. Never would it be her own child holding the hand of her husband. No matter how much she tried, it was a pang she could not put aside entirely.

She moved to stand, but Mr. Jenkins waved her down. "Why do you not sit and visit with Grace? I imagine you have much in common." As if sensing her uncertainty, he nodded toward the stables. "There is my mother. She will help with the children also. You need not worry after them."

Elle saw the woman in the distance and nodded. Mr. Jenkins set off with the two children. She knew she should feel more trepidation about it, but something about him and his family set her at ease. Perhaps it was Sophia's instant taking to him, or maybe it was Winston. She did not rightly know.

"Thank you for a lovely afternoon, Miss Jenkins."

Miss Jenkins leaned forward. "Is it too soon to ask you to call me Grace? When I first saw you approach, I could not help but feel we would become dear friends." She looked at her hands. "Miss Martindale says we're not yet close enough to call one another by our Christian names." She shook her head. "I beg your pardon, I should not have mentioned it."

"No. I do not mind at all." Elle smiled and placed a hand on Grace's arm. "I should like that very much, Grace. And please, call me Elizabeth."

She helped Grace clean up the tea set and settle the cups in the hamper. Then, because neither seemed to know what else to do, they folded up the rug and Grace draped it over her arm. She bent to pick up the hamper, but Elle grabbed it first.

"Please, let me take this." Then she reached out and grabbed hold of Katie's hand.

"If you do not mind my asking . . ." Grace folded her arms across her chest and allowed the rug to hang down in front of her. "How did you come to meet Philip?"

Elle smiled even as her face heated. Why was she blushing over the simple question? It was not as if she had something to be embarrassed about. "I can place that squarely at the feet of Lady Sophia. She is rather fond of your brother's horses. We were admiring one at the cricket match when your brother spotted us."

"He is very proud of his horses." Grace did not seem to share the fondness.

"As well he should be. While I am no expert, I think his horses are very fine." The two set out at a leisurely pace across the field toward the house. "You do not agree?"

Grace shrugged. "Sometimes it feels as if he cares more about the horses than he does about his own family."

Elle nodded. "Ah. I understand feeling as if you are second in affections to something else. I have not heard from my brother in over a year. And even then, it was only to request that I send him part of my income."

Grace's lips pinched together, then opened before quickly pinching shut again. "I know I am being improper, but was your father really a viscount or was that only said to quiet Miss Martindale?"

Elle nodded. She must have lost much of the demeanor her mother had taught her if no one actually believed she could be the daughter of a viscount. "It is the truth."

Grace looked at her from the corner of her eye. "Then why are you a governess?"

Elle felt the similar sting of heat on her face and ears. She had known the question would come at some point. It always did. "For the same reason most ladies seek employment. There was no money."

When she had first become a governess, it had embarrassed her to answer. It felt as if she were betraying her father by making him appear careless. She had even felt a misguided need to relieve her brother of fault. But over the years, all of that had faded. She had come to realize her father and brother had both failed her. Her answer was the truth, and she need not feel any guilt for it, even if she did still try to downplay her father's role.

"My father made some imprudent investments before his death and my brother only increased the debt." Her voice lowered as she felt the sting of betrayal.

Grace's brow crinkled. "But how did you not even have your dowry? Was it not protected?"

Elle shook her head. "It would seem it was not. I was to have a small estate as my dowry. While I do not know the particulars, I was told after my father's death, that the estate was gone. My brother had no notion how it happened." She smiled, even though she felt anything but happy. "Tell me about yourself, Grace. Your brother says you like to paint."

Grace's face lit. "Oh, indeed, I do." She started into an animated debate about whether oils or watercolors were more desirable. It was an entirely one-sided conversation, but that suited Elle's mood. She was content to listen and pretend that she had not any other responsibilities—no other cares in the world—at least for another moment or two.

They walked around the far side of the house and Elle looked over, a startled sigh escaping her lips. "What happened to this wing of the house?"

Grace stopped talking and looked at the blackened stones surrounding the now windowless frames. "There was a fire here, many years before we acquired the property."

"How long have you lived here?"

Grace sighed. "Nearly eight years."

Elle stared, unable to hide her surprise. This had happened years ago? Why had they not yet repaired the damage?

Grace continued walking. "It is as I said. Sometimes it feels as if Philip cares more for his horses, than he does for us. They are the reason the repairs have not been made." Grace's voice lowered. "He says he must use all of the money to make the horses profitable. But surely there is some left to make repairs or buy a few new gowns."

Elle looked back up at the scared rock face. Perhaps Mr. Jenkins was simply a gentlemen with his pockets to let. She frowned. She had not thought this of him, although it did explain a great deal.

But it was precisely what she did not need. If she had harbored any affections toward Mr. Jenkins, she must surely stop them now. She already knew what it meant to be poor. She wished to escape that life, not mire herself deeper in it.

CHAPTER SEVENTEEN

M r. Jenkins stepped out of the stable as Grace placed the rug on the stone balustrade leading up the stairs to the front door. He looked at the direction they had come, and a look of uncertainty fell over his face. He swallowed and licked his lips. "You have seen *all* of the house on your walk about the grounds?"

Elle glanced up. Her eyes followed his tongue as it slid across his lips and she noticed again how perfectly shaped they were. Her cheeks burned. It was likely why he had such a pleasant smile.

"Perhaps you would like to see a more pleasing part of the estate. There is a little garden on the other side of the house that my mother and Grace have cultivated over the years. Would you care to take a turn with me?"

He wished to walk with her? Alone? She bit her lip, thoughts of a stolen kiss passing through her mind. Or was it implied his sister and Katie would join them? What was she thinking? Had she not, only moments ago, decided there was nothing for her here? There was no sense in thinking on kisses when she knew nothing could come of it. Even if it did flatter her to think he might hold some interest toward her.

"As a painter, Elizabeth, I look forward to your opinion of the garden." Grace stepped forward. "Lady Katie, do you like to paint? Perhaps we could find a flower in the garden for you to sketch."

Katie shook her head. "I am not at all proficient with oils."

Grace held out her hand. "Have you tried crayons?" She bent low, lowering her voice by Katie's ear. "I find them easier to control than oils. Perhaps you might too."

Katie dropped Elle's hand in favor of Grace's, and Elle felt a slight pang. Was it jealousy? She did not like to admit she could feel such emotions. Especially for someone she was employed to teach. But she could not deny the feeling.

Katie did not take to many people. It seemed significant that she should embrace Miss Jenkins so quickly.

Mr. Jenkins motioned Elle forward, then clasped his hands behind his back and followed his sister and Katie toward the far side of the house.

He did not speak at first, and Elle wondered if this might be the quietest turn she had ever taken.

Grace pointed out different things to Katie, their whispered voices barely drifting back to Elle's ears.

"I am sorry for Grace's friend, Miss Martindale." Mr. Jenkins glanced over at her.

Elle shook her head. "There is nothing to apologize for. I have encountered many such ladies." She grinned. "In point of fact, many even less pleasant. Miss Martindale is young still. Hopefully, she will learn to act in a more restrained manner."

Mr. Jenkins chuckled. "I confess, I did not think it possible. But after Lady Katie's set down, it seems she might learn yet." His smile fell away. "I only wish she was a better influence on Grace."

"I do not think you need worry after your sister. From my perspective, she is a delightful young lady."

Mr. Jenkins shrugged and looked ahead to his sister. "She can be delightful. However, more and more I am seeing her behave selfishly, thinking only of herself and her desires. I believe Miss Martindale has put too many unrealistic notions in her head."

"She too, is still young, Mr. Jenkins. I am certain she will come around."

Elle shook her head. "Though I must say, I have no notion what came over Lady Katie. She is usually such a shy child."

"I believe she was defending you." He glanced over at her. "Those children love you, you know. It is quite obvious."

Elle shrugged, uncomfortable with the notion. "I am there to teach and take care of them, not be loved by them." She swallowed. She should surely not mention that she loved them in return. It was most improper. "I was fortunate Lady Kirtley hired me without any references."

Mr. Jenkins looked at the path ahead of them. "I confess, I still do not understand much of the workings of the upper class. But that seems unusual."

Heat moved up Elle's neck and into her face. Why did she still feel so much humiliation when speaking about finding a paid position? "It is most unusual. But we met at a ball in London when I had my come out. We spoke for a time. Her mother and mine were friends." Elle sighed. "When my situation changed, I knew she had recently given birth to her third child. I sent a letter inquiring after her health and mentioned that I was looking for a position, if she knew of one available." Elle put a hand to her throat, rubbing her thumb over her collarbone. "I confess, I had little hope *she* would hire me. I had little to recommend myself. But she is a kind lady and offered me the position. I am in her debt."

Mr. Jenkins glanced over. "Lord Kirtley came to see me. He seems an amiable man. You are fortunate in your employment."

"Yes, I am."

Though I should not have been in this position to begin with. She knew she owed a great deal to Lord and Lady Kirtley. Yet she still could not help the burning in her stomach when she thought about it. Miss Jenkins's question about her dowry had brought up many questions. Questions Elle had had for years, Questions she had put aside for lack of any answers. Why had her dowry not been protected?

"Then you truly are the daughter of a viscount?" His voice was lower, tentative.

Elle nodded. "Yes. I am."

His brow furrowed. "And that is how your father was acquainted with the Duke of Larmont?"

The duke, again? What was Mr. Jenkins's fascination with the duke? "Yes. They sat in Lords together. But they have been friends since they were boys. They attended Harrow together and then went on to Cambridge."

"I see."

They entered a walled garden through a stone archway. Color filled the space and for a moment, Elle was transfixed. She had seen nothing like this at Briarwood.

There did not appear to be any plan regarding the location of each plant, but as Elle took in the garden, she realized she was mistaken. It must have taken a great deal of thought to intersperse the colors so precisely. "Oh, this is simply lovely," she breathed out.

"It is, isn't it?" There was pride in Mr. Jenkins's voice. "As I said, my mother and Grace have been working at it for years."

"Has your sister painted it? This garden needs to be painted." Elle would choose this exact spot for her first picture. But one painting would never be enough.

Mr. Jenkins sucked in a deep breath and smiled. "I believe she has from nearly every vantage point. Perhaps one day you will return and see her work. I am certain she would love your opinion on them."

Elle looked over at him. "Your sister mentioned you have lived here for nearly eight years." How had they come to possess such an estate? And where had they lived before?

"Yes. It will be eight years come January."

Elle stopped and bent to smell a flower. She did not have the slightest notion of the name of the beautiful bloom. She painted flowers often enough, she really should learn their names. But her lack of knowledge did not stop her from appreciating their beauty and lovely fragrance.

"How did it come to be in your family?"

Mr. Jenkins was the master, yet his father still lived. She had never heard of a son inheriting over a father. Unless the father had done something so terrible as to be cut out of the inheritance or entail altogether. But those extremes usually ended in Newgate or transportation.

"This estate belonged to Lord Downings."

Elle looked up at him from her crouched position. "You inherited from Lord Downings? But why did his son, Lord Monteclaire, not inherit this estate?"

"You are familiar with the family?" There seemed a hesitation in his tone.

Elle nodded. "Yes, some. We did not visit each other's estates, but we often attended the same house parties. Lord Downings and my father held similar political views, so they met often. How had we not been introduced before? Especially as you were to inherit from him."

Mr. Jenkins squinted at his sister's back. "I did not *inherit* the estate. He gave it to me as a sort of...reward."

Elle's brows rose. A reward? What did one do to earn such a reward?

"There was no entail on this estate," Mr. Jenkins continued. "Lord Downings could do with it as he pleased."

She nodded, but when he sighed, she put out a hand to him. "You need not explain. It was improper of me to ask such intimate questions. I apologize."

"You need not do so." He shook his head and paused. "Lord Downings has a daughter—"

"Yes, Lady Dorothea. She is several years older than I, so we were not close friends. But I know of her. Lord Monteclaire and I were closer in age. He was friends with my brother." Elle paused, realizing she was not allowing him to tell his story. "Pardon me, please continue."

He nodded slowly. "Lady Dorothea found herself in a dangerous situation, and I was there to help her. Lord Downings gave me this estate as a thank you for my actions."

Elle's brow creased. There were surely details missing from the story, but what were they? And was he leaving them out for brevity or for another reason?

Elle tried to recall hearing of some dangerous situation Dorothea had encountered. It would likely have been shortly before Mr. Jenkins moved to Greystone. He said it had been nearly eight years . . . Elle's eyes widened. "It was you."

He looked at her with furrowed brows.

"I remember hearing a story about Lady Dorothea falling through the ice of a frozen pond. You are the one who saved her."

He swallowed, but he nodded, his steps quickening. "There was a reason I asked you to take a turn with me, and it has nothing to do with Lady Dorothea. I wish to ask a favor of you."

Why was he changing the subject? And why was he so reluctant to speak more on saving Dorothea? Was he not proud of his actions? Or was he simply being humble? She wanted to ask him more questions about the story, but the look on his face told her he did not wish to speak on it more. What was he hiding?

"You wish a favor?" What could she possibly offer him?

"His Grace, the Duke of Larmont expressed interested in buying one of my horses. He came to look at Black Thunder, but I have heard nothing from him since. I am concerned he changed his mind."

Elle nodded, but she had no notion how this concerned her.

"His recommendation would go far in spreading the reputation of my stables across the country. I *need* him to buy this horse." There was an undertone of desperation in Mr. Jenkins's voice. He ran a hand through his hair. "You said you knew him well. I know I have no right to ask, but would you speak to him on my behalf? Perhaps he will tell you if he plans to buy Black Thunder. Or if he does not, I hope he will at least offer his reasons."

Elle opened her mouth, but he continued.

"Please, Miss Carter. You do not understand how important this is to me . . . to my family."

Elle pulled her lower lip between her teeth and then released it. "It is not that I do not wish to help you, Mr. Jenkins. I just don't know how I can be of assistance. I am not a guest at the party, I am simply a governess—a position the duke does not think highly on. I do not socialize with those attending and have no notion when I will have the opportunity to speak with His Grace."

Mr. Jenkins's shoulders dropped. "I had only thought after I saw you walking with him yesterday that perhaps you might see him more often." He shook his head. "But you are correct. I had no right to ask it of you. Please, accept my apology." He dipped at the waist and turned on his heel.

"Wait, Mr. Jenkins . . ." Elle called after him, but he did not turn back before passing through the archway. That was it, then? He was abandoning her in the garden because she could not help him?

Elle swallowed. How had she been such a dolt? To think he might have had an affinity for her when all he wished was to ask for her help. And why could she not stop thinking his situation was better than her current one?

Elle closed her eyes. Perhaps it was because she could not deny that she held a small affinity for him, even if he did not return her affections. The disheartened look on his face pierced her heart. This sale was important, and she had offered him no help.

But what could she do? She had not been lying when she said she had little access to the guests at the party. And after the dinner she had attended, she had little hope of Larmont seeking her out again. Her only hope was if she encountered him by accident. That would mean he would need to come to the school room, which seemed unlikely.

But she had to do something. If for no other reason than to see the sparkle in Mr. Jenkins's eyes and the creases that formed around his mouth when he smiled.

She would think of something—some way to see the duke and talk to him. But what if he did not intend to buy the horse? What would Elle do? That was something she was not sure she could fix.

She reached up and twisted the hairs at the back of her neck. She needed to leave—be away from this garden that she had thought so lovely. She needed to be away from Mr. Jenkins.

"Grace," Elle called. "It looks as if a storm is gathering. I think it best if I gather the children and return to Briarwood."

"We could move inside the house." Grace sounded hopeful. "Must you go?"

Elle nodded. "I fear we must." She held out her hand. "Come, Lady Katie. We must fetch Lord Culpepper and Lady Sophia. Make haste, please."

They left Grace standing in the garden as they hurried through the arch and across the side lawn to the stables. Had Grace known the real reason for Elle's hasty departure?

She pulled open the door and slipped inside. "Lord Culpepper. Lady Sophia. There is a storm coming. Please, come along. We do not wish to be caught out of doors when it arrives."

Winston let out a groan, and Sophia stomped her foot, but both children came to Elle's side immediately.

"Must we go already?" Winston whisper-whined.

"I am sorry to cut your visit short. But the weather does not seem to be cooperating." She glanced over to Richard. "Thank you, sir. We had a lovely time."

She placed her hand on Winston's back and led him out the door, then picked up Sophia's hand and hurried to the path that led back to Briarwood.

As she crossed through the gate in the wall, Elle glanced over her shoulder at Greystone one last time. Mr. Jenkins stood at the edge of the lawn, staring after her. He was surely regretting his decision to invite her to tea.

CHAPTER EIGHTEEN

The school room was quiet as Winston worked on his geography and Katie practiced her words. Elle stood at the window and stared out at the grounds. If only the school-room faced the opposite side of the estate, she would be able to see the grounds of Greystone. Perhaps even the stables.

She crossed her arms in front of her and sighed. Not that it mattered. Mr. Jenkins was only interested in her associations.

Her lips pushed out as she recalled the look on his face when she'd told him she could not help him. Had it only been yesterday? It felt much longer. Why was she so disappointed with the way things had turned out anyway?

The man was hardly more than a groom himself. Three years earlier, she would not have given him a second glance.

The thought disappointed her. When she thought back on her life before her father died, she found she did not always like what she saw. Perhaps, in some small way, her new life had made her a better person. Allowed her to be more sympathetic towards those of the lower classes.

Elle's eyes were drawn to several couples strolling around

the gardens below. A breeze fluttered the ties of the ladies' bonnets. It looked pleasant enough, but Elle knew better. It was early May, but the weather still felt more like late February.

Still, watching the couples stroll around the garden made Elle think of her turn with Mr. Jenkins. It had started out lovely. They had spoken of things that made it feel as though they were coming to know each other more intimately. But then . . . she let the thought fall off.

She leaned forward slightly and squinted. Was that His Grace strolling below? Could this be her opportunity to speak with him on Mr. Jenkins's behalf? Lud, it would mortify her mother to know Elle's thoughts. But what did Elle care? She was not a lady of Society any longer. She need not worry so much after propriety.

Elle bit her lip and turned away, darting through the door into the nursery. "Nurse Jones, could I prevail upon you to watch over the children while they do their studies for a moment?"

Nurse Jones looked at the door leading to Sophia's room and nodded. "She has not been abed long. I have a moment or two until she awakens."

Elle smiled. "Thank you."

She grabbed her skirts and hurried from the room, racing down the back stairs, stopping only long enough to grab her spencer and bonnet. Shoving her arms into the sleeves, she flew out the door as she tied the strings under her chin.

She moved around the side of the house and slowed her pace, taking a few steps to calm her breathing and her racing heart. She had never acted in such a rash manner. It was rather exhilarating when it was not completely terrifying. What would the duke think of her?

She fastened her buttons as her gaze swept the grounds. A

slow smile curved her lips as she found him. Now how to approach him without it looking intentional.

He was in the garden with Miss Perdy. It would be wholly improper to interrupt the couple. Especially as she intended to take the duke away so she might speak to him privately. But if she did not, when would she speak with him? It was now or never. But just what would she say once she interrupted them?

Perhaps she would think of something before she *accidentally* bumped into him. Miss Perdy could not be too angry with Elle if it were an accident, could she?

She watched Larmont from beneath her lashes as she walked toward him. He was still at the midpoint of the garden.

Elle slipped through the vined archway and looked around for something to feign interest in. A large lilac bush sat to her right, the first few blooms of the season just starting to open.

She glanced down the path. The duke and Miss Perdy chatted quietly, the younger lady giggling at every word he said.

Elle's nose scrunched up. Such immaturity must surely be taxing. It was distasteful what a man would endure for a pretty face.

Standing in front of the bush, Elle waited until the duke was only a few rods away. Leaning over, she pretended to smell the lilacs and waited until the duke came closer. When she felt him behind her, she stood up quickly and took a step back, smiling as she stumbled into him.

"Oh, my apologies." She lifted her hand to her mouth, then widened her eyes as she pretended to have only just recognized him.

The duke reached out to steady her. "Easy there, Miss Carter. Are you injured?"

Elle ran her hands down her skirt, hoping she looked properly embarrassed. "No, I am well. Only startled." She dropped her eyes. "I only pray I did not cause you any injury, Your Grace."

He shook his head. "No, no. It would take much more than that to set me off-kilter." He smiled down at her and held his hand out for her to precede him on the path.

He was dismissing her. What was she to do now? She placed her hand upon his arm and smiled up at him. "Oh, thank you for offering your arm. I had not thought to take a turn with anyone, but I find your offer quite acceptable." Elle dropped her gaze. He would surely see the dishonesty there.

The duke looked from Elle to Miss Perdy and then back again. "Why do you not hurry along to the house, Miss Perdy? I believe I see your aunt waiting for you on the terrace."

"But—"

Elle did not miss the narrowed-eyed glare from the girl. Although, in Elle's estimation, she was doing Miss Perdy a favor. The duke was nothing but arrogant and condescending. And while Elle had not noticed it in her younger years, she had noticed it plenty here at the house party.

"I said hurry along." He cast a disapproving look at Miss Perdy. "I do not appreciate repeating myself."

The girl cast her gaze downward and moved away.

Elle's brows rose. It seemed he treated everyone with disrespect, not just Elle. How did the girl not see the kindness Elle was paying her?

She pushed her concerns away. Miss Perdy and her disappointment were not Elle's worry. She had concocted this charade for a reason, and she may as well see what she could discover.

"She is a sweet girl, even if she has little sense." The duke sniffed. "But I dare say her appearance will help a gentleman overlook her deficiencies."

"I do not know her well, but she does seem rather young."

Elle cringed at the negative assessment she was adding to the duke's. It was unkind and beneath her.

The duke shrugged. "Perhaps."

Elle looked at the back of the retreating girl, and her stomach turned. She could not be much older than Lady Mary, the duke's youngest daughter.

Elle sighed. "I am sorry if I cut your time with Miss Perdy short, Your Grace. But I thank you for your assistance."

He grunted. "I find your company tolerable, so it is not so much of an inconvenience."

She clenched her teeth tightly. He found her *tolerable*. Such a compliment from the duke would charm many ladies, but Elle found it difficult to be anything but irritated.

She wanted to walk away and forget she had even attempted this farce. But it was doubtful another opportunity would present itself. She simply needed to find a way to broach the subject with him. It was not as if she could ask his intentions toward the horse outright. A more subtle approach was necessary.

"Have you taken your morning ride, Your Grace? If I remember correctly, you used to ride every morning, did you not?" Would just the mention of a horse be enough? Elle bit her lip.

"Indeed, I have. I find it clears the mind and body." He tipped his head toward her. "Your father and I were of like minds in that regard."

She did not wish for the conversation to move to her father.

Elle puffed out her lips. Perhaps if she mentioned Mr. Jenkins's stables, the duke would mention the horse on his own. She heaved out a sigh. "Lady Sophia is quite excited. We were to visit the stables at Greystone this afternoon. She loves to see the horses there." Was it really a lie if the event had happened, just not at the time she mentioned? Surely, if it was, it was a much lesser lie. If there were such things as degrees of lying.

The duke nodded. "I remember her enjoyment from the Cricket match."

Elle waited for him to mention more about the stables, but he did not. She nearly stomped her foot in frustration. Was the man going to force her to ask outright?

"It is one of the things I miss most in my current situation. I do not have the pleasure of riding fine horses anymore." She swallowed. She had hoped not to have to remind the duke of her lowly state—not that he had likely forgotten about it. But she could think of nothing else to bring the conversation around. And surely, it would be worth it if she obtained the information Mr. Jenkins needed. "I have heard that Mr. Jenkins has a fine racer." She placed a finger to her lips. "Did not Mr. Jenkins mention at the cricket match that you were meeting with him about a horse?" She looked heavenward. Could she have been more obvious?

The duke looked straight ahead. "Yes, I met with him that very afternoon."

Elle smiled. Finally, he was cooperating with her. She waited for him to mention his decision. But he remained quiet beside her.

Her hand fisted at her side. Why would this man not give up the information she needed? It was as if he knew what she wanted and was refusing to give it to her.

"Hmm. It must not have impressed you. I have not seen you on a new horse." She clamped her mouth shut. Why had she said that? It made it seem as though she were watching him and keeping track of his every move.

He smiled and raised a brow slightly as he patted her hand. "You watch the stables often, do you?" His hand stayed on hers, making hers moist inside her gloves.

Elle's face heated. "The schoolroom overlooks the stable yard. It is difficult not to glance out the window when I am instructing the children in their lessons." Perhaps bringing up her employment was precisely what she needed. Hopefully, the duke would take his hand from atop hers and put it back at his side.

This was not working out as she had planned. Perhaps she should simply excuse herself and return to the schoolroom. Nurse Jones was surely wondering at how long Elle had been away.

But she was so close to obtaining the information. She could not give up yet. "Then the horse was not anything special? Mr. Jenkins had led me to believe it was a rather fine horse."

The duke looked ahead. "It was a fine horse. Finer than I expected to find in such a small stable."

Elle looked up at him, even though she thought better of it. "Then why did you not buy it? Are you simply waiting until the end of the house party?"

Larmont shrugged. "I am uncertain I need another horse at present."

Elle let out a laugh. "When have you ever waited until you had a need before you bought something you desired?"

He stared down at her, his tongue running across his lips.

She pinched her mouth shut and looked away. There was nothing remarkable about the duke's lips. Nothing that made Elle wish to linger on them.

He nodded, staring at the path ahead. "It is true. I always end up with what I want."

She closed her eyes and shook her head, knowing he would likely take her next words completely wrong. "I have seen the horse, Your Grace. And I cannot imagine anyone could look so well upon it as you surely will."

155

He tilted his head to the side and studied her as if he were truly seeing her for the first time. "Yes, well, I still have some time yet before the house party ends, and I take my leave of Somerset."

Did he plan to buy the horse or not?

Why was she doing this? Mr. Jenkins clearly had no intentions toward her and yet, she still felt compelled to help him. And it was surely to be a great expense to her.

A soft smile turned his lips. "You like the horse, Miss Carter? You said you have missed riding fine horses. Is that horse one you wish to ride?"

What was he implying? It was difficult to know how to answer such a question when she did not know what he meant by it.

She missed a step and stumbled, but he moved a hand around her waist. This was all so inappropriate, and she could not continue on, no matter how much she wished to see the sparkle in Mr. Jenkins's eyes.

She had done her best to discover the information, but she needed to put a stop to the conversation before it led to something Elle was not prepared for. "I am sorry to have stumbled into you, Your Grace, and I do appreciate your help, but I have been away too long. I need to return to the schoolroom. Please, excuse me." She pulled away, his hand coming off her waist, and dipped a curtsy.

"If you are certain you are well?" he asked.

Elle nodded. "I am very well. Thank you again for your help, Your Grace." Lifting her skirts, she hurried back toward the house and the safety of the schoolroom. She did not know that she had any answers for Mr. Jenkins, but at least he would know she had tried. She only hoped her actions were enough to bring the crinkle to the side of his eyes.

CHAPTER NINETEEN

W hy had he asked her? And then left her standing in
the garden when she refused him? Philip reined in his
horse and looked out over the fields on the east side of his
estate. He should have known she would not be amiable to the
idea. They hardly knew one another. It was completely inappropriate to have asked for such a favor. But he had only made
the situation worse by leaving her. What must she think
of him?

Philip placed his knuckled hand to his brow and thumped
it several times. What had he been thinking? Was he so
desperate as to use a governess to achieve his goals?

He shrugged. He was not desperate. Not anymore. But that
did not mean he did not need the sale. And he wasn't ready to
forsake his goal. A goal in which Larmont played a large part.

But using Miss Carter was not the solution. He needed to
figure out another way.

Why did his thoughts always come back to Miss Carter?
How was he to apologize to her? To send a note to Briarwood

would be even more inappropriate than it had been to ask her to intervene.

Would she bring the children to visit the horses again? It had happened several times over the last week. But he had muddled things so badly yesterday, it seemed unlikely she would venture over of her own accord.

He scrubbed a hand over his face. Maybe he could convince Gracie to send another invitation for tea. Although, if she would not bring the children to see the horses, would she accept an invitation for tea? It seemed doubtful.

He shoved his hands in his hair, pulling at the roots. It brought tears to the corners of his eyes, but he did not mind it. He deserved much worse for what he had done to Miss Carter.

Releasing his hair, he tried to put it back in place as best he could. Why was he so concerned about Miss Carter? If she never came back to Greystone—he swallowed hard—would it be so terrible? His chest tightened, and he rubbed at it.

He had thought a good bruising ride would clear his head, but it had done nothing of the sort. What was wrong with him that a hard ride could not set things to rights? Or at least provide him with a clear path?

He leaned forward in his saddle and rubbed a hand down the horse's neck. It was not acceptable to Philip's way of thinking to let things stay as they were with Miss Carter. He would not think clearly until he had fixed things with her. Perhaps if he rode home slowly enough, he would think of the right way to go about it.

All the other times he had seen her, save the invite to tea, he had been working outside in his fields or paddocks. Perhaps that was the answer. He simply needed to work more in those places where she would see him easily. Or, as he did not think her inclined to seek him out, where he could easily see her.

Philip nodded. That was it. That was how he would find

his chance to speak with her. The children would likely be with her, but he could pull her aside easily enough. Then he could say what he needed to say and have no regrets. She could return with Lord Kirtley's family to whichever county they called home, and Philip would never wonder after her again.

He would never have to worry if she thought ill of him or if she was angry with him. He would never have to wonder if she missed speaking with him over the fence rail or bringing the children to the stables. No, he would not have to wonder about any of that.

He dug his heels into his horse's sides and set off at a gallop. If he was to see Miss Carter, he did not wish to wait any longer than he had to. It was already late in the morning. For all he knew, he had already missed his opportunity for today.

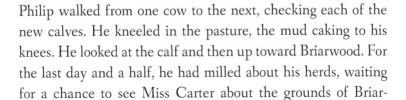

Philip walked from one cow to the next, checking each of the new calves. He kneeled in the pasture, the mud caking to his knees. He looked at the calf and then up toward Briarwood. For the last day and a half, he had milled about his herds, waiting for a chance to see Miss Carter about the grounds of Briarwood. But to no avail.

The weather had been foul and cold, so it should not surprise him she had not been out. But that did not stop his disappointment. Why was it when he desired to speak with her, she was not about?

He glanced up at the gray sky and reached a hand up to keep his hat from blowing away. No one was walking about the grounds of Briarwood. He glanced behind him at the stables. He should make his way back before the heavens opened and soaked him to the skin. He lingered among his herd a moment longer, staring at the large house in the distance. It was a futile hope that she would magically appear before him, yet he still held out.

He ran a hand through his hair and turned his back to Briarwood. He bent to examine the last calf in the herd. He would ensure it was well and then return to the stables.

Poking and prodding, the little calf let out a low bellow.

Philip smiled. There was much to be satisfied with this year. His herd was strong and as long as the fields produced enough to feed all the stock, he did not see why next year should not see some vast improvements to the estate.

Taking in a deep breath, he pushed himself to standing and headed toward the stables.

"Mr. Jenkins."

He stopped. Was he daft, thinking he'd heard her voice on the wind?

"Mr. Jenkins." Her voice was more insistent.

Philip stopped and turned around. He smiled without even thinking.

She had come out. He had imagined it, and it had happened. Perhaps he had a bit of magic within him.

He glanced again at the darkening skies. But now that she was here, apprehension seized him. "Miss Carter, what are you doing out here? It is likely to rain any moment."

She lifted her skirt a little higher and hurried toward him. "Yes, I know. But I knew of no other way to tell you what I discovered. I saw you through the windows, and knew I had to speak to you at once."

"Do not rush so. The ground is still quite slippery with all the rain we have had." Philip moved toward her.

She looked up at the sky. "I will be we—" Her legs slipped out from under her, and she landed with a thud on the ground.

Philip launched himself over the rock wall, running until he came to where she lay. Kneeling beside her, he looked down at her. Was she hurt? Was she even conscious? "Miss Carter, are you all right?"

Her eyes stared at the sky above, unblinking for a moment. But then she nodded. "Yes," she wheezed out. "I believe it just knocked the air from my lungs."

He reached forward and placed his hand on her arm and the other on her shoulder. "Here, let me help you up."

He slowly lifted Miss Carter's back off of the ground. Mud clung to her spencer and clumps hung onto her hair.

"Do you think you can stand?"

She nodded.

He moved to his knees so he could help her up.

She pulled her feet under her and made to stand but cried out as she crumbled to the ground.

Philip looked at her. "What hurts?"

Tears pooled in the bottoms of her lids, and he thought his heart might tear in two. He did not know how to handle a woman in tears.

"It is my ankle. I must have twisted it."

He looked down at her slipper-clad feet. It was no wonder her legs had slipped out from under her. These were not the shoes to wear on a day like today. "Why did you not put on walking boots?"

She grimaced. "I told you. I saw you from the window. I did not know how long you would be about. I had no time to change into my half boots."

He lifted her skirt enough to see her feet. It did not take any investigation to discover which was the injured ankle. Her right one was already the size of a cricket ball. "Zounds! This is not good, Miss Carter. You cannot walk back to the house on that ankle."

He crouched down. "Here, put your arm about my neck. I will carry you back to Greystone. It is closer.

Then we can decide how best to transport you to Briarwood."

She pulled back. Did she dislike him so much now she could not even stand the thought of his help?

"No, Mr. Jenkins. I am certain you are mistaken. It is not so bad. Surely, I can walk on it."

He shook his head. "No, Miss Carter. You cannot. I am afraid I must insist." He scowled at her. Did she not understand her predicament? Or that he wished to be of service? It was the least he could do after putting her in such a difficult position the other day.

He slid his arm around her back, ignoring the uptick in his pulse. When he slid his hands beneath her knees, his skin heated. He frowned at himself. He did not have time for such reactions. If he did not hurry, they would both be caught in a downpour that could easily see *him* with a twisted ankle also.

"I need you to put your arm around my neck."

Miss Carter held back.

"Make haste, Elizabeth. Those storm clouds will await no one. Not even a handsome governess with a twisted ankle."

She sucked in a breath, a small smile on her lips, but her hand slid around his neck.

He made certain she was securely in his arms before pushing himself up to standing. He paused for a moment, enjoying the feel of her against him. Even the cold mud seeping from her back through his coat and shirtsleeves did not dampen the enjoyment.

"I thought you said we must make haste?" Her voice was quiet next to his ear.

A shiver tingled down though his body. He readjusted her in his arms, mostly so he could take in a deep breath without her noticing. Even wet and muddy, she still smelled faintly of orange flowers.

Philip smiled. Never had he found the scent so appealing. "Now, hold on, please. This terrain is full of dips and holes."

She nodded, but he felt her flinch with each footfall. The pain in her foot must be growing. It grieved him to know that he was causing her pain.

They had only made it halfway across the field when the first drops fell. Miss Carter—had he really called her Elizabeth back there—tucked her head into his chest, as if trying to keep the rain off her face.

He hoped she could not feel the thudding of his heart, which only increased with her face in the folds of his coat. He cautioned a glance down at her but could not see her face over the brim of her bonnet.

What must she think of him? First, he called her by her Christian name, without permission, and now she was witnessing his rapid heartbeat? It would not surprise him if she called for Ryecombe's servants to fetch her immediately.

The rain came faster and harder, running down his face in rivulets. He squinted, trying to keep the water from blurring his vision. The last thing he wished was to trip and send them both sprawling across the field.

The house was in view, but the stables were closer. It did not seem the most comfortable stop for her to rest her sore ankle, but would it not be better to get out of the rain? Or would it be better to push on to the house where she could warm herself by the fire?

If he entered the house through the terrace doors instead of going around the house to the front, it would cut the distance drastically.

But the terrace led to the ballroom. And that room was sorely in need of repair. What would Elizabeth think of it—think of him—should he take her inside through that door? She had already seen the charred remnants of the west wing.

Lightning flashed across sky and Philip no longer cared about the condition of the ballroom. He needed to get Elizabeth to safety and the stable was closer.

He moved toward the stable yard. They could wait there until the rain and lightning stopped. Then he could move her to the house where they could enter through the front doors and go directly to the parlor. The finished parlor.

Philip blinked the water from his eyes as he stepped up to the door of the first stable building. He shifted Elizabeth in his arms as he grasped hold of the handle and yanked it aside.

She let out a whimper, and he realized he must have hit her foot with the door. "I'm sorry, Miss Carter."

She shook her head in his chest. "I thought it was to be Elizabeth now."

Philip smiled. That she could still find humor in this situation said much about her character.

"Just a moment and I will see you settled." He stepped inside the stable and waited for his eyes to adjust to the darkness. This stable only held five horses at present. Once the foal was a little older, he would move both mother and foal into the other building.

He moved to the first stall and lowered Elizabeth into the hay. She curled into him. It was likely because she was warmer next to him, but he preferred to think she was simply reluctant to let him go.

He stood up and moved toward the door, pulling it shut behind him.

He paused with his hand on the handle. What was he doing? Calling her Elizabeth? Thinking her partial to him? Had he not been through this before? Why was he allowing himself to be hurt again? If he had learned anything from Lady Dorothea, it was that ladies of the *ton* were not to be trusted with a man's heart. But was Elizabeth a lady of the *ton* anymore?

He took in a slow breath. Did anyone ever completely quit the *ton*? He would see to her injuries, and that was all. That was the wise decision.

He moved to the end of the aisle and pulled several heavy blankets off the railings. They were not particularly clean, but they were thick and warm. And that seemed of more import at the moment.

He threw them over his shoulder and grabbed a lantern off the shelf.

Thunder shook the stable as he kneeled beside Elizabeth.

Her arms hugged her shaking body, her teeth chattering loudly.

"I'm sorry there is no fire. I probably should have taken you to the house. But I thought it better to be protected from the lightning." He rubbed at his brow. "That was likely the wrong decision." Why did he second guess everything with this woman?

Unfolding the first blanket, he draped it over her shoulders. "Here, pull this tight. It should help to stop the shivering."

Shifting, he glanced back at her. "I am going to check your ankle unless you disagree."

She nodded.

He lifted her dripping skirt just enough to see her injured ankle and sucked in a breath. It had at least doubled in size on their walk to the stable. What if she had done more than twist it?

"I think a doctor should be called. This looks to be more than a twist."

"Are you certain?" She shifted to see for herself, wincing before her eyes widened. "How did it grow so large?"

Philip nodded. "That is my concern." He stood up. "I will

send for Mr. Cooper. He is a surgeon but is more likely to come out in this kind of weather."

"I don't want to put anyone to any trouble. If you help me to Briarwood, I am certain they will take care of it there."

Philip shook his head. "No. This was my fault. I will see to your care." He moved to the door. "Stay where you are. I will return shortly."

Elizabeth gave him a wry look. "I was considering taking a turn about the stable. But after your caution, I suppose I shall save it for another day."

Philip grinned and ducked out the door. How could she both scare him and excite him at the same time?

Philip squinted into the pouring rain. He jogged to the next building and pushed open the door. "Jim. Are you within?"

The stable boy peered around the corner of the farthest stall. "Yes, sir."

Philip waved him forward. "I need you to take a horse into Bath and fetch Mr. Cooper, the surgeon. Then on your return, stop at Briarwood and inform Lord Kirtley that Miss Carter is here at Greystone with an injured ankle."

Jim nodded. "Yes, sir, Mr. Jenkins."

Philip walked over to the peg on the wall and removed the worn greatcoat hanging there. "This will be too big on you, but it should keep you dry. Try to keep to the cover of the trees as much as you can. I have not heard thunder in a while, so hopefully it has passed." He guided Adonis out of his stall and saddled him for the ride. He would help take care of Jim in this weather.

Philip did not wait for Jim to move to the mounting block. He grasped the boy around the waist and placed him in the saddle. "Give Adonis his head and he will get you there safely and quickly."

"Yes, sir."

Philip moved to the front of the horse and whispered instructions to him. Adonis was the only horse Philip trusted with this task. "Be quick about it."

He opened the stable door and swatted the horse on the rump, sending it grudgingly out into the rain.

Once they were clear of the stable yard, Philip moved back to the other building to check on Elizabeth.

"How are you feeling?"

Her whole body shivered as a gust of wind blew in. "I was well until you opened that door."

"I have sent for Mr. Cooper. And Jim will stop at Briarwood on the way back and tell them what has happened."

Elizabeth nodded.

Philip came over and lowered down beside her.

"Why do you not change into warmer clothes? There is no reason we should both be cold and wet out here."

He scooted in next to her. "It would not be gentlemanly for me to leave you here alone."

"Did you not do just that?" She gave him a shaky smile.

"It was necessary. But I will not leave again." He opened the blanket laying on the ground next to her. "Now, what was so important that you had to come outside in this weather?" He was not about to admit he had been hoping she would do exactly as she had.

"It was not raining when I came out. And I had not intended to stay out so long." She rubbed her hands together. "I had the chance to speak with the duke, as you requested. I wanted to tell you what I learned."

He turned toward her. "You spoke to the duke? About me? But I thought you could not."

"I had thought it near impossible. But then I found him walking in the gardens and I sort of . . . ambushed him."

CHAPTER TWENTY

Now that she could think back on it, it was rather an amusing story. Elle had never ambushed anyone in her life. Let alone a duke.

Philip's—surely if he called her Elizabeth, she could call him by his Christian name—eyes widened. "You ambushed the Duke of Larmont in the gardens?"

A quiet giggle escaped Elle's throat. Or it could have been a verbal shiver. "Can you believe it?"

Philip's face lit up, his eyes sparkling and the dimple in his chin growing shallower as the skin on his face stretched tight. It was just as she had expected when she told him her news. Or rather, the news she had hoped she would be delivering.

"I find I am rather sad to have missed that. I have never seen a duke ambushed in a flower garden." He tilted his head toward her. "Tell me, Elizabeth, how exactly does one do such a thing?"

Elle shivered, as much from hearing him say her name as from the cold. "Well—"

Philip reached over and tucked her hands between his own.

Warmth spread instantly through her hands and made its way up her arms. How were his hands so warm?

"Well?" he asked.

Elle swallowed. "Yes, well, I spotted him from the schoolroom window—"

"You must have very good eyesight, Elizabeth. You seem to spot a good many things from the window." He pulled a knee up and balanced his elbow on it. He was teasing her.

"Do you wish to hear the story or not?" She gave him her sternest look, one she reserved only for those times when the children were being the most difficult.

He leaned slightly back. "Begging your pardon. Please, continue."

She nodded. "I raced down the stairs and out to the garden where I pretended to be smelling a lilac that happened to be right in his path. When he walked behind me, I stood up suddenly and *accidentally* bumped into him." She smiled widely. It *had* been a rather good plan.

Philip grinned. "You are rather impressive, Elizabeth. I confess I had not thought you the ambushing sort."

She shrugged even as a smile tugged at her lips. "I am certain there are many things you do not know about me."

"Perhaps we could change that."

Elle swallowed. What did he mean?

He stared at her for a moment. Was he waiting for her to share what she had discussed with Larmont? Could that be what he had meant by his comment about knowing things about her?

She bit her lip, hesitating so she could enjoy his crinkles and dimples a little longer. But she knew the moment was ending.

Philip licked his lips. She followed the trail with her eyes. He did it so much better than Larmont. It was easy for her to imagine kissing Philip. But Larmont? Her stomach recoiled.

"Once you successfully ambushed Larmont, what happened next?" Philip smiled, a hopeful look in his eyes.

"We talked of many little things." She paused. "But eventually, I managed to steer the conversation to Black Thunder."

Philip's eyes lit again. "And? What did he say? Does he plan to buy him?"

Just the thought of telling him this news made Elle's stomach twist. Why had she not tried harder to convince Larmont to buy the horse? In truth, it might still happen. There was still a chance he would decide to make the purchase. After all, there were still four days left of the house party.

It might be best if she *gradually* broke the news to him. "He said that Black Thunder was an impressive horse. Much finer than he had expected."

Philip let out a whoop. "I knew it to be true, but to hear someone of his status agree? That is wonderful news." He leaned forward. "When shall I expect him to come and fetch him? Is he waiting until he leaves Somerset?"

Elle sucked in her bottom lip. This would not do. She must just tell him, rather than allowing him to believe it was a sure thing. "He also said he has not decided if he is to purchase the horse." The words spilled out rapidly, tripping over each other as if none of them wanted to be the last one uttered.

"What?" Philip's shoulders dropped, and the light in his eyes disappeared. His handsome face creased with confusion. "But why? If he thought Black Thunder impressive, why would he not purchase him?"

Elle raised a shoulder. "He is not certain he needs a new horse just now." She dropped her eyes, unable to look at the disappointment in Philip's eyes any longer. "His horse is still rather spry and—"

"Since when did a man like Larmont settle for just one horse? It makes no sense. And why would he contact me if he were not intent on buying?" Philip raked a hand through his hair, then scrubbed it over his face. "I could understand it if I had contacted him. But I didn't."

Elle reached out a hand. She felt helpless to make the situation better, even as there was nothing she wanted more. "I'm so sorry. I will try to speak with him again. Perhaps I can make him see it is best for him to buy Black Thunder. Perhaps if I appeal to his vanity . . ."

Philip looked up. "No. I am sorry. I have done it again. I turned my troubles into your troubles. And that is not right. You are a good friend, and I am grateful for what you did."

She was a good friend. Why did those words sting so badly? She should be grateful to boast a friendship with Mr. Jenkins. But her heart wanted more from Philip. It wanted . . . *Philip*.

"I am a man and can handle this on my own. You need not think on it a moment longer." He picked up her hands again, covering hers with his. "I thank you for all that you have done. Truly, I do."

She did not feel relieved. Indeed, her stomach felt jumpy and her muscles taut. Some of it may be because of the cold, but she could not place all of it there. She should have done more. And if the opportunity presented itself, she would.

A full body shiver shook her, even though her hands were warm.

Philip's brow creased again. "You are still cold?"

Elle shrugged.

He hesitated a moment. "Come here. It is not entirely proper, but I think keeping you warm is of more import than propriety." He opened the blanket draped around his back and scooted closer to her, wrapping his arms around her and encircling her with his blanket.

Elle's neck warmed, and her face flushed. He was right. This was most improper. But she could not bring herself to reject his offer. Already, she could feel the effect of his warmth.

She wanted to lean into him—rest her head on his chest and perhaps even close her eyes. But she knew she should not. "Why did you not tell me everything about Lady Dorothea?" It was none of her concern, she knew, yet she could not stop wondering about it.

"How do you know I did not tell you everything?" His voice was gruff, but not angry.

"I cannot put my finger on it. But it felt as if there was something left unsaid." She paused. "I know many gentlemen who would crow over their bravery. Yet you passed it over as if it were nothing."

He sighed.

She leaned in sightly. It would only keep her warmer, she told herself.

He tightened his hold on her, and Elle finally gave in, dropping her cheek onto his chest. The sound of his heartbeat thrumming in her ear brought a sense of safety she had not felt since she was a child. A part of her wished to push away from him so she did not grow accustomed to the feeling. But the desire to stay and embrace it, even knowing it was only for a fleeting moment, kept her in place.

"My father was the stable master at Severdale. As was his father before him. It was expected I would take the position when the time came for my father to retire. I had lived at the estate for the whole of my life. I knew Lord Downings's family as any servant knows his employer. We attended to them and saw their comings and goings. They lived in their sphere, and we lived in ours. It was not an unpleasant life." He sighed. "But then Lady Dorothea grew up."

Elle smiled against his chest. "My mother said she was an unrepentant flirt."

A wry chuckle vibrated through his chest. "Yes, that is a very accurate accounting. And for a young boy, unfamiliar with the ways of society, when she turned those flirtations on me, I thought myself in love. And perhaps even worse, I thought she reciprocated the feelings."

Elle could imagine a younger Philip thinking himself in love with Lady Dorothea. Her own brother had thought himself in love with Dorothea at one point in time. Elle smiled, but then her brow furrowed. Could it have been true love? Did Philip still hold a tendré for Lady Dorothea? Was that why he could not see Elle as anything but a friend?

He shifted underneath her cheek and pushed out a breath. "I do not crow over saving her because it was not happenstance that I was there. I knew where she was going. I had told her my father did not think the ice thick enough for skating yet. But she laughed and said her father thought it plenty thick. I followed her to the pond, hoping I might have the chance to skate with her. I planned to tell her how I felt about her. I even thought to offer for her." He puffed out his lips.

"It seems absurd and very naïve of me, looking back on it now. I knew her father would not approve, but had others like us not defied social barriers before? I thought we could be together. I thought we could be happy. When she dropped through the ice, I saw my dearest love disappear. I raced to save her. When I carried her back to Severdale Hall, I explained what had happened to her father. He was genuinely grateful and asked what he could offer me as a reward."

Philip frowned. "I told him all I wished for was his daughter's hand." He lowered his voice, whispering in Elle's ear. "You see, I thought saving her life was enough to prove my love."

Elle knew Lady Dorothea well enough to guess what had happened. "But she rejected you, did she not?"

He nodded. "Most adamantly. She begged her father not to consent. Then she made up terrible lies about me following her and trying to . . ." He cut off and cleared his throat. "Anyhow, Lord Downings did not believe his daughter's lies, thankfully, but he was also not about to allow the stable master's son to marry her either. Instead, he offered me this estate and two horses to begin my business." He looked around the stable. "Looking back, I can see I received the better part of the deal."

Elle looked up at him. She could see why Lady Dorothea would flirt with him. What she could not understand was how she could treat him so ill. He was a better man than any gentlemen of Elle's acquaintance. He was kind and worked hard—a trait she knew would not endear him to most of the *ton*. But it was who he was, and it made her love him more.

Her breath shook in her throat. She loved him? It felt foreign and odd to think about it, but not so much as to make it untrue. At that moment she realized that she did not care that he did not have money or status.

He looked down at Elle. "You are still shaking." He fingered a limp strand of hair at the side of her face and gently tucked it behind her ear. "I do not believe I can hold you any closer." His voice was low, and his breath dusted along her cheekbone.

She looked up into his face. "I'm not very cold. I must look a wreck, though."

"You could never look anything but lovely." He stared at her, and she held his gaze, unable to look away. He lifted his hand and untied the ribbons of her bonnet. It fell away, tumbling into the straw behind her. "That is better. It keeps rubbing against my skin."

She lifted her hand and ran her thumb over the dimple in his chin. "I'm sorry. Does it hurt?"

His breath stilled, and he shook his head. "No," he whispered. He paused only a moment before he dipped his head and brushed his lips lightly over hers.

Elle's eyes fluttered closed. Tiny, colorful lights danced behind her lids—it's what she had always imagined magic would look like if it were real. But this *was* real. Did that mean magic could be too? With Philip's lips against hers, she could almost believe anything was possible.

He shifted and his lips pressed harder, his arms pulling her closer to him.

Thunder cracked outside, but Elle hardly noticed it. Philip was kissing her, and she would not allow any distractions.

"What the devil?"

Philip jerked away, and all the magic disappeared.

Elle realized it had not been thunder she'd heard but the stable door slamming into place. She turned to see a stranger standing in the aisle, his mouth slightly agape.

"I was led to believe this was an emergency, Jenkins." The man raised a brow.

Philip jumped to his feet. "Uh, yes, well, it is an emergency. I was simply trying to keep Miss Carter warm until you arrived." He raked a hand through his hair. "Thank you for coming, Cooper. I am afraid she may have broken her ankle." He turned to Elle. "This is Mr. Cooper, the surgeon I told you about."

The surgeon. Oh, he was here about her ankle. Elle frowned, only now noticing the throbbing pain in her leg.

Cold air surrounded her, bringing on nearly uncontrollable shaking.

Mr. Cooper narrowed his eyes at her. "She looks to be freezing. I think it best if we move her to the house. The rain has not stopped, but it has let up. We should be able to get her there without soaking her more." He bent down. "Here. I can help you move her."

"No," Philip shouted, putting himself between Mr. Cooper and Elle. "I can manage."

Mr. Cooper raised a brow, but swept his hand in front of him, motioning Philip to proceed.

Elle hardly knew what to think. One minute Philip looked mortified to have been caught kissing her, and the next he seemed so protective. She could not begin to interpret what it all meant.

She lifted her hand so Philip could help her stand. But he did not take it. Instead, he stooped down and lifted her effortlessly into his arms.

"If you will man the door, Cooper." Philip held her tightly against him as he waited for the surgeon to open the stable door.

Mr. Cooper had been correct. The rain was still coming down, but not with the force of earlier. Philip breathed deeply then tucked his head and hurried across the lawns to the front door of Greystone.

Mr. Cooper ran ahead and opened the door, allowing Philip to turn sideways and slip inside.

Elle may not have become more wet, but the winds had chilled her right down to the bones.

"Mama," Philip called in the entryway.

A small girl, not much older than Winston, came around the corner. "Did you need something, sir?"

"Yes, Anne. Please find my mother and Grace and have them meet me in the parlor." He moved down the corridor. "Oh, and please have your mother warm up some soup and tea. We will need lots of tea."

The girl curtsied. "Yes, sir."

He stopped in the corridor and Mr. Cooper stepped forward and swung the door open. Philip stepped inside and walked directly to the couch in front of the fire. "Cooper, throw that rug over the couch, will you?"

Once the couch was sufficiently covered, he deposited her, then moved to the fire and dropped another log in the grate. Sinking down to his haunches, he poked at the coals until the log caught fire.

Elle tilted her head to the side, hoping for a better view of the defined shoulder and back muscles straining against his coat. She had never realized how pleasant it could be to watch someone stoke a fire.

"While we wait for Mrs. Jenkins, let me look at your ankle."

Elle grudgingly pulled her eyes from Philip's back and lifted her hem for the surgeon.

Mr. Cooper whistled low. "How did this happen, miss?"

"I was hurrying and slipped on the muddy ground."

He leaned to the side, examining the mud still caked on her elbows and back. "It must have been very important for you to be out in weather such as this." He flicked a glance at Philip and raised his brows.

"I brought you here to assess her ankle, not to make assertions." Philip folded his arms across his chest.

Mr. Cooper shrugged, but his grin stayed firmly in place. "Very well." He turned to Elle. "This may hurt a bit, miss. But I must assess if you broke the bone." He pressed his fingertips around her ankle.

Elle sucked in a breath as tears sprang to her eyes.

In three long strides, Philip was on the couch next to her. He took her hand in his. "Here, squeeze my hand when the pain becomes too strong."

She nodded and immediately tightened her grip.

The surgeon poked, and she clenched her teeth tightly.

Philip winced.

Elle looked over at him. "I'm sorry. Am I hurting you?"

He smiled and shook his head, tucking a hair behind her ear. "Not at all."

"What is going on in here?" Lady Kirtley's voice echoed through the quiet room.

Elle jerked her gaze to the doorway. Pulling her hand from Philip's, she momentarily forgot about the pain in her ankle. Lord Kirtley stood behind his wife, an amused look on his face.

"May I finish my assessment before we start the explanations? It is almost complete." Mr. Cooper pushed at the back and side of the ankle, and Elle fisted her hands at her side, missing the feel of Philip's hand in hers. It may not have cured the pain, but it had made her feel better all the same.

Mr. Cooper sat back and looked around. "The good news is her ankle isn't broken. However, it is severely sprained. She will need to stay off it for at least a month." He looked at Philip. "I believe we can forgo soaking it in cold water. It was subjected to the cold for long enough while you were waiting in the stable for the rain to let up."

Elle glanced at Lady Kirtley in time to see her eyes widen.

"I will apply a poultice and wrap the ankle. That is about all I can do. Rest will be the best medicine in this case."

Lady Kirtley stepped forward. "Thank you for your help, doctor, but I think we will take Miss Carter back to Briarwood."

"You should apply the poultice quickly. It is a simple recipe of vinegar and oatmeal. Although, stale beer is acceptable, also. It should help with the swelling."

Lady Kirtley smiled. "Yes. I will see to it once we have her settled at Briarwood." She motioned to Lord Kirtley. "Hugh, please help Miss Carter up."

Philip stepped forward. "She cannot walk. I can see her to your carriage if you will allow me."

Lady Kirtley narrowed her eyes. "You have done enough, Mr. Jenkins. We cannot impose on you further." She nodded to her husband.

Lord Kirtley placed Elle's arm around his neck and his around her waist. "Can you hop, Miss Carter?"

Elle nodded. She looked at the ground, unable to look Mr. Cooper or Philip in the eyes. Now that the ordeal was over, mortification flooded over her. She currently had her arm around her employer's neck. But more than that, she had allowed herself to be kissed rather thoroughly, and she had liked it. She had more than liked it. She wanted it to happen again and again. What had she become? How had she allowed herself to be so compromised? What would her mother think?

What if Lady Kirtley discovered the truth?

She would surely be out of a job. And then she would truly have nothing.

CHAPTER TWENTY-ONE

E lle stared out the carriage window, her whole body shaking, as Greystone disappeared behind a large stand of trees. Was Philip still watching from the open doorway, or had he retreated inside to warm himself in front of the fire? He was likely eating the soup he had ordered from his kitchens.

Elle's stomach growled, and she placed her hand over it.

"Miss Carter. I am uncertain how to think of what we saw when we walked into that parlor. I should think you very fortunate it was us and not someone else." Lady Kirtley shook her head. "And look at you—soaked through and caked with mud."

Elle pulled her eyes from the window. "It was nothing untoward, my lady." If Lady Kirtley was scandalized by what she had seen in the parlor, she would surely require smelling salts for what had happened in the stable. "Mr. Jenkins was simply allowing me to squeeze his hand when the pain from the doctor's prodding became too much. He was a perfect gentleman."

Lady Kirtley grunted. "And just how did fingering the curl at the side of your face help ease the pain?"

Elle turned back to the window. What could she say? Besides, the smile curving her lips would give an answer Elle did not wish to discuss further.

Lady Kirtley turned to her husband. "Hugh, please remind me the next time I am injured to have you tuck my hair behind my ear. It seems Miss Carter has discovered a new cure for pain." In the reflection in the glass, Elle saw Lady Kirtley raise a brow.

Lord Kirtley smiled. "I think she may be onto something, my dear. I believe there was a time when all I needed to do was touch your hair and you would have been too distracted to feel anything unpleasant."

Lady Kirtley scowled at her husband. "We are not speaking of us, Hugh. We are husband and wife and carry ourselves with great decorum." She looked back at Elle. "I cannot say the same for you, Miss Carter."

"Eleanor, leave the lady be. Can you not see is she half frozen? I dare say your lecture is having little effect. Perhaps you could save it for when she is warm and not suffering from a severe sprain." Lord Kirtley patted his wife's hand.

Lady Kirtley looked heavenward. "What in the name of Zeus were you doing out of doors in this dreadful weather, anyhow?"

Elle sat silently. She could not tell the truth—not with what Lady Kirtley had already seen. Perhaps Elle should have been coming up with an excuse instead of kissing Philip.

But she could not wish *that* had never happened. Even if it meant she was in the briars with Lady Kirtley and thoroughly confused as to what it meant to Philip. "I thought I saw Lady Sophia's spencer on the lawn. I remembered her removing it when we played outside earlier. I did not wish it to be ruined by the rain."

Gah! Elle was a terrible liar. There was no doubt Lady

Kirtley would see it for what it was and then, considering all that had happened today, send Elle on her way without a reference. "Mr. Jenkins must have seen me fall because he was at my side almost immediately. We were closer to Greystone, otherwise, I am certain he would have returned me here."

"Hmm." Lady Kirtley's gaze bore into Elle from across the carriage. And then moved to Elle's large ankle propped up on the bench. "For future reference, a child's spencer is not worth a month without an able-bodied governess."

Elle nodded. "I shall keep that in mind . . . next time." Was there even to be a next time?

"We are here. A footman can assist you to your room. I will send Heath to assist you in changing your gown and in applying the poultice." Lady Kirtley moved to the door and waited for her husband to hand her out.

"You really must not go to any more trouble, my lady. I am certain I can manage fine on my own." She scooted as close to the carriage door as possible and stood, balancing on one foot. "You see? I am well."

Lady Kirtley tilted her head to the side and gave Elle a bland look.

The footman reached up. Elle eyed his hand. How was she to manage the steps from the carriage? Why could Lady Kirtley simply not move into the house and leave Elle to bear this embarrassment alone?

"Miss Carter, you should practice your storytelling. I do not believe a word you have said."

Elle frowned. From the whole of the ride back from Greystone? Or just about being well? Not that the lady catching Elle in *any* sort of lie was desirable.

"I can see you are not well. Now I will not brook any opposition." Lady Kirtley looked at the footman waiting for Elle.

"Can you not see she needs assistance? I can see the size of her ankle from here."

The footman looked from Lady Kirtley to Elle and back again. "How should I assist her, my lady?"

Lady Kirtley waved another footman over. "Perhaps if you each stand on either side of the steps, she can use your shoulders as support as she hops down." A look passed between the two men, but they did as instructed.

Elle's face heated. It seemed red was the permanent color of her skin of late. She placed her hands on each man's shoulder and hopped down the first step. But the men were much too tall for her to hop to the ground in the same manner.

"Why must you stand there? She requires your arms now." Lady Kirtley shook her head at the footmen, obviously disappointed in their inability to see what needed to be done.

Elle held tightly to their arms until she made it to the ground. "Thank you," she muttered to each of them.

Lady Kirtley pointed to the footman on the left. "Now, if you would please help Miss Carter to her room."

He nodded and slipped an icy hand around Elle's waist. It immediately reminded her of how warm Philip's hand had been. Even after carrying her through the pelting rain. It was so different from the ice resting on her back now.

She looked over her shoulder at Lady Kirtley as they passed through the front doorway. Suddenly it occurred to Elle that she might never see Philip again.

Elle and the footman hobbled up the staircase. Tears had pooled in the corners of her eyes by the time she reached the first floor.

The footman deposited her at the door to the schoolroom, and Elle hopped inside, closing the door behind her.

"Miss Carter. What happened?" Lady Katie came to Elle's side and slid her hand down Elle's arm. "You're all wet."

Elle smiled down. "Yes. And you will be also if you continue in this way." She moved Katie away from her. "Let me put on a dry gown. And then we can talk."

Katie looked as if she were about to protest but simply nodded and stepped away.

Winston's brow furrowed. "Is Mr. Jenkins responsible for this?" Anger flashed across his features.

Elle smiled, even as her heart squeezed. Had Philip been correct? Did these children love her? The thought nearly caused the tears to spill over. "No, my lord. It was all my doing. It is what happens when one runs on muddy ground."

Winston nodded, satisfied. Although Elle wondered briefly what Winston would have done if she *had* blamed Philip for the accident.

She moved to her adjoining room—closet would have been a better description—and pulled a fresh gown and underclothes from the wardrobe with shaking hands. Oh, what she would not give for a chance to soak in a tub of hot water. But such was not her life anymore.

She fumbled with her buttons, taking twice as long as usual to unfasten them. She pulled the sodden dress over her head and laid it over an old chair next to the small firebox. Her mouth dropped open. Muddy brown stains covered the back of her gown. Lawks. How would she ever remove it all? She did not have enough gowns to dispose of this one. Letting out a heavy sigh, she sat down on the bed.

She would worry about that later. For now, she had lessons to teach. She pulled a white chemise over her head and then a gray gown. She twisted on the bed so she could put her ankle up while she tied the ribbons at her back.

A knock sounded at the door just as Elle tied the last one. "Come in," she called.

Heath kicked the door open with her foot and then

bumped it wider with her hip. "Lady Kirtley asked that I come assist you. I have a tisane for you to drink and a poultice for your ankle." She set the tray on the small bedside table.

Elle looked at everything. "I am sorry to cause you more work, Heath. I am certain my ankle will be fine. For now, I really must see to the children."

Heath looked at Elle's foot up on the bed. "You are wrong, miss. We must address your ankle immediately." She tilted her head from side to side. "Is the swelling worsening?"

Elle nodded. "I believe it is."

The maid poured out a liquid into a teacup and thrust it into Elle's hands. "Drink this."

Elle looked into the cup. It was much paler than the tea she was used to drinking. "What is it made of?" She thought she smelled lemons.

"Rosemary and cinnamon for the swelling. I mixed it with some of the lemonade in the kitchens to add some sweetness."

Elle sniffed at it again. It did not smell terrible. But it did not smell delicious either. She sipped it slowly. The warmth was as pleasing as the taste, which was sweeter than she had thought it would be. It must be from the sugar in the lemonade.

Heath applied the poultice to her ankle and then produced a long swath of cloth. She wrapped it around Elle's ankle. It was not so tight as to add to Elle's pain, but just enough to add support.

Elle relaxed into the bed. "Thank you, Heath. I feel better already."

Heath stood up. "You should. I added a few drops of laudanum to your tea. It is not full strength, but it should help to take the worst of the pain away." She held out her arm. "I will help you into the schoolroom."

"Thank you, Heath. For everything." She leaned heavily on

the smaller lady, hoping she had never treated the abigail poorly. "How did you learn such things?"

"My mother's father was an apothecary. She learned much from him and then passed the knowledge to me."

Elle patted the woman on the arm. "My ankle is very grateful to your mother and her father."

Heath nodded, her lips pushing up in the barest hint of a smile. "You are welcome, miss." She helped Elle settle into a seat near the children's table and then moved toward the door. "I will return in the morning to redress your ankle and apply more of the poultice. You need to drink *all* the tisane."

Elle nodded dutifully.

Nurse Jones sidled up next to Elle. "You all right, miss?"

Elle nodded. "I will be." The more she thought on the accident, the more irritated she was with herself. How had she been so stupid?

But then she would think on the kiss she shared with Philip, and she could not think herself so stupid after all.

"I hope he was worth all this, miss." Nurse Jones waved her hand above Elle's ankle.

Elle stared up at the woman. "What? You hope who was worth it?"

"That groom you ran out to meet. I could not see you with him out the window, but when I saw you hurrying across the lawn, I knew where you were going."

Elle pulled at the now straightened lock of hair lying on her cheek. "He is not a groom." Her voice came out more defensive than she intended. Although Nurse Jones was not so very wrong. Philip seemed to act as master, groom, and gamekeeper all in one. But Nurse Jones need not know that. "He is the owner of Greystone Manor. And he rescued me after I fell and injured my ankle."

Nurse Jones chuckled. "Perhaps the blind, or those preoc-cupied by something else, might believe your claims."

Elle's cheeks warmed. Was it so obvious to others that she loved Philip? How had it not been so obvious to her until today?

She turned her head toward the window, a grin slowly curving her lips. He had kissed her. She believed it must mean something because he did not seem the type of man to kiss a lady without having intentions toward her. But precisely what those intentions were, Elle was not certain.

What did she wish to happen? Elle bit her cheek. He was hardly the kind of gentleman society expected her to marry. She looked down at her gown. But then, society expected little of her anymore.

She squeezed her hands together. Why was she ques-tioning if she should marry him or not? He had made her no offer. Nor had he indicated he had any such plans. The only thing he had asked of her was that she speak to Larmont. As far as she knew, that was all he wanted from her. She frowned. That and a kiss.

Elle sighed and looked back out the rain-streaked window. It would be good to return to Dovehaven where there was no one who made her daydream or increased her pulse. No one she desired to see out the windows.

She had only to endure a few more days and then Lord and Lady Kirtley would take them all back to Kent.

Elle picked up her teacup and closed her eyes as she drank the tisane, allowing it to warm her. She turned back to the older woman. "Thank you for overseeing the children's studies, Nurse Jones."

The nurse shrugged. "Heaven knows you have done it for me more times than I can count." She gave Elle's arm a squeeze and whispered, "I didn't intend to embarrass you, miss. I wish only the best for you. You are a good person, and I hope that young man knows how fortunate he is to have secured your affections."

Elle jerked her head up. "What?" The other governesses and children in the room looked up, and Elle schooled her features. She dropped her voice to a fierce whisper. "I never said he held my affections. He simply acted as any other gentleman would. There is nothing more to it, I can assure you."

Nurse Jones raised a brow and nodded. "Very well, Miss Carter. I didn't intend to rile you."

"I am not riled. I only do not wish for false rumors to start." It surely wouldn't bode well should Lady Kirtley hear such rumors.

"No rumor will start with me, dear. You have my word." Nurse Jones smiled and stepped out of the schoolroom.

Elle ran her hands up and down her skirt several times. She sucked in a deep breath. "Children, where did you leave off with Nurse Jones?"

CHAPTER TWENTY-TWO

E lle leaned toward Winston and looked over his arm. "Very good, my Lord. I dare say you will be much ahead when your tutor arrives."

Winston's body stiffened. "Have you not yet chosen your path, my lord?"

Winston shrugged. "I have. Or rather it was chosen for me."

Elle patted him on the hand. "I believe what you must choose is the perspective with which you will travel the path chosen for you." She leaned in close. "I can tell you from experience that a poor perspective never helped me in the least."

"Miss Carter, might I have a word with you?" The Duke of Larmont stood in the doorway.

Elle frowned. What could he want with her? It must be important for him to lower himself to fetch her from the schoolroom.

She held up a hand and leaned down to offer Katie a kind correction. "I think you should try this one again, my lady."

Breathing in slowly through her nose, Elle pushed herself to standing, using the back of the nearby chair for support.

"Your Grace." She dipped a shallow curtsy.

He eyed her, his gaze dropping to her foot. "May we speak in the corridor, Miss Carter?"

Elle frowned. "I do not believe I can make it that far, Your Grace."

He stepped up beside her and put his arm around her waist. "I did not realize you had injured yourself so badly in the garden."

Elle's brow furrowed. "Oh, no. This was not from the garden. I slipped in the wet mud yesterday."

"You went out of doors yesterday?" His voice sounded doubtful. As if he could not believe someone would do such a thing. "Lean into me, Miss Carter, and I shall help you into the corridor."

What was so important that he could not discuss it with her in the schoolroom? They could move off to the side if he wished for privacy. Although, what he needed to discuss with Elle privately, she could not fathom.

They stepped over the threshold, and Larmont pulled the door closed behind them. Whatever it was he wanted to discuss with her, he was certainly causing more of a stir by removing her from the schoolroom than if he had just pulled her to the side. Did he plan to raise his voice?

He moved Elle to the opposite side of the corridor and released her, allowing her to lean against the wall. Clasping his hands behind his back, he moved several paces away from her and then back. "Elizabeth." Elle's brows rose on her head. He was using her Christian name? What could that possibly mean? "I have thought about this for some time—almost from the first day I saw you here. You are a handsome woman, one I should not feel any hesitation in having upon my arm. And you hail from nobility."

Elle squinted up at him. She had no notion where he

planned to take this conversation. Had he heard the rumors about her feelings for Philip? Was he here to caution her against such an alliance?

"While I do not know the particulars of your situation, I *do* know that this life"—he swept his hand up and down in front of her gray dress— "is not what your parents intended for you. Your mother raised you to be a lady, not some paid servant teaching someone else's children."

Elle swallowed, her cheeks instantly aflame. She'd had similar thoughts nearly every day since becoming a governess. Yet to hear the duke say them out loud felt even more degrading than when she'd thought them herself.

"As such, I would like to make you an offer of marriage." He stopped his pacing and stood in front of her.

Elle's mouth dropped open. "You what?" She could not have heard him right.

"I am offering for you, Elizabeth. I am offering to make you the Duchess of Larmont."

Elle blinked once. Twice. Then a third time. Surely, he was not in earnest. How could he be? He was as old as her father. But that was not the only problem she could see with this situation. What of her reputation? Why her?

She glanced up at him. Did he love her? She searched his face for anything that might show some partiality on his part. It seemed a far-fetched notion, considering they had hardly spoken in the last fortnight. They had hardly spoken in all of Elle's three and twenty years. It was not as if the duke made a habit of speaking to the children of his friends. Especially when those children were girls. So why? Why was he doing this?

She looked around the dusky corridor. Love seemed hardly likely, as this was the place he had chosen to make his proposal. It was not the most romantic of places to offer for a lady. Although now that she knew his designs, she was very glad he had removed her from the schoolroom. This was not something she wanted all the other governesses to witness.

She looked up at the man in front of her. He was not what she had imagined when she had dreamed of an receiving an offer. Her dreams usually had her in a garden, perhaps in the evening, just before darkness consumed the light.

She had even imagined it once or twice in a London ball-room after a scandalous waltz. But in the corridor outside the schoolroom? Never had her mind considered such a wholly unromantic place.

Where were the declarations of love and adoration? Where was the stolen kiss she had always dreamed of? Where was Philip and the dimple in his chin? For that was truly the offer she wished for now.

Larmont cleared his throat, and Elle looked up at him. "Well? What have you to say?"

Elle swallowed. What did she have to say? "It is a generous offer, Your Grace. May I have a day to think on it?"

His brow furrowed. "*If* you need such time. I will wait for your answer, but I shall not wait for long." He dipped a shallow bow and turned on his heel. He only took two long steps before he stopped and partially turned back. "You *do* realize the honor I pay you, do you not?"

Elle nodded. "Indeed, I do, Your Grace."

He raised a brow. "Very well. I will leave you to your charges."

Elle sucked in a deep breath. What had just happened? How was she to return to the schoolroom now?

Elle hopped across the corridor and swung open the door.

Winston jumped from his seat and moved to her side, putting a small hand—especially when compared to the duke's or Philip's—around her lower back. She hobbled beside him, trying not to put too much weight on the boy's shoulders.

He helped her into her seat, a proud smile on his lips.

Elle's chest tightened. It had been many months since she had seen such a genuine look on his face. She missed it but was at a loss about how to keep it there.

She placed her throbbing foot onto the chair next to her and sighed. She looked over at the children's work. "I apologize for the interruption, children. But it looks as though you did not need me for this task. You both did very well." She placed the next assignment on the table in front of them. "Let us see how you perform on this one."

Her gaze wandered to the window. The Duke of Larmont had offered for her. She wrapped her arms around her middle, a knot forming in her stomach.

There were obvious advantages to marrying Larmont. The most obvious being she would once again move about the *ton,* not as a servant, but as a member of Society. Larmont was one of the few men in England whose reputation could withstand Elle's fallen one. And she would be a duch—

"Miss Carter, I am finished." Katie looked up at Elle.

"That was quick, my lady. Did you do it proficiently?" Elle pushed her thoughts of Larmont and marriage aside. She could think on them once she had retired for the evening, or when she and Katie were painting. But for now, she had responsibilities that took priority.

Elle ran her finger next to the sums on Katie's slate as she checked the girl's work. "Well done, my lady. And I see you learned from the mistake I pointed out earlier." Elle used a rag to wipe the slate clean. "I think you have done enough studying now." She looked at Winston. "And how are you doing, my lord? Are you nearly finished with your assignment?"

Winston nodded and pushed his paper forward. "Yes, I am finished." There was no color or animation to his tone.

Perhaps if they went outside and played some games, he would forsake this solemn, melancholy boy that had taken over once again.

"It looks as though the rain has ceased now. How about we go outside and play a game?" Elle asked. She saw a spark of anticipation in Winston's eye, but it quickly vanished when he glanced down at her ankle.

"Oh, yes. That would be very diverting. We could play Blind Man's Bluff." Katie clapped her hands and pushed out of her seat. "Hurry, Winston. The last person out is the blind man!" She grinned and hurried toward the door.

Elle smiled. She should scold Katie for such unladylike behavior. But if Elle were being completely honest, she had a great urge to pick up her skirts and run after the girl—if only she could.

"How will you get outside, Miss Carter?" Winston looked far too concerned for someone his age. Elle stood up, making certain to hide the grimace of pain.

"I will have a footman come and help Miss Carter outside." Lady Kirtley stood just inside the doorframe, her mouth set in a firm line. "Although, would not an inside game suit Miss Carter's injury better?"

Both children's faces fell.

"I can make it on my own, my lady." Elle did not know how she would make the statement true. All she knew is she had to try. For Winston's sake.

"Nonsense. I will not risk having your recovery delayed any longer than necessary. Wait here and I will send up a footman to help you."

The schoolroom felt especially stifling when they returned from their games. The children immediately collapsed on the settee, but both had smiles on their faces.

The footman Lady Kirtley had commandeered to stay with Elle while they stayed outside deposited her on the window seat. "Thank you, Thomas."

She looked around the room. They were the only ones within. It seemed they had been an influence—whether for good or bad would depend on which governess you asked—on the other children. It had only been a short time before all the children were out on the grounds playing games.

From Elle's point of view, it had been enjoyable having all the children play together. It had made her feel less guilty about sitting on the chair and simply watching them. There were few children at the house party but having any other children involved in playing surely enhanced the pleasure.

She closed her eyes and smiled. In a few moments, the schoolroom would again be full, and the peacefulness would flee.

Nurse Jones poked her head in from the nursery. "There is a note for you on that table over there."

Elle's brow furrowed. "For me?" Was it from Philip? Her stomach fluttered. "Who could it be from?"

Nurse Jones shrugged. "I have no notion. A maid brought it up while you were out with the children."

Katie moved over to the table and snatched it up. "Here you are, Miss Carter." She handed the note over.

Elle turned it over in her hands. There was no wax seal. The letter stayed closed simply by the intricate folds. There were also no directions on the front. Only Elle's name. *It did not come by post, then.*

She unfolded the paper.

Her stomach flopped again when she took in the masculine

writing. Her eyes dropped to the signature and the hill of ants inside her stomach scattered. It *was* from Philip.

She smoothed out the creased paper on her lap, allowing her eyes to scan the letter. A smile curved her lips. It was short and did not boast any declarations of love. Even so, Elle could not stop her heart from racing.

Dear Miss Carter,

Elle dropped the letter to her lap. Miss Carter? Not Elizabeth? Surely, he was using such formalities in case anyone else saw the letter. It was most improper for him to be sending a letter at all. But for it to contain Christian names would only make the scandal worse should someone intercept the note.

I know this is highly improper, but I saw no other way of assuring you were well and to thank you for the information you provided me. It has proven most helpful. I am forming a plan even as I write this letter.

Please send a quick reply so I might know you are well.

Yours,

P Jenkins.

Elle read through the letter again. The contents were not so scandalous. It was simply the letter itself that would cause people to judge.

"Who is it from?" Nurse Jones stood at Elle's elbow and raised her brows as if she already knew the answer. Which she likely did. But Elle did not intend to let the nurse know she was right. "Miss Jenkins, from Greystone. She was asking after my ankle." It was only a partial lie. And one Elle did not feel bad about. It was no one's business that the letter was from Philip.

And while she did not believe Nurse Jones would tell anyone if she knew the truth, Elle did not wish to share Philip or his letter with anyone. It was hers and hers alone. She swallowed, wishing she could say as much about him.

She folded the paper up and tucked it in the sleeve of her

gown. Philip was thinking about her. That was enough, was it not? Even the thought of him thinking about her made her grin like an idiot. She pulled one knee up to her chest, tucking her gown around her, and dropped her chin onto it.

If he was thinking on her, surely that meant there was some partiality. And if he was partial to her, could she even consider marrying the duke? She did not love the duke, nor was there much chance she ever would. But she would have status again. And money. But what was that to love?

She leaned her head against the glass. They would return to Kent in a few days. A tightness formed in Elle's chest. Would she return with them? Or would she be heading to her brother's estate in Oxfordshire to prepare for her wedding? Her stomach roiled. If only she could speak to Philip again.

"Miss Carter, I am hungry." Katie stood at Elle's side.

"Then I will ring for tea and a bite to eat."

Winston stood and tugged at the bell cord in the corner.

"Who was the letter from?" Katie's soft voice sounded at Elle's elbow.

"It was from Miss Jenkins at Greystone. She inquired after my ankle." Elle felt guilty lying to Katie. Even more so than she had when she lied to Nurse Jones.

Katie clasped her hands together. "Oh, I wish we could visit Greystone one last time before we return to Kent."

"As do I." Winston appeared next to his sister. "Mr. Jenkins thought they may have another new foal in the next day or two. I should like to see it before we leave."

Elle nodded. She felt precisely the same way. Although, her reasons were very different. She closed her eyes, trying to picture Philip's face. Trying to feel the warmth of his hands on her back and his breath on her cheek as he moved in to kiss her.

Her face heated, and she jerked open her eyes. What was she doing? Such remembrances were for when she was alone.

Not when others were there to witness her blush. "Lady Katie, why do you not fetch our book, and I will read to you while we wait for tea."

Katie grinned and scampered toward Elle's closet-room.

———— ⟨∽⟩ ————

Elle shut the book just as the door to the schoolroom opened and a maid entered with a tea tray.

Placing the book on the bench beside her, Elle put her feet on the floor. She bit her cheek against the pain and hobbled the few steps to the table.

Elle shook her head. If she could not even make the few steps to the table, it seemed one last adventure to Greystone was out of the question. Her eyes drifted out the window. Even though she could see none of his estate from this window, she still somehow knew that Philip was out there. She could picture it as easily as she could picture her childhood home. But would the pictures be enough? Or would they merely be a torturous reminder of what she could not have?

CHAPTER TWENTY-THREE

Philip looked at his reflection in the mirror and ran a hand through his hair. He scowled. That had not helped in the least. With a cleanly shaven face, and wearing his best tailcoat and waistcoat, Philip still felt as if something was amiss.

Straightening the misplaced hair with his hand, he shifted his shoulders, settling his coat into place.

"You look very handsome, Philip." Grace stood in his doorway. "Where are you going looking so fine?"

Philip pointed to the bonnet on the chair next to the window. "Miss Carter left her bonnet behind in the stable."

Grace's gaze stayed firmly on him. "You have feelings for Miss Carter, do you not?"

Philip cleared his throat but did not return her stare. "I cannot say I have feelings for her, but I will admit to enjoying her company." His nose scrunched up. He did not believe his own words. If Grace were even remotely thinking of anyone but herself, she would surely see the lie. But Grace thought very little of others lately, so it was possible she would not notice.

She chuckled. "You enjoy her company? Really, Brother?" She leaned against the door frame. "The house party is nearly over. I suggest you decide your feelings before Miss Carter leaves for good."

"Yes, well, perhaps her removal would be for the best. I have neglected a great deal while they have been visiting the earl. I should be much further along on the repairs of the tenant cottages than I am."

Grace crossed her arms. "Why are you so reluctant to admit that you find Miss Carter amiable and might wish to court her?"

Philip narrowed his eyes at her. "It is none of your concern, Gracie. I have not the time nor inclination to discuss such things."

"Is it because of Lady Dorothea?"

Philip's shoulder twitched. "No," he snapped. His voice sounded much louder than he had intended, and he regretted the outburst immediately.

Grace stared at him for several heartbeats. "Very well. I shall only say one thing and then I shall speak of it no more." She raised a brow that reminded Philip so much of their mother. "It has been eight years, Philip. You need to let go of the hurt and move on. Not all women are like her, you know." She tilted her head to the side. "Unless it is not hurt but love which you still harbor for Lady Dorothea."

How did Gracie even remember Dorothea? She had only been eight years old and had little to do with those in the main house back then. That Gracie knew of Philip's feelings—past feelings—for the lady was surprising.

"There is no lingering love for Lady Dorothea, I can assure you."

Grace nodded. "Then it is only hurt and resentment that remains."

She said it as if it were easy to push aside. As if it were a mere fly to be swatted away. No one had ever betrayed Gracie. She had no notion what it felt like, how deeply it cut into one's soul. The soul was not so easily mended.

"Yes, that is all that remains." Perhaps if he agreed with her, she would leave him alone.

"Then let it go, Philip. The lady is not worth eight years of your life. She is not worth your unhappiness."

Philip swallowed. "I know, Gracie." Where had this observant Grace been for the last few years? He would have been happy to see her return if she were not directing her perceptiveness at him.

She gave him a single nod and turned away, leaving him staring at his reflection once again.

Philip fidgeted with his coat. Logically, he knew his sister was right. He needed to let go of his anger. And he could not deny the draw he felt toward Elizabeth. Nevertheless, there was something about her that held him back, something that made him leery to profess his love for her. Wait. He squinted at himself. Was it true? Did he love her?

He swallowed as the truth of the words settled over him. But how? How had he allowed it to happen? He had worked so hard to guard against it.

Somehow, she had found a weakness in his defenses.

But now what was he to do? She was to quit Briarwood in a few days' time and return to Kent with Lord and Lady Kirtley. Could he allow that to happen? How could he stop it?

An urgency he had never felt before, not even in those moments when he'd searched for Lady Dorothea in the icy water, tightened his chest and caused his muscles to twitch with tension. He was to go to Briarwood to return her bonnet, but should he try to speak with her or just leave the bonnet with a servant?

His chest squeezed, and he knew he could not leave Briarwood without seeing her. What would he say? He did not feel ready to make an offer. And yet, what else would keep her from returning to Kent? Would she even accept him if he offered for her?

He shook his head. He had no notion how she might feel about him. She had seemed willing when he had kissed her in the stables. Philip ran a hand through his hair again. Why he had done such an impulsive thing, he did not know. He had chastised himself nigh onto a hundred times for the action, even as the thought of it brought a smile to his face. Could it be he had done it because a part of him had already realized he loved her? Had his brain simply not yet figured out what his heart had already known?

When he thought on the kiss itself, he could think nothing but pleasant thoughts. The memory of the feel of her fingertips brushing over his chin. The smooth skin of her hands as he held them between his own rough, calloused ones. And her lips . . .

He did not allow himself to think on them often, afraid that if he did, he might go mad knowing he might never taste them again.

But it was more than just her lips. He loved her goodness.

As a servant, he had been mostly invisible to those of the higher class. Through the years, he had watched nurses and governesses for both Lord Downings's children and those of his guests. Never had he seen one like Elizabeth.

While she might deny it—Philip believed it was the proper thing to do—he was certain she cared for the children in her charge. Perhaps even loved them. She was kind and patient, offering correction quietly so as not to draw embarrassing attention to the child. She answered their questions and attentively listened to them.

Philip saw the way Lord Culpepper watched out for her

and beamed under her praise. It was not the attentions of a boyish fancy but more like the respect and adoration one might have for an older sister.

Elizabeth would make a wonderful sister to Grace, who needed such an example. And in time, a good mother.

And Elizabeth made him laugh. She may not be outwardly witty to most, but he found her most entertaining. Simply watching her cheeks change color could entertain him for hours. He smiled as he thought on her story of ambushing the Duke of Larmont. But could he offer for her? He had nothing to give her, nothing to make his offer appealing.

Philip straightened the knot on his cravat. The more he thought on it, the more certain he was that it would be impossible for him to live without her.

But to make an offer meant he must take a risk. And he was not certain he was up for the task.

Papa, please do not force me to live a life of servitude simply for disobeying you. Lady Dorothea's words from that day eight years ago, echoed in his mind. He had been quite certain she returned his affections. What if he was wrong again? Could he recover from a broken heart a second time?

Perhaps he should start by seeing how Elizabeth's ankle faired. If the visit went well, then he could gather the courage to ask for her hand.

That was what was best. He would go to Briarwood and inquire after her wellbeing.

Philip scowled at himself. *You are a coward, Philip Jenkins.* But coward or not, he could not bring himself around to the notion of an offer without some assurances.

He gave his jacket one last hard tug, straightening it and shaking himself at the same time. He moved away from the mirror before he found something else to find displeasure in.

Walking down the steps, he looked down into the entryway

and followed the walls up to the high ceiling above him. It was a fine house—a fine entryway. But was it desirable enough for a young lady to wish to be mistress? Perhaps not Lady Dorothea. But as Gracie had pointed out, not all ladies were like Dorothea.

Philip stepped through the door of the parlor, and his mother glanced up from her stitchery. Her brows rose. "You look very handsome, Son."

Philip tugged at this waistcoat and looked down. "Do not raise your brows at me, Mama. I have already received the look from Grace." He frowned. "Why must everyone take notice simply because I changed from my work clothes? I had rather thought it would please you."

His mother smiled. "Oh, I am pleased. Make no mistake about that. It is simply unusual." She looked back to her sampler. "Perhaps it is because you are always working. I am happy to see you take a break from the stable chores."

"Thank you, Mama." It surprised Philip she had not questioned his reasons for changing.

"Are you making a trip into the village?" She continued to study her needlework, yet Philip could hear the curiosity in her voice.

"No. I thought to go to Briarwood. Miss Carter left her bonnet here the other day. I wished to also make certain her ankle is healing well." He cleared his throat when his mother smiled. "When she left here, she was soaked through. I should feel quite responsible should she develop a cold and become gravely ill."

His mother nodded. "Yes, that would be terrible. Do you wish for Grace to accompany you?"

Philip shook his head. "No. I am certain my presence will put the earl off enough. I do not wish for him to speak harshly in front of Grace."

The smile slowly faded from his mother's lips. "Yes, you are likely correct. The earl is not so very fond of our family. It would be better for Grace to remain home."

Philip knew it pained his mother that those in the neighborhood still thought of their family as no better than servants. The earl was more than willing to point this out to anyone who would listen.

She looked up and smiled. "Please pass along my regards to Miss Carter, will you, dear?"

Philip nodded. "Of course, Mama."

Striding to the stables, Philip guided Adonis out of his stall and quickly saddled him for the ride to Briarwood. Normally, he would have just walked on the path between their estates. But with the unpredictable weather they'd had of late, he did not dare. The last thing he wished was to appear at Briarwood, dripping wet.

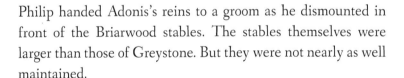

Philip handed Adonis's reins to a groom as he dismounted in front of the Briarwood stables. The stables themselves were larger than those of Greystone. But they were not nearly as well maintained.

There was not a nail or board loose within the Greystone stables. Briarwood could not boast as much. Philip's pride in his stable was second only to his pride in his horses.

The groom dipped his head. "I will take him from you, Mr. Jenkins, sir."

Philip smiled. "Thank you, James."

Walking up the wide front steps, Philip patted his pockets, feeling for the calling card he had tucked in there before he left Greystone. The earl was rather adamant about calling cards, even though most of the staff knew Philip by name.

Philip knocked on the door and took a step back, running a hand down his coat sleeves and checking his pants. Was there anything the earl would find lacking? Philip shrugged. Likely. The earl always found Philip lacking. And if there was nothing to find, he would surely make something up.

The butler opened the door and Philip thrust his card forward, his other hand tightening around the bonnet ribbons. "Miss Carter dropped her bonnet yesterday. I came to return it."

The butler reached forward. "I will see she receives it."

Philip put the hand with the bonnet behind his back. "I, uh. I also wished to check on her recovery. When last I saw her, she was badly injured."

The butler nodded, looking Philip up and down. "Please come in. I shall see if she is available." He turned his back to Philip. "It is likely she is teaching the children at present."

Philip nodded. "Yes, I understand."

"Wait here, Mr. Jenkins." The butler sounded mildly irritated as he motioned to a corner of the entryway. He moved to the coatroom doorway and began whispering to a footman. Their eyes flicked to Philip many times during the brief conversation before the footman nodded and walked up the staircase.

Philip clasped his hands behind his back, the brim of Elizabeth's bonnet bouncing against the backside of his knees. Perhaps he should have just given the bonnet over to the butler. Elizabeth was surely busy.

Hours ticked by. Or perhaps it was only minutes.

Philip shifted from one foot to the other. He glanced at the butler several times, offering a weak smile each time. This seemed less and less like a good idea. Perhaps Philip had romanticized his time with Elizabeth in the stable. She had been cold and hurt, which had likely made her vulnerable. Had he taken advantage of her vulnerability? Philip frowned.

"Mr. Jenkins, if you will follow me. Miss Carter asks that you meet with her in the schoolroom as it is too difficult for her to use the stairs."

Philip nodded, sucking in a quiet breath through his nose. This was why he had built up his defenses against women. He hated feeling weak and dependent upon another for his happiness. Could he be happy without her? The thudding in his chest made him wonder.

However, when he stepped through the doorway into the schoolroom and saw Elizabeth sitting at the child-sized table, his apprehension fell away. She was here, and she was smiling up at him. That had to mean something, did it not? Lady Dorothea had never looked at him as Elizabeth did.

She smiled and motioned to a chair across from her. "Mr. Jenkins. Please, have a seat."

Philip moved over and sat down, his knees coming up to his chest in the child-sized chair. He slid the bonnet across the table. "Your bonnet must have fallen off when you fell."

He smiled when her face turned crimson. Was she thinking back on how her bonnet had really come loose? He had relived that moment more times than he could count.

She pulled the hat toward her, and the silken ribbon slid through his fingertips. "Thank you for returning it. I was uncertain where I had lost it and it is one of my favorite bonnets." She glanced up from the tabletop, and her gaze met his. The smell of orange blossoms filled the air between them. How had he believed this was not worth the risk? Now that he was here, he was ready to risk everything if it meant being with her.

This was right. This was what he wanted.

She shifted. "Was there something else, Mr. Jenkins? Shall I ring for tea?"

Philip shook his head. He knew he wished to offer for her, but he could not do so here in the schoolroom. It was the least romantic place he could think of to profess one's love. Except for perhaps the corridor.

At the very least, a parlor would do, if the gardens were unavailable.

He shook his head. "No. I did not intend to disrupt the children's studies for an extended time. I simply wished to know how your ankle faired. And to assure myself that you had not taken ill."

She blushed again. He did not know why, yet it did not stop him from enjoying the sight of it. "As you can see, I am well. The poultice Heath has been applying is working wonders. The swelling has gone down, and the pain is decreasing."

Philip stood up, even as his heart told him to stay there forever. "I am pleased to receive such a report and to see with my own eyes that you are well."

Elizabeth nodded.

Philip stood there, staring down at her. Neither spoke for what must have been a full minute.

Elizabeth cleared her throat.

"Oh, I almost forgot to pass along my mother's regards." He nodded his head like an idiot. "Yes, well. I must be on my way. Good day, Miss Carter."

She smiled and awkwardly stood up.

He put his hands out to steady her. "You mustn't stand, Miss Carter. The doctor said you were to stay off your ankle."

She looked down at her single foot standing on the floor. "I am not on my injured foot, Mr. Jenkins. You need not worry." She looked around the room at the other governesses, all of whom looked to be far too intent on their charges to truly not be listening to his conversation. "Thank you, Philip. It was pleasant seeing you again. I had not thought I would before we returned to Kent." Her voice was low and the sound of his name on her lips warmed his belly and chest.

"If I do not see you before you leave, safe travels, Ellie." He had no intention of allowing her to return to Kent. But with all the listening ears in the schoolroom, it seemed best to pretend she would leave.

She tilted her head to the side. "My mother used to call me by that name."

Philip frowned. "I'm sorry. I should not have been so presumptuous."

She shook her head. "Please, do not apologize. I find I rather like it, coming from you."

If he had any doubts before about his feelings for her, they were gone now. She seemed more than amiable to him, and he could no longer deny he loved her. He loved Ellie. And he would see that she knew it before she removed herself to Kent.

CHAPTER TWENTY-FOUR

E lle wrung her hands, twisting so hard the blood seemed to leech from them. Philip's visit had been unexpected, but in no way unwelcome. It had thrilled her when the footman told her Philip was at Briarwood to see her. Surely if he cared nothing for her, he would have simply left the bonnet with the butler and returned to Greystone. But he had wished to see her.

She bit her lip to keep the cry of happiness inside.

"Miss Carter. His lordship wishes to see you." A maid dipped a curtsy. "Please follow me."

Elle looked at Katie and Winston, her brows raised. "Please continue reading. I shall return shortly." She looked at Winston. "If Lady Katie does not know a word, please help her, my lord."

Winston nodded.

She stood up gingerly, grabbing the walking stick Lady Kirtley had procured for her. It did not keep Elle from walking on her injured ankle, but it helped to take some of the weight off it.

She followed behind the maid, wincing with every step she took. Where were they going? And why did Lord Ryecombe wish to speak with her? Her stomach twisted. Had she done something wrong that he thought to reprimand her for?

They stopped outside a door. Thankfully, they had traversed no stairs, but Elle was certain they had moved to the opposite side of the house. Wherever they were, it had taken hundreds of painful footsteps to get there, and Elle was no closer to discovering the reason for her summons.

The maid curtsied and left Elle standing alone in the corridor. She raised her hand and rapped lightly on the door.

"Come." Not even the door muffled the terse order from inside.

Elle pushed on the door and limped inside.

The earl looked up from the papers on his desk. "You are Miss Carter?"

Elle nodded. "Yes, my lord."

He eyed her up and down. "Do come closer. I can hardly see your face in the shadows."

Then perhaps you should light another candle, Elle thought but kept her mouth pinched closed. She took several steps forward, clenching her teeth. The long walk had put her in a foul mood. Not only did pain pulse up her leg, but her shoulders ached, and her head pounded at the temples from bracing herself against the footfalls.

She looked longingly at the chairs in front of his desk. There was a time when she would have been invited to sit down. Although, most gentlemen would still offer upon seeing her current condition.

"I heard you were injured. What is wrong with your foot?" Ryecombe asked, lacking any concern in his voice.

"A severe sprain, my lord. I slipped on the wet grass." It was mud, in actuality, but this man did not seem concerned about the particulars. Indeed, knowing it was mud would likely only make him think less of her than he already did.

"I am certain it was no fault of mine or my staff."

Elle's eyes narrowed. Was he trying to place blame elsewhere? She had not inferred it was anyone's fault, yet he made certain to remove it from himself. It only proved to irritate her more. The man had made her walk all this way on an injured ankle simply so he could shirk responsibility?

"I believe it was only the fault of the rain, my lord." Elle said through clenched teeth.

He grunted. "I understand Mr. Jenkins came to see you."

Elle nodded.

"Why?"

What business was it of his? He was not her father, nor her employer. Why did he care who came to visit her? "My bonnet slipped off when I fell. He was simply returning it to me."

Ryecombe gave her a bland look. "But he came to see you, did he not? If he was simply returning a bonnet, why did he not just give it to Hollings?"

Elle shifted on her feet. She was not comfortable with this conversation. It seemed the earl knew the particulars but wished for her to tell him of them anyway. "He wished to see that I was not ill after being out in the rain." Why did she feel compelled to give him the information? Perhaps it was because he sat at his desk, scowling at her. Suddenly, leaving Briarwood the day after tomorrow did not feel too soon. "He was acting as a gentleman."

"Mr. Jenkins is no gentleman," Ryecombe scowled. "It has come to my attention that Mr. Jenkins has taken a personal interest in you, Miss Carter. And as a friend of your late father, I feel it my duty to warn you away from him. The man is no better than a servant. I know he thinks himself a gentleman, but it is not the truth."

"Why are you telling me this now, my lord? I am for Kent with Lord and Lady Kirtley the day after tomorrow. Do you think Mr. Jenkins intends to do something untoward in the short time we have remaining here?" She shifted, leaning heavily on the walking stick, trying to relieve some of the throbbing in her ankle.

"I have no notion concerning Mr. Jenkins's motivations or thoughts. I was simply offering a warning. He should raze that house. It is nothing but a dangerous, burned-out shell. Making a few public rooms presentable, does not change what the house really is. He would do well to sell me the land and quit the estate all together."

Ah, the earl desired Philip's land. It explained the ill-will the earl held toward Philip. But why was he telling *her* all this? The earl seemed to know all the particulars concerning her and Philip. Except for those surrounding the kiss. She pushed down her grin.

Perhaps Ryecombe had heard something Elle had not. "I must confess my confusion, my lord. I have no notion why you should feel compelled to expose Mr. Jenkins's true nature to me. I am certain my father would have appreciated what you are doing for me. But I have seen nothing to warrant your concern."

He steepled his fingers in front of him. "Very well. I only wished to make you aware that his motives might be questionable."

The earl was right. She had learned much from their meeting. But it had more to do with the earl's true nature, rather than Philip's.

"If that is all, my lord, I must return to the schoolroom."

She dipped a curtsy and turned from the room, limping painfully into the corridor.

Once the door was closed behind her, Elle leaned her back against the wall. Tears stung at her eyes. How was she to make it all the way back to the other side of the house? The pain in her ankle was quite unbearable after standing on it for so long. She slid down, sitting on the floor with one ankle propped on top of the other. How long would it take before someone came looking for her?

"Elizabeth?" Henry—or rather Lord Amesbury—stopped midstride. "Good heavens, what are you doing there on the floor?"

Elle choked on a sob. She pounded a fist into the carpet, angry at her lack of control. "I cannot make it to the school-room. The pain in my ankle is too great."

Henry stooped down. "Yes, I heard about your mishap." He leaned forward and put an arm behind her back. "Let me help you up. Then you may lean on me until we return you to the schoolroom."

"No. I do not wish to be an inconvenience. You were on your way somewhere, just now. I do not wish to make you late."

Henry sighed. "You are not an inconvenience, Elizabeth." He supported her as they moved down the corridor. Elle leaned her head against his shoulder. She had missed her friendship with Henry.

"Henry?"

He looked down at her. "Yes?"

"Do you believe in marrying for love?"

His brow creased. "I think everyone thinks on it at least once in their life."

Elle sighed. "But if given the choice, would you marry who you loved or who had the greatest wealth and status?"

Henry paused. "What I would do is not the same as what you should do, Elizabeth. I am a man. I have more options in this life than you."

Elle made an unladylike sound. "You are no help at all, Henry."

He squeezed her waist lightly. "You are right. You asked for my opinion and I shall give it to you." He stopped as if organizing his thoughts. "If I were a lady, I believe I would marry for wealth and status."

Elle's chest tightened. "You would? But why?"

He shrugged. "You should know better than anybody, Elle. Your father died and left you unprotected. If you marry someone of less standing because you love them, and then something happens, what becomes of you? You must take on the task of finding a position as a companion or a governess again." He frowned and Elle frowned too. "On the other hand, I am certain the Duke of Larmont will provide you with a sizable jointure, should he die before you."

Elle flicked her gaze up. "What have you heard?"

"Only that he offered for you." He shrugged. "I know it was not the answer your heart wished for. But it is the answer your brain should understand. You need security, Elle. And Larmont can offer you that."

Elle nodded. "Thank you for your honesty, Henry. You are still a dear friend."

They reached the end of the corridor where a footman stopped them. "Ah, Miss Carter. The Duke of Larmont requests you to join him for tea. He is in the yellow parlor."

Elle sagged. What was it with the nobility attending this party? Could none of them leave her in peace?

And Larmont? He was the last person she wished to see. She did not have her answer for him yet. And she would much prefer to return to the schoolroom and take tea with the children. Heath had delivered a new tisane earlier and the thought of drinking it, even cold, was much more appealing than tea with Larmont.

Henry turned her around.

"What are you doing? The schoolroom is that way." She motioned over her shoulder.

"Yes, but the duke invited you to have tea. Surely you do not intend to turn him down." Henry looked at her as if she might be daft.

"Yes, that was my plan. My ankle needs rest, not tea with the Duke of Larmont."

Henry shook his head. "What happened to my sensible friend? The Elizabeth Carter I knew would never have turned down such an opportunity."

Elle shrugged but continued to allow Henry to lead her away from the schoolroom. "I am afraid you do not know Elizabeth Carter anymore. She had to change in order to survive."

Henry looked at her with sad eyes. "I am sorry for her. But I am her friend and will not allow her to miss this chance—this chance to do more than just survive."

They stopped outside the door to the yellow parlor. "Do you think you can make it the rest of the way on your own?"

Elle sighed. She wanted to say no, but she knew Henry could take her no farther. "Yes, I will manage. Although, how I will return to the schoolroom I do not know."

Henry smiled. "I am certain the duke will escort you."

She raised a shoulder. "I do not think you can be so certain. After all, he did not come to fetch me."

"If he does not offer, stay here. I will check in this room on my way back to my chambers."

It was not the offer she wished to receive. She would rather return to the schoolroom now. But it was better than nothing.

At least she knew someone would come for her eventually if Larmont did not help her back.

"Very well." She pulled her hand from his arm and leaned onto her stick. "Thank you for helping me, Henry."

He dipped his head. "It was my pleasure, Elle."

Elle hobbled into the yellow parlor. Larmont was sitting on the sofa, a tea tray already on the table in front of him. He looked up, and a hint of a smile crossed his face. It was the first time she had noted any indication he was pleased to see her. "Good afternoon, Elizabeth."

When Henry said her name, it brought back memories of joy and happiness from their childhood. When Philip said her name, she thought butterflies might fly out of her stomach and her heart might beat out of her chest. But when Larmont said her name? She felt nothing. Surely that should give her the answer to his question, should it not?

He motioned to the chair across from him. "I expected you sooner."

She sat down and closed her eyes as the intense pain faded into a dull throb. "I am sorry if I kept you waiting. Lord Ryecombe wished to speak with me, and the footman found me in the corridor as I was returning to the schoolroom." She motioned to her ankle. "And I am moving much slower of late."

Larmont nodded. "Ah, yes. I should have taken your injury into account." He motioned to a servant girl standing to the side, and she stepped forward, pouring out a cup of tea for Elle.

Elle smiled. "Thank you."

The maid dipped a curtsy and moved into the corner of the room. It seemed she was to act as chaperone.

"I hope you come with good news." He sipped from his cup, but his gaze stayed on her.

He wanted an answer. She had known this moment would

come. She had only hoped he wanted to discuss something else because she was still uncertain of her answer.

She did not want to marry Larmont. But Henry's words came again to her mind. *You need security, Elle. And Larmont can offer you that.* Would Larmont give her the security she longed for?

She had told Winston that everyone had to pick a path. Did she not think that notion applied to her? Which path was she to follow? Which path was best for her and her future?

"You do not have an answer for me yet?" Irritation laced his words.

Elle left her teacup on the tray. "Do you love me, Your Grace?"

"Do I love you? What a notion." He raised a disdainful brow.

Elle frowned. She had not expected him to admit he loved her, but she had not thought he would find the notion so distasteful. "And I do not love you, Your Grace. I find it difficult to accept knowing that to be the case."

Larmont looked at her as if he might be reconsidering his offer. "Love is for poets and silly young girls, Elizabeth. If I had wished to marry a silly young girl, I would have made an offer to Miss Perdy. But I wish for a wife with some sense and decorum, which is why I offered for you."

Elle licked her lips. "But why, Your Grace? Why would you choose me when I have nothing else to offer?"

He nodded. "That is true enough. But I do not need a wife with a large dowry. I have plenty of money. And I do not need an heir. I already have an heir and a spare."

Elle swallowed. If she had come here thinking to hear overtures of love and affection, she was to be disappointed. "You have only told me what you do not need. What made you choose me? Surely there are other young ladies with sense, decorum and dowries, whose reputations are intact."

"You are very handsome, Elizabeth. I wish to enjoy looking at the person sitting at the dinner table with me each night. Your mother raised you to be a nobleman's wife, and I believe you very well-suited to the task." He sighed. "Perhaps I also feel a small sense of obligation to your father."

Elle picked up her tea. Obligation and beauty. That was to be the basis of their marriage?

"I cannot offer you love, Elizabeth. But I can offer you a title, a sizable jointure, and enough pin money to buy what a lady desires. Is that not enough to convince you? I should have thought it an easy decision. I am offering you a way out...a chance to forsake your paid position."

Elle looked around her. Her mother had taught her how to be a lady and a mistress. This offer would return her to her former social position. Indeed, it would elevate her beyond what she had been before. Henry was right. She needed security. And as much as it broke her heart to admit, this should be her path.

She looked out the window and saw Greystone in the distance. Why did she have to be in a room that had a clear view of that estate? The black charred rocks of the west wing stood out, as if they were confirming what she already knew. She needed to marry Larmont. She only hoped it was possible to be happy in a marriage without love.

Larmont cleared his throat. "I am certain, in time, we might grow fond of each other. But until then, we get on well enough. You are intelligent enough. I should not think I will avoid conversations with you."

Elle blinked. She supposed he meant it as a compliment, even if it sounded like a slight.

"Your Grace, may I ask what you decided regarding the horse you thought to buy from the Greystone stables?"

He shrugged. "I think I shall wait and look at Tattersalls next time I am in London."

Philip was not to have the sale, then. Was that not what was most important to him? She thought of the look on his face when he had learned that Larmont was not going to buy the horse.

Elle sucked in a deep breath. In for a penny, in for a pound. "You asked for my answer, and I am ready to give it. I accept your offer, Your Grace. But I wonder if I might make a request?"

He looked at her, and the corners of his lips turned up in a small smile. "I have not offered you enough?"

She grinned. Did this mean he might have some wit within him? "Your offer is very generous, and I know I have no right to ask any more of you."

"But?" He drew the word out.

She looked at the tea in her cup. "I hoped you might consider buying Black Thunder for me as a wedding present. I have not ridden such a fine horse in a very long time." She was making a deal with lifelong repercussions. A deal that might hurt Philip almost as much as it hurt her. But was it not worth it to see that he made the sale? The weight of Larmont's recommendation could ensure the success of Greystone stables. And she would do all she could to ensure his success and happiness.

She swallowed. He may hurt for a time, but he would overcome it when his dreams became a reality. For her, she doubted the hurt would ever fully fade.

"If that is what you desire. But do you think you can handle such a powerful horse?" The duke set his teacup on the tray and looked Elle over.

"I think, Your Grace, it will surprise you just how much I

can handle." Had she not lowered herself to take a paid position? Had she not endured the looks and whisperings of those she had once called friends? Was she not even now, committing to a marriage of convenience?

"I am certain I will discover many surprising things about you, Elizabeth." He dipped his head to her. "I shall go see Mr. Jenkins before I leave tomorrow."

Elle nodded, swallowing back the tears hovering at the back of her lids. "It looks as if we have reached an agreement."

CHAPTER TWENTY-FIVE

Philip held loosely to the reins of the horse following along behind him. Lord Kirtley was leaving on the marrow and asked that Philip deliver the horse before he left.

Philip planned to make the most of the trip. He was determined to see Ellie and ask for her hand while he was at Briarwood.

His stomach twisted in a knot. He was confident that she loved him, but there was a small amount of doubt that still left him uncertain of her answer.

But there was no time left to become certain. He needed to ask her before she left for Kent, or he would have to propose through a letter, which made the schoolroom look very romantic in comparison.

He turned onto the lane leading to Briarwood, rehearsing in his mind what he would say to her—how he would ask her such a question. He smiled as he pictured her nodding her head and twisting the hairs at the back of her neck, as she did so often. In his most fantastical dreams, she would throw her arms around his neck as she told him yes repeatedly. But in his more reserved imaginings, she would simply say yes with blushing cheeks and earlobes. He knew he would find it difficult not to pull her into his arms and continue their kiss from the stables.

Philip supposed the location and privacy of their conversation would be what dictated which of his dreams became the reality.

Briarwood came into view. The lawns were full of people, even though the sun was not out and there was a chill in the air. But the rain had stopped and that seemed to be enough to bring the guests out of the house.

Groups played battledore and pall-mall. There were even easels set up for those leaning toward more artistic endeavors.

Philip did not look closely at the people. It was doubtful Ellie would have come outside with her injury. But he was ready to risk irritating Ryecombe to visit Ellie inside the house.

He would head for the stables first, then he would seek Lord Kirtley and inform him that his new horse had arrived.

"Mr. Jenkins, may I take your horses?" The stable master stepped out of the stables.

Philip handed over both sets of reins. "Yes, thank you." He looked out at all the people milling about the lawn. "That gray one there belongs to Lord Kirtley. Please see she is placed near Kirtley's other horses."

The stable master nodded. "Yes, sir." He led both horses away as Philip walked slowly toward the front lawns, looking for Lord Kirtley among the gentlemen. Philip smiled when he saw the light-colored hair standing out above those around him.

Philip picked up his pace, walking directly toward the man. He would inform him that the horse was in the stables and then go inquire after Ellie at the house.

"Mr. Jenkins?" Her voice stopped him in his tracks. He looked over to see Ellie sitting on a stool in front of a canvas, her foot propped up on a second stool to the side of the easel.

Philip smiled at the sight of her. Her cheeks held the slightest pink hue, most likely due to the chill in the air. Her dark brown eyes sparkled. "I came to deliver Lord Kirtley's horse and then I planned to seek you out. But here you are."

She nodded. "Yes, here I am." There was a tightness to her voice he had not heard before. And he thought the sparkle in her eyes had suddenly dimmed.

Philip folded his arms across his chest and studied her painting. "Your work is very good. I was correct in assuming you could help Gracie improve."

Ellie let out a quiet sort of snort. "I hardly think so. My proportions are incorrect. Having my foot up like this makes it difficult to see things correctly when I lean in close." She switched her lips to the side and placed the end of her brush to them. "I should stop now before I make this painting irreparable."

"I do not care what you say. I think the painting is lovely." Where were the children? They were always close by Ellie. He saw Lord Culpepper running beside a large hoop, while Lady Katie was jumping a rope with another girl of a similar age.

"You are being kind, Mr. Jenkins. Of that I am certain." She smiled at him, but it did not reach her eyes. And why, when no one else was around them, was she calling him Mr. Jenkins?

"I am very glad I found you." He pulled over an empty stool from the easel next to her.

"I believe it was I who found you, Mr. Jenkins."

There it was again. Why was she not calling him Philip? He stared at her for a moment, trying to determine what had changed. Because something had certainly changed since he'd seen her yesterday.

"Yes, I suppose that is true. I had not thought you would be outside with your ankle as it is."

She nodded. "I planned to remain inside. I spent far too

much time on my ankle yesterday and it was rather sore this morning." Her brow creased. Was that what had changed? Was she simply acting differently because her ankle was causing her pain?

"But Lady Kirtley insisted I come outside and enjoy the break in the weather." She looked up at the sky. "And I find I am rather glad she did. It is colder than one would expect for May, but we have spent far too much time in the schoolroom of late."

Philip stared at her long neck and the delicate line it made to her shoulder. It tempted him to pull the ribbons of her bonnet and free her neck from their tether. But he held himself back. There were far too many witnesses, and he loved her too much to compromise her.

Although had he not already done that in the stables? He frowned. But Mr. Cooper was a discreet man. He was the only witness to that incident, and he would say nothing about it.

Once they were engaged, it would not matter in the least. *Once they were engaged.* To become engaged, Philip would need to ask her the question, and his time was running out quickly.

He felt as if worms wriggled about inside his stomach, crawling over and under each other. He sucked in a breath. Surely the only way to rid himself of the feeling was to ask Ellie to marry him. It would not become easier if he waited longer.

"Ellie? I have thought long and hard about this and I cannot wait any longer to speak to you about it." He took in a deep breath and surged ahead. "I love you and I cannot see my future without you at my side. And so I must ask if you will consent to be my wife." He held his breath as he awaited her answer.

She tilted her head to the side and all the air whooshed from his lungs. All the weight pressing down on his shoulders evaporated, making him feel suddenly light. He had done it. He had asked her. Now all he needed was to hear her acceptance.

But she gave no answer. She did not say she returned his love. She did not fling her arms around his neck and whisper her acceptance in his ear. Nor did she nod her head with her usual knowing smile on her lips. She did nothing he had imagined she would. Indeed, she did nothing at all as she sat on the stool, twisting at her fingers.

Say something, Philip willed. The silence was far worse than if she declared she did not love him in return. He swallowed, his brow furrowing deeper the longer she stayed quiet.

What did this mean? He shifted on the stool. Was she playing a game? He had not taken her for a lady to trifle with a man's feelings. Why was she not answering?

At last, she took in a stuttering breath. "I am sorry, Mr. Jenkins, but I cannot accept your kind offer. I am already engaged to the Duke of Larmont."

Philip's eyes widened. She was engaged? To Larmont? How was that possible? When had it happened? He stared at her, waiting for her to answer his questions. But she only chewed on the side of her lip, and he realized the questions had only been shouted in his mind.

"When? Were you engaged when we waited out the rain in the stables?" Had she kissed him, knowing she was already engaged?

She shook her head. "It happened yesterday after you returned my bonnet."

Philip shook his head. "Why? Why would you accept him?" A gut-turning thought pushed into his brain. "Do you love him?"

Ellie looked at a spot just in front of her. "Love is for poets and silly girls, Mr. Jenkins."

What did that mean? Did she love Larmont or not? Because Philip had been almost certain Ellie loved him. And if that were true, how could she marry another? Especially once Philip had declared himself to her.

"How can you marry him if you do not love him?"

"You do not know the particulars, sir, and should not ask such things." She tucked her bottom lip between her teeth. "But he is to buy Black Thunder, so you will have what you wished for."

Philip stared. "I do not care about Black Thunder. Between the earl and Lord Kirtley's purchases, I am not so desperate for the money."

"But you still need Larmont's recommendation. That has been your goal for as long as I have known you. Your family depends on you and your horses. You cannot let anything else take precedence." Her voice wobbled.

"I will find another buyer. Someone with just as much influence. Please, Ellie. Don't marry him just so he will purchase Black Thunder."

She looked away. "It is not just Black Thunder. I need security, Mr. Jenkins. And the Duke of Larmont can provide it." She turned pained eye to him. "It is something you cannot promise me."

He felt as if the ground beneath him might open and swallow him whole. How could this be happening...again?

She reached a hand out and placed it on his arm. He jerked it away as if he had been scalded.

"You don't understand. My reputation is such I will only add to your troubles. Your neighbors will never see you as a gentleman with me at your side. Can you not see that?"

Philip stepped toward her. "I don't care about society."

She looked up, meeting his gaze for the first time. "But I do." She picked up her walking stick and hobbled away.

He could have stopped her, she moved so slowly. But what was the point? She would not have him.

———— ⟨∽⟩ ————

It should have been an extraordinary day, yet it was the worst day of Philip's life. He had delivered the dappled horse to Briarwood, and he should now be an engaged man. If things had gone according to his plan. But they had not.

His hands fisted around the reins. How had he been so daft? He had known how this would end, and yet he had allowed himself to be vulnerable. Allowed himself to believe this time would be different. And look where it left him. Broken and angry.

His father sauntered out of the stables, and Philip tossed the reins to him. "I'll be in my study if you need me."

"Son? Is everything all right?" His father's eyes dimmed with concern.

Philip waved him away and continued into the house. What was he to do? How was he to purge her from his mind? From his heart?

He had thought her different from those of the *ton*. He had thought them well suited to each other. He had thought she loved him.

He pushed the door to his study open hard, banging it into the wall. Sitting at the chair behind his desk, he scrubbed his hands through his hair. He had *thought* a good, many things. And all of them were wrong. But just how he had been so wrong, he could not say. He went over their interactions in his mind and still could not come up with where his faulty notions had begun.

Had she been playing a game with him the whole time? Did she do this with all the men she encountered? She must be a temptress who thrilled in capturing men's hearts and then casting them aside. She was Lady Dorothea all over again.

A soft knock sounded on his door. Philip did not answer. Whomever it was, he did not wish to see them.

The knock sounded again.

"I am busy. Come again later." He knew it sounded harsh, but he did not care. He felt harsh and raw and beaten.

His mother stuck her head inside. "Son, your father mentioned you might need tea."

Philip shook his head. "I am fine, Mother." He snapped. "I only need to be alone so I can balance these ledgers. If I am to finish the repairs on the tenant cottages, I must see where I can take money from other endeavors." It was not precisely the truth. With the sale to Lord Kirtley, Philip had the money to make the repairs without having to sacrifice something else. It was a freedom that should make him proud and happy. Yet, he felt neither.

"Did you deliver the horse to Briarwood?"

Philip nodded. His mother did not seem to understand that he did not wish to have a conversation. He wished to be alone so he might brood over his failure at love. Perhaps Miss Carter had the right of it. Love *should* be left to poets and silly young girls. It had done nothing for him but bring pain and self-doubt.

"Did you see Miss Carter while you were there?"

Philip heaved out a great sigh, not caring in the least if it hurt his mother's feelings. "Yes. And I gave her your regards."

"And how was she? Is she well?" There was a tentativeness in her voice. One that said she knew she was moving into dangerous waters, yet she would not turn back.

"She seems very well, Mother. I suppose becoming engaged is helping her to feel better."

His mother's eyes lit, and she smiled. "She is engaged? Oh, Philip. And what a good joke you played, pretending to be out of sorts." She gave him a knowing smile. "And to whom is she engaged?"

Philip gripped the arms of his chair until his knuckles whitened. "The Duke of Larmont."

His mother's smile fell, and her mouth dropped open. "But I thought—"

"Yes. As did I. But it is not to be. Now, if you will leave me to my ledgers, I have work to do." She turned from the doorway and nearly collided with Anne in the corridor.

"Mr. Jenkins, sir, there is a man here to see you. He says he is the Duke of Larmont."

Philip ran a hand through his hair again. What did the duke want? Philip was in no mood to deal with entitled nobility today. Especially the man who had ruined his future.

He sighed and pushed away from his desk. He may as well see what Larmont wanted. And the sooner he did, the sooner Philip could return to his wallowing.

The duke sat in the parlor, his eyes roving around the room, as if he were making a list of every way it was lacking.

Philip cleared his throat, and the duke looked up. "Ah, Mr. Jenkins. I came to purchase the horse I looked at last week. I trust he is still available?"

Philip had the urge to lie and say he had sold Black Thunder to another. While it might have felt good, in the moment, to do so, he knew that feeling would lessen as the days went on. Especially if Black Thunder did not sell quickly. And with few other potential buyers waiting, it was not a risk he could take. No matter how much his pride hurt.

"Yes, I held him back from other buyers until I knew of your decision." Philip fervently wished he could punch the smug look off the duke's face. The man was so used to getting everything he desired. He had decided he wanted Miss Carter, and he was to have her.

Waves of anger and resentment surged through Philip. "Let us move out to the stables so you may have another look at Black Thunder."

"There is no need." Larmont held out his hand. "Here is the price we settled on, I believe."

Philip stared down at the banknote for two hundred and twenty-five pounds. On any other day, this paper in his hand would have brought great satisfaction. Joy, even. But today he could barely stand to look at it. "Do you wish to take him with you now? Or wait until you leave Briarwood?"

The duke put a finger to his lips. "He is a wedding present for my betrothed. She asked for Black Thunder specifically. And while the wedding is not for several weeks yet, and her ankle would prohibit her from riding, I do believe I will take him with me now. I believe it will overjoy her to see him."

Philip's jaw clenched. "Yes, I heard congratulations are in order."

The duke raised a brow. "Oh? I have not yet made the engagement public."

"I saw Miss Carter when I delivered Lord Kirtley's horse to him earlier."

The duke nodded, but his brow stayed close to his hairline. "Oh, yes. I did you see you speaking with her." He sighed. "While I am certain she wishes to tell everyone of our engagement, I must ask her to wait until they have posted the banns before she spreads the news."

Philip swallowed. How could Ellie—he closed his eyes—Miss Carter have accepted this man? Were money and status so much more desirable than love? He looked down at the note in his hands. It seemed it was for Miss Carter.

CHAPTER TWENTY-SIX

Sophia sat on Elle's lap, her head resting against Elle's chest. Katie sat on the bench, nearly stitched to Elle's side. Even Winston was closer than usual. She had told them nothing of her engagement, yet they seemed to sense that something was amiss.

But were they sensing her impending departure or the unease Elle felt? Indeed, she had hardly slept the night before. The hurt and betrayal she had seen in Philip's eyes haunted her dreams.

She looked out the window as the carriage bumped along toward London.

She had spoken harshly to Philip, but what choice did she have? He had been willing to sacrifice the sale of Black Thunder for her. It was too much. It was a weight she could not bear. While he could not see the shortsightedness of that decision, she surely did. And she could not allow him to do it. If she allowed it, it would surely become a source of resentment in years to come.

She wished she could say that her situation was her only

reason for rejecting Philip's proposal. But it was not. When she was alone with her thoughts in her room, she wondered if she was being selfish. But what choice did she have? Henry had been right. Her father and brother had not provided her with any security, and looking at Greystone, Elle did not think Philip could either. And after three years of serving as a governess, she needed security.

But she was having trouble reconciling how love fit into the picture. Was it not a part of security? She had never felt as safe as she had with Philip.

Elle grunted quietly. She needed to stop thinking on him or the ache in her chest would surely never go away. She had chosen her path and it would do her no good to look back at where she had come from.

The fields of the countryside faded, and the busy streets of London filled her view. Unlike others of her acquaintance, Elle disliked London. There were far too many people, and the air was too thick for her liking. She much preferred the quiet of the countryside. But this was only a stopover until she could return to Oxfordshire.

Familiar sights flowed past the windows as Elle dropped her chin onto the top of Sophia's head. They were almost at her family's London townhouse. There had been no time to inform her brother she was coming. She was uncertain he was even in London.

The carriage stopped, and Elle looked out the window at the pale-yellow exterior.

"Why are we stopping here, Mama?" Katie looked out.

"This is where Miss Carter's brother lives. She is going to stay here with him."

Katie's brow creased. "How long is she staying?"

Lady Kirtley looked at Elle and raised a brow.

"I have accepted an offer of marriage to the Duke of

Larmont, Lady Katie. I am to return to Oxfordshire to prepare for my wedding."

Katie scooted closer, her hands wrapping around Elle's arm. "But who is to be our governess?"

Lady Kirtley cleared her throat. "We will find you a new governess, Katherine. For now, you need only offer Miss Carter your congratulations and well wishes."

Katie's lips turned down, the corners trembling. "Congratulations, Miss Carter." The tremor in her voice held no felicitations.

For the second time in a week, Elle thought her heart might break into pieces.

"I had thought if you left us, it would be for Mr. Jenkins." A tear slipped over the corner of Katie's lid and down her cheek. "I like him better than the duke."

"It is not proper for a lady to cry over such things, Katherine." The quiver in Lady Kirtley's lips made Elle wonder if she really meant the reprimand only for Katie. Lady Kirtley turned back to Elle. "What will you do if your brother has already left for Oxfordshire?"

Elle shrugged. "Then I shall secure passage on a mail coach." She smiled. "I am not a duchess yet, so it should not be too scandalous."

Lady Kirtley put a hand on Elle's knee. "If you find yourself in need of employment, you will always have a place with us." She smiled. "Although, that seems unlikely, given your betrothed."

Elle lifted Sophia onto Nurse Jones's lap and looked over to Winston. He looked very stoic and gave her a firm nod.

Elle smiled, wishing she could drop a kiss on the top of his head. She moved to the open door. A footman stood on the walkway, waiting to hand her out. Using her walking stick in one hand and the footman's arm in the other, she gingerly stepped out of the carriage with a heavy heart and stood looking up at the house. Was Robert within? Would he be happy to see her? She turned back just long enough to offer a final wave to the children.

Swallowing the dry lump in her throat, she slowly made her way to the door. Knocking firmly, she looked back over her shoulder, wishing she could return to the Kirtleys' carriage and forget about everything—about the marriage, about Philip. But the carriage was no longer there. It had pulled away and was now making its way down St. James Street.

Placing both hands on the top of the walking stick, she leaned into it and bit at her lip to keep the tears at bay.

The door opened and Johnson, their London butler, dipped his head to her. He looked much older than when she had left. "Miss Carter. It has been a long time."

Elle smiled at him, the air racing from her lungs. "Good day, Johnson. Is Lord Crammer at home?"

Johnson motioned her inside, slightly raising a brow when she hobbled forward.

Elle took in the entryway, noting how bare it was. The antique tables no longer sat around the perimeter. They moved a short way down the corridor before Johnson motioned Elle into the parlor. "Wait here, Miss Carter, and I will see if his lordship is at home."

"He is still in London, then?" Elle had never been close to her brother, but knowing someone was in residence made her sag with relief. She would not have to travel home alone, or with strangers on a mail coach. "Thank you, Johnson."

Elle sat on the nearest couch, propping her foot up on the low table in front of her. After the bumps of the carriage ride, and being unable to prop it up, her ankle throbbed with pain. Hopefully, she could send someone to the apothecary for something to help with the pain before they left for Oxfordshire.

"Elle? What are you doing here?" She could hear the disapproval in her brother's voice. She closed her eyes and gathered her strength before turning to greet him, pushing down the hurt that he was not as happy to see her as she was to see him. She smiled brightly. "Good day, Robert."

She stood up and limped over to him.

His brow furrowed as he watched her labored walk. "What has happened to you?"

She shrugged. "I slipped on wet grass and sprained my ankle."

His face softened slightly. "Yes, that does sound like something you would do." He quirked a half-grin before wiping it away. "You never answered my first question. What are you doing here?"

Elle finally reached him. She stood up to her full height and lifted her chin. "I am to be married. I thought if you had not yet left for the country, I could accompany you home so I might prepare."

Robert shifted on his feet and clasped his hands behind him. "I had no plans to return home in the near future."

Elle frowned. Would he change his plans now that she had arrived? "I see. I am sorry if my arrival comes as an inconvenience. But I must return home so I might fetch the things mother left for me for my wedding." She may not have a dowry, but there was at least a lovely brooch and the veil her mother had worn when she married Elle's father.

Robert shrugged. "Well, I am *not* going at present."

Elle stomped her foot, and immediately regretted her rash decision as pain radiated up her leg. She swallowed and glared up at her brother. "Then I shall make the arrangements myself. I have become quite independent." She did not need him. She could arrange for a seat on the mail coach herself.

"You cannot go. There is no place for you to stay."

She looked at him. "Why can I not stay in my room?"

He frowned. "I have let the house for the year."

Elle stared at him. He could not be in earnest. He had let the house? And what of the things she had left behind?

"But what of my trunk? How am I to fetch it if someone else is living there?"

Robert heaved a sigh and looked at the ceiling. "There is no need to return to Oxfordshire for your trunk. It is not there."

Elle sighed. He had brought it with him to London. She would be sad not to see Blakely Hall, but she could visit once the renters had left. "You brought it to London, then?" She looked around. "Is it in my room or in the attics?"

Robert shrugged uncomfortably. "There is no trunk, Elle. I sold its contents long ago."

Elle sucked in a breath. "What? How could you do that?" He had sold the contents? What of the brooch? It had been handed down from mother to daughter for generations.

He grumbled. "You had entered service. I did not think it possible that you would marry. And why should an old trunk take up space when you were not to use any of the contents? If it was so precious to you, you should have taken it with you."

Elle blinked several times. He had sold off the only things she had left of her mother. And for what reason? Because it took up too much space? She was a governess. She'd had no room for a second trunk in her small chambers.

Elle clamped her mouth shut and clenched the top of her walking stick tightly, afraid if she let go she may slap her thoughtless brother. "I see. I suppose there is no reason to make the trip after all." She took several steps back, unable to look up at her brother any longer.

He flashed a smile at her, but it held no warmth. "Precisely." He unclasped his hands and stepped to the side. Was he to let her stay here? From the look on his face, she thought it likely he would turn her out. "Just who did you trick into marrying you?"

Elle felt a tear prick at the back of her eyes. "The Duke of Larmont offered for me. We shall wait for the banns to be called and then we shall wed."

Robert's brows shot up. "The Duke of Larmont? That is who you are to marry?"

Elle's own brows rose in challenge as she nodded.

He moved in next to her and put a hand around her waist. "You look tired, Elle. Let me help you to your room. Perhaps once you have rested, we can talk more." His voice softened, the words flowing from his lips like honey. He led her to the staircase.

She squirmed out of his hand, despising the feel of it on her waist. He had sold her brooch and her mother's veil. She could not forgive him for that. "I can make it on my own. Thank you for the offer." She hopped up the first two steps, wishing for distance between them until she could control her emotions. But with every step, she felt his eyes on her back.

"Are you certain I cannot help you? You are moving very slowly." There was impatience in his voice, and it made Elle grin. Robert had never been patient, which might explain why he was in trouble financially. But it was not for her to assuage his impatience. No, he could stand there and watch her trudge up the stairs. It could be the beginning of his penance for selling all of her treasures.

CHAPTER TWENTY-SEVEN

Elle walked gingerly down the staircase. She had been at her brother's London home for more than a week, but she had yet to have the conversation with Robert he had promised when she had arrived. Which was fine with Elle. She was still angry with him for selling her mother's brooch.

Her ankle was feeling much better, though. So much so, she had discarded the walking stick two days ago and was only slightly limping when she walked.

Now that she could walk without the thump of the stick giving her away, she felt freer to explore the house and see what changes Robert had made. From what she had seen so far, he had simplified the decorating. The furnishings were sparse and held few ornamentations, if any at all. It was an interesting decorating style. Although Elle had suspicions it had little to do with style.

She had made it to the landing between the first and second floors when she heard Johnson open the front door. "Good afternoon, Mr. Yates."

Elle slipped into an empty alcove on the landing and

pressed herself against the wall. Perhaps the lack of furniture was a good idea.

She listened for footsteps. Mr. Yates was a barrister and one of Robert's dearest friends. Surely Johnson would show Mr. Yates to Robert's study, which was on the floor below where Elle stood plastered against the wall.

Sure enough, Johnson and Mr. Yates stopped climbing the stairs at the first-floor landing and disappeared down the corridor.

Elle stepped out of the alcove and straightened her dress. She still wore her serviceable gray gowns. Robert had made no mention of buying her new ones. If he were so low on blunt that he'd sold off the furniture, it seemed doubtful he had the money for new gowns. After all, if he had the money, she would not have had to take a paid position.

She moved to the first floor, wishing to see the gallery. It had been an age since she had seen the likenesses of her mother and father. She tiptoed past Robert's study door. They had not shut the door tightly, leaving a narrow crack between it and the doorframe. She did not wish for him to hear her. Although she did not believe Robert would take the time to introduce her to Mr. Yates again, not while she wore this drab gray gown.

She cleared the door, just as her name drifted out of the crack. Elle paused. What would her brother say to his friend about her?

"Elizabeth is back?" Mr. Yates asked.

"Yes." Robert's chair creaked. "I had the same thought you surely are. But it is not so bad as I initially thought. Indeed, I believe it may work to my advantage."

Mr. Yates let out a chuckle. "And how do you figure that? What if she has discovered what we did?"

"No, that is not a worry anymore." Robert sounded irritated. What had they done? "She is to be married. I had never thought it possible. Especially once she took the position as a governess. But she has accepted an offer, and it is very advantageous."

"How do you figure?" Mr. Yates asked.

"She is engaged to the Duke of Larmont." She had never heard such excitement in her brother's voice. What did he have to be excited about? She was the one marrying the duke. She was the one to have all that came with it.

One of them whistled. Elle assumed it was Mr. Yates. "A duke? Surely this is the answer to your problems. And it comes at the perfect time. There is no money left from the sale of her estate and you have nothing left to sell. But perhaps your new brother-in-law will allow you to hang on his sleeves. After all, if he learns your pockets are to let, it could scandalize his new bride." The barrister laughed. "Although perhaps I should begin practicing the duke's signature?"

Robert grunted. "If only she had another estate I could sell, I would not need the help of the good duke." He let out a breath. "But this situation might be just as good. Even if the duke will not give me the blunt, I am certain his name will be enough to open many doors that are presently closed to us." He let out a chuckle. "But you may be right. It might be prudent for you to perfect his signature. I am certain his will be harder to pass off as legitimate than hers was."

Elle put her hand to her mouth. Robert had sold her estate? Her dowry? How had he done such a thing? He had led her to believe her father was the one to lose the estate. But it had been Robert? She swallowed, regretting every ill thought she'd had of her father.

Her stomach lurched, and she thought she might be ill. How could her own brother do such a thing to her?

A part of her wished to charge into the room and demand answers, but she knew her brother. Such rash actions would only lead to him removing her from the house. And then what would she do? Oxfordshire was no longer an option. Besides, it was doubtful she could keep her breakfast down. And she would not allow herself such an embarrassment.

She quietly picked up her skirts and hurried away from the study before she alerted Robert to her presence. She took the servants' staircase, finding comfort in the plain, unadorned area. Moving to her room, Elle tried to sort through what she had just heard. But she could not make any sense of it. How had Robert sold her estate without her knowing it?

She closed her bedroom door behind her and moved over to the window, looking out at the gray skies. The London smoke and fog made the weather feel much more ominous than it had in the country.

She had to speak with someone. Find out if there was anything to be done. Grabbing her bonnet and pelisse from her wardrobe, Elle moved quietly down the stairs.

Robert and Mr. Yates stood in the entryway speaking in hushed tones. They were planning something nefarious, no doubt.

Robert looked up when Elle stepped onto the marble tiles. "Elle, you remember my friend, Mr. Yates, do you not?"

Elle dipped her head, unable to meet either of the men's gazes. "Yes, I do. It is a pleasure to see you again, Mr. Yates."

"And you, Miss Carter."

"Where are you off to, Elle?" For a moment Elle thought Robert might volunteer to come with her. Which would not do. She smiled. "I have set a bonnet to pieces so I might make it anew for my wedding. But I need some ribbon. Would you care to come with me?" She hoped the invitation would make her seem less suspicious so her brother would decline the offer.

"While I enjoy shopping for ribbons, I have not the time today." He waved her off. "Do not stay out too long."

"I could escort you, Miss Carter." Mr. Yates stepped forward. "If you are in want of company."

Elle gave him a small smile she did not feel in the least. She trusted this man even less than she trusted Robert. "Thank you for the offer, but it would not be proper. And I am certain you have better things to occupy your time than the milliner's shop."

She moved toward the door before either Robert or Mr. Yates could change their minds. It did not escape her attention that Robert did not offer her the family carriage. Was that because they no longer had a family carriage or because he cared so little for her? Neither option left her feeling loved or safe, not like she had with Philip. It was odd she felt something so strongly from a man she had only known a fortnight, yet she could only feel betrayal and indifference toward the brother she had known the whole of her life.

She motioned to a passing hackney and walked toward it as quickly as her ankle would allow. She had little money, but she surely had enough for the ride to the solicitor's office and for a single ribbon from the milliner's shop.

The ride to her father's solicitor was faster than she remembered. She pushed into the anteroom and looked around. Was he a part of her brother's plan? If so, it seemed likely Robert would learn that Elle knew what he had done. Which surely meant he would turn her out. But she could not think of that yet. Perhaps Mr. Ludlow was the honest man she had always believed him to be.

She knocked, and a muffled "enter" sounded.

Elle opened the door and stepped inside.

"Miss Carter? To what do I owe the pleasure of your visit?" Mr. Ludlow motioned her inside.

Elle limped to the chair facing his desk and waited until he had taken the seat behind it to start the conversation. "I came to inquire about the estate my father left for my dowry. I had been led to believe my father lost it before his death. But I am now doubting that information."

Mr. Ludlow frowned. "What are you speaking of? Your father did not lose the estate, you sold it after his death."

Elle licked her lips. "It was sold without my knowledge. That is why I am here."

He looked affronted. "I did not sell the estate without your knowledge, miss. You signed the papers. You wrote to me and asked for me to sell it on your behalf. Do you not remember? I suggested you simply let it for a year or two, but you would brook no argument."

Elle shook her head. "I never wrote to you, sir. Nor did I sign away my right to the estate."

He frowned. "But you did. Both you and your betrothed signed."

"My betrothed?" She leaned forward. "Do you still have the papers?"

He moved to a cabinet on the wall next to the desk. "Of course. They are right here." He removed a stack of papers and brought them over, placing them in front of Elle. Flipping over several pages, he pointed to a paper with two signatures. Elle's name was scrawled across the bottom, along with the signature of a man Elle had never heard of.

"I have no notion who Mr. Hugh Winthrop is, but this is not my signature." She pointed to the quill sitting next to Mr. Ludlow's arm. "May I?"

She scribbled her name on the back side of the next paper. "That, sir, is my signature."

Mr. Ludlow's face blanched. "I did not know. How am I just learning of this?"

Elle shrugged. She would never have thought such deceit possible from her brother. "I only learned of it today."

"But who would do this? Is it this Mr. Winthrop?" Mr. Ludlow straightened his glasses on his puce face. Now that the initial shock of the discovery had passed, he looked as though he might explode. "I will contract a runner and see that we discover the scoundrel."

Elle sucked in a deep breath. "I overheard a conversation with my brother which leads me to believe he is—" She could not bring herself to discredit him, although why he deserved her loyalty she did not know. Regardless, Mr. Ludlow seemed to take her meaning.

Mr. Ludlow pursed his lips.

"Is there anything to be done? Any recourse I may take to reclaim the estate?"

Mr. Ludlow shook his head. "No. Your only recourse would be to bring charges of fraud against," he cleared his throat, "the forger. But he is a peer, and you are a woman . . ."

There was nothing for it, then. The estate was lost to her, and there was nothing she could do about it.

She nodded. "Thank you, Mr. Ludlow."

He stood and shook his head. "I am sorry, Miss Carter. I wish there was something more I could do for you."

"I have had my questions answered. That is something." She turned and left the office, pausing on the walkway outside. Her circumstances were the same as before she met with Mr. Ludlow, yet her stomach churned and her head ached as if she had just received devastating news.

"Miss Carter? What are you still doing in London? I had thought you were to return to Oxfordshire until the wedding?" The Duke of Larmont stood in front of Elle, a disapproving look on his face. Why was he disapproving? Should not a person feel some degree of excitement at seeing their betrothed? Yet he looked at her as if she had done something wrong.

"That was my intention. But my brother is not yet ready to return to the country. I thought it better to remain with him than to take the post without a chaperone." Elle knew the notion of the mail coach would appall the duke, but to do so without a chaperone was nigh unto shocking. But was it shocking enough to withdraw his offer?

A very large part of her hoped he just might. Then she could return to the Kirtleys. At least she knew they loved her at Dovehaven.

"Well, I am happy to see you. Perhaps you could come around for tea and I could introduce you to my son, Lord Ragsdale." If this was his happy voice, Elle was certain she did not wish to hear his unhappy one.

Elle nodded. "Yes, I should be delighted." Her voice was completely devoid of emotion. The stiffness of her spine gave way, and she slumped slightly. Was this what her life would entail once she was married? Verbal sparring with her husband? The thought exhausted her.

"You seem out of sorts, Miss Carter. Is there something wrong?"

Elle shook her head. "No, I received some disappointing news, is all. It will pass, and I will be well."

"May I be of assistance?" His brow creased and she thought she may detect a hint of concern.

Elle shook her head.

"We are to be married. If there is something I can do to help, I wish to be of service to you."

Should she tell him? It would likely only cause him to think less of her family and, in turn, her. But the duke was one of the few people with enough power to see her brother punished for his actions. Was it worth the risk of having Larmont know the truth? If she did not tell him, her brother would have no punishment for what he had done. And was she not obligated to inform Larmont of everything she had overheard in her brother's study?

"I just learned that my brother falsified documents in order to sell the estate that was to be my dowry."

The duke's jaw clenched. "And you just discovered this? How did you not know before?"

He was going to lecture her? He was not her father. Nor was he her husband . . . yet.

And how was she to know? She only knew what Robert had told her. He was her guardian, and she had believed he had her best interest at heart. "Robert had told me my father somehow lost the property before he died." She stood to her full height, which brought her almost level with his nose. "Why should I not have believed him? He was my brother and guardian. It is not as if I had access to the estate ledgers to know who mishandled our fortune." Now that she thought about it, she wondered just how much she could blame on her father. Perhaps most of their misfortune had been Robert's doing.

The duke nodded. "You are right. My apologies, Miss Carter." He looked at the office Elle had just left and nodded. "I will send a card around with a date for tea." He dipped his head. "Good day."

Elle nodded. "Good day to you, Your Grace." She turned her back on him, walking in the opposite direction even though she had no notion where she was going. She would figure out how to find the milliner's shop once she knew the duke was far away.

She sighed. If it were Philip she was marrying, would she feel this much unease? Was it the thought of the wedding or the man that made her stomach turn?

Philip's face came to her mind. His crinkled eyes and dimpled chin. Just thinking about him settled her mind, even as her stomach fluttered and her heart ached.

CHAPTER TWENTY-EIGHT

Philip sat at the breakfast table, reading the paper. Although, if questioned, he could not recite a single detail of a single story. Miss Carter consumed too much of his thoughts for him to concentrate on such mundane stories as what the newspaper contained. It seemed everything he read or saw reminded him of her.

He grunted. It had been more than a fortnight since she had declined his offer and left Briarwood. Even so, he could not push her from his mind. And every time he thought about her, his chest ached. He would have thought the pain would lessen with time, but it seemed to only increase. Lud, why had he been so careless? Why had he allowed himself to care for her?

"Good morning, Philip." Grace fluttered into the room and picked up a plate. "I thought you sold Black Thunder."

Philip looked over the top of his paper. "I did."

She frowned, placing an egg on her plate. "Did you not say once you sold that horse that we would have finer food? This is not much better than what we ate when papa was a stable master."

The paper crinkled in Philip's tightly fisted hands. "Then you do not remember when father was a stable master. We never had ham for breakfast."

Grace shrugged. "I suppose. I just expected things to change, and they have not." She glanced at the paper. "When can we go to London? Miss Martindale is to have her come out next Season. And I am one year older." Grace placed a hand on her hip.

Philip sucked in a breath. "Why should you want to participate in such a ridiculous display? Surely you can see the falseness of it all."

Grace pouted. "I am starting to believe you do not wish me to marry well, Philip. If you did, I am certain you would take me to London for the Season. How else am I to find a gentleman of quality?"

"And what traits does a gentleman of quality possess, Gracie?"

"He must be rich and handsome. I should prefer he had a title, but I suppose if he is wealthy enough, it should not matter." She leaned forward. "Do not tell Miss Martindale, but I should not like someone in trade. There are many in the *ton* who look down on money that comes from trade."

It was obvious Grace had been spending her days in the company of Miss Martindale. His sister had not shown such presumption after her time with Miss Carter. Miss Carter brought out the kinder more thoughtful side of Grace. But Miss Carter was no longer here to guide Grace.

Philip slammed his hand down on the table, and Grace jumped in her seat. "Who do you think you are, Grace? Do you not remember what your father is? How can you possibly think that any gentleman of title or wealth will seek after you?" He threw his paper to the side. "Why do you not wish for a man who loves you and wants what is best for you? A man that

254

places your needs and comfort above all else? I doubt you will find such a man among the *ton*."

Grace dropped her gaze to the napkin on her lap. "I think you are wrong."

He shook his head. "I regret sending you to Mrs. Bootle's. It seems all she did was fill your head with unrealistic expectations." Philip stood up and leaned over the table toward her. "*You* are a stable master's daughter, and you would do well to remember that. Several men of genuine quality have shown an interest in you, yet you cannot seem to pull your nose down far enough to see them. You are a selfish, shallow girl and I am ashamed to call you my sister."

Fat tears dripped over the edge of Grace's lids, trailing down her face. Her lips quivered.

Philip shook his head and threw his napkin on the table. "Good day, Grace." He strode out of the room, yanking his hand through his hair as he walked. What had he done? While Grace was rather selfish and her expectations skewed, did she deserve the tongue lashing he had given her? Perhaps it would make her think, and if it did, surely it was of benefit. But if that was so, why did his stomach burn?

He clenched his fist at his side, throwing open the front door. He looked at the gray skies. Perhaps it would be best to stay indoors today, but he could not. He needed to work, to exercise the frustrations, the disappointments, the hurt, out of him.

He stopped by the small outbuilding and grabbed the supplies he needed for the tenant cottages. He would work Elle out of his mind if he had to build a whole new stable. Slamming the door closed with his foot, he stomped toward the east side of his property.

Climbing onto the roof of the second cottage, Philip set to work replacing broken boards and shingles. Despite his best effort, he could not seem to keep his eyes from drifting toward Briarwood. Which was completely bacon-brained. She was no longer there. But reason had no hold and his gaze still flitted over as if he might catch sight of her.

"There you are, Son." His father's head appeared just above the edge of the roof. "Do you need some help?"

Philip shrugged. "If you wish."

His father grunted as he climbed up next to Philip. "I am not a young man anymore."

Philip grinned. "I should like to see other men of your age complete the tasks you do."

His father picked up a hammer and quietly set to work. But Philip could feel his father was holding something back. There was something he wished to say, but he did not know how to broach the subject.

Normally, Philip would start the conversation, but today he didn't feel like talking. He had talked to Gracie and look at what had spewed forth. No, he was better off keeping his mouth shut and finishing his work.

"I understand you had some words with your sister."

Philip sighed. Anger and guilt warred inside him. "Yes, we shared several words this morning."

His father sighed. "You hurt her, Son. I cannot imagine it was your intention, but you did it all the same." Philip's stomach burned at the disappointment evident in his father's voice.

"She has changed, Father. And not for the better. Someone had to tell her before she is beyond redemption."

His father quirked a brow. "Perhaps, but could you not have done so in a kinder way?" He paused. "Did you really tell her you were ashamed of her?"

Philip's face heated. Why had he said such things? They were not entirely true. Yes, her misguided superiority frustrated him, but to say he was ashamed of her? That was untrue. Indeed, on the few occasions he had escorted her to the village assemblies, he had been proud of the looks he had received from those gentlemen who saw her on his arm.

"I was angry. She thinks herself quite above her station . . . acting like—" He cut himself off before he said too much.

"Lady Dorothea?"

Philip attacked the shingle, shattering it with the force of his hammer strike. "She was not who I was thinking of, but yes. Lady Dorothea fits the description as well."

His father sat back on his heels and looked at Philip. "What has happened? For weeks you have been out of sorts. What has caused this?"

Philip's gaze flicked toward Briarwood without thinking.

His father nodded. "Ah, I see."

Philip chuckled mirthlessly. He could not. No one but Philip and Miss Carter knew about the proposal. Which also meant no one else knew she had turned him down in favor of the duke. He should not feel the sting of embarrassment—who would not choose a duke over him?—but he did. He had convinced himself that she felt the same for him as he did for her, but he had been wrong. So very wrong.

She had not cried and begged not to be aligned with him, as Lady Dorothea had. But the outcome felt very much the same.

"If you love her, Philip, go after her. I can manage the stables for a fortnight or two. Go. Tell her how you feel."

"No. There is no need for you to manage the stables, Father. I am not going anywhere."

"But—"

"She knows how I feel." The words spilled out of him before he could call them back. "I told her just before I offered for her. She rejected my offer in favor of the Duke of Larmont."

"Oh." His father sat silently, his hammer still at his side.

"I will apologize to Gracie when I return to the house. Now, may we work in silence for a time? Words have done nothing but make matters worse."

His father nodded, leaning forward and placing the next shingle.

They worked quietly for hours until they completed the cottage roof. Philip moved down the ladder first, just in case his father slipped on his way down.

Once both men were on the ground, Philip leaned forward to brush off his pants.

"Excuse me. I am looking for the owner or stable master. I have heard this stable produces fine horses, and I wished to see for myself before I left the county." A finely dressed man stood several rods off.

Philip stepped forward. "You have found him. How may I help you?"

The man came forward and dipped his head. "Lord Amesbury. And you are?"

Philip rubbed his hands together as he offered a shallow bow. "Mr. Jenkins, my Lord, and these are my stables."

Lord Amesbury looked at the ladder leading to the cottage roof and then back.

Sweat dotted Philip's brow and soaked the collar of his shirt. He ran a handkerchief across his forehead. "If you follow me, I will show you what we have available. We recently birthed three racers. I am certain each will appear in the General Stud book. They will not be available for sale for another few years, but it shows the quality of the horses you can expect."

Lord Amesbury nodded. "I caught a glimpse of what looked to be a fine jumper when I handed off my horse to the stable boy. He told me where to find you."

Philip breathed a sigh of relief that Jim had been around this time. "What kind of horse are you looking for?"

They spoke about what Lord Amesbury was looking for and what other kinds of horses Philip had available. Their brisk pace saw them at the stable doors in only ten minutes. Once inside, Philip pointed out each horse, giving the man a brief description of the horse's abilities and temperament. When they reached the end, Philip clasped his hands behind his back and straightened. "What do you think, my lord?"

Amesbury smiled and his eyes brightened. "I confess, when Lord Kirtley told me how magnificent your horses were, I thought him exaggerating. But I must admit he was correct. Your horses are superior to what I have seen of late."

Lord Kirtley had told this man of Greystone's horses? Perhaps Philip had underestimated the man's influence. Could it be he did not need the Duke of Larmont's recommendation? He let out a grunt. That knowledge did him little good now. He had already lost Miss Carter over it.

Lord Amesbury stared at Philip. "How is it I have never heard of you before? I thought I knew all the top breeders in England."

Philip shrugged. "We have been rather small until recently —only selling to those within the county. But I am eager for others to know of our stables."

Amesbury nodded. "I will see you are not kept in obscurity any longer." He moved back down the aisle. "Although, it might be better for me, if I was the only one to know of you." He pointed to a black mare with white front legs. "I would like to buy this horse and that one there."

Philip smiled. Two horses?

Philip had sold more horses in the last two months than he had all of last year. His luck had turned. He frowned. Was it luck? Or something else? He shook it off. "Let us go to my study and we can discuss the price."

Lord Amesbury nodded, giving one last pleased look at his new horses.

Philip stood outside Grace's bed chambers and raised his hand to knock. He rapped three times before clasping his hands behind his back and bouncing on the balls of his feet.

"Yes?" she called from inside.

"Gracie, it is me. May I speak with you?"

"I believe you have said quite enough to me today, Philip." The hitch in her voice made him believe she was still crying or had started up again. Lud, how did a woman have that much water in her?

"Please, Gracie? I wish to apologize and perhaps even explain myself."

The door cracked open, and Grace's face appeared, red and blotchy. Lawks, she had been crying for quite some time. "Nothing can explain away your words, Philip. They were very hurtful." Her lip quivered and her eyes dropped. "But perhaps only because they are true."

Philip sighed. "They are not completely true, Grace. While you do think yourself too far above your station, I have never been ashamed of you. I only wish I could say the same for myself."

Grace opened the door wider and motioned him inside to the couch in front of her fireplace. "If you did not mean it, Philip, why did you say it?"

He sat down. Putting his elbows on his knees, he ran a hand through his hair. "I was angry, and I lashed out at you. You didn't deserve it and I'm sorry. It was wrong of me."

Grace slid into the chair opposite him, pulling her feet up underneath her. This was the Grace he saw too little of these days. "What made you so angry?"

Philip looked at his hands. "You were speaking as a lady of society, one who cares not for anyone but themselves. One who thinks only money and titles are worth your interest. I hate to see you become one of those ladies."

"You think I was acting like Lady Dorothea." It was a statement. Why did everyone assume it was Lady Dorothea he was thinking about? Perhaps because she had been the object of his disdain, the symbol of all that was undesirable in the upper tiers of society.

"You would rather me act like Miss Carter, would you not? That is why you invited her for tea—so I might see how a proper lady should act?"

Philip shrugged. "That was not the only reason I wished for her to come. But I had thought it a good idea for you to see another side of society."

Grace tilted her head to the side. "But you do not now?"

"I have come to realize she is not so different from Lady Dorothea. I wonder now if it is not born in them to act as they do. Perhaps they know no other way."

Grace shook her head. "I cannot agree with you. While my memories of Lady Dorothea are few, I have some. And Miss Carter is nothing like the lady. Miss Carter is kind and sweet and genuine."

Philip nodded. Yes, and her eyes sparkled and made his stomach feel out of sorts. But even more, she had made Philip's goals change. Perhaps not the goal itself, but the reason behind it. He still wished to be successful, not for his sake, but for hers. He wished to make her proud. He wished to make her feel safe and loved. He wished for her to feel secure.

He sighed and closed his eyes. He wished he were a better man. Perhaps then she would have chosen him.

But she was not his to make proud or safe or secure. She belonged to another—by her own choice.

The usual ache in his chest throbbed with each beat of his heart. He was blasted tired of feeling this way. While he had held onto his anger with Lady Dorothea for years, the actual hurt of her betrayal had faded rather quickly. Why was it not the case for Miss Carter? Why could he not stop thinking on her, dreaming of her, smelling her on the wind? Why could he not rid himself of her as easily as he had Lady Dorothea?

He raised a brow and stared into the fireplace. Could it be he had never really been in love with Lady Dorothea? It was an interesting thought, one that seemed to melt away the anger he'd felt toward her for years. If he had never been in love with her, then she had not hurt anything more than his pride.

Was such the case with Miss Carter? Was it simply his pride that stung?

Philip frowned, his hand coming up to rub at his chest. No. It was not his pride that hurt. It was his heart.

CHAPTER TWENTY-NINE

Elle stayed mostly in her rooms for fear she would encounter her brother in the corridors. She did not think she could look him in the face without revealing everything she had learned.

But midway through the second day, she could not stand it any longer. Grabbing her pelisse and bonnet, she took the back stairs—Robert would never use the servants' staircase—and left the house by the back door.

She needed fresh air—or as fresh as one could find in London—and exercise. All she had done while sitting in her rooms was think on Philip and wonder what he was doing. Was he happy? Had he forgiven her? And what of his sister and parents? Had she helped him by asking for Black Thunder as a wedding present? Did he despise her after she had treated him so badly?

She walked through the side gate and slipped into a passing crowd until she was out of view of the house. She had no destination in mind, only wished to be away from her brother.

There were times she had been certain she had heard him

outside of her room, but he had never knocked or asked to speak with her. Nor had he requested she join him for dinner.

Elle was perfectly amiable to taking a tray in her room.

She walked until her ankle throbbed in pain. It would have soothed her soul more were she strolling along a country road rather than a crowded London street. But it was better than torturing herself inside the house.

Would Philip enjoy London? Elle could not think he would. He seemed better suited to the country, just as she was. She supposed it was one thing that had drawn her to him.

What about Larmont? Elle's mouth twitched to the side. He loved London. Loved the balls and card parties. He loved to be *seen*. Elle knew that from their years of association. There had been a time when Elle enjoyed a party or two, but they always left her mentally and emotionally exhausted. But now? She could not muster any enthusiasm for it, even if she had wished for it. Although, wishing to be accepted by society and wanting to take part in it were two different things.

Marrying Larmont would require Elle to spend a great deal of time in London. With parliament in session from before Christmastide until late June, the duke would need to be in London for more than half the year.

Elle sighed. Yet another thing to look forward to with this marriage. She knew of wives that stayed at their country estates instead of traveling to London with their husbands. Perhaps that would be an option. But that seemed an unlikelihood. Had Larmont not said one of his reasons in asking for Elle's hand was so people could see her on his arm? Surely, he meant for that to happen in London.

The wind blew through the narrow alleyway between houses, and Elle pulled her pelisse tighter. She looked up at the darkening sky. Another storm was coming. Elle grudgingly turned and retraced her steps back to her brother's townhouse. When would summer finally arrive?

The rain started just as she passed the corner of the house. She had planned to enter the same way she had left, but the front door was closer, and Elle did not wish to become any wetter. Nor did she wish to slip and injure her ankle again. She knocked at the front door and waited under the small balcony overhang for Johnson to answer.

The poor man was being run ragged. Her brother only employed Johnson, one maid, and a cook, which was hardly enough staff to manage a house of this size, even if she and her brother were the only ones living within.

Johnson opened the door and raised his brows. Dark circles shadowed his eyes. "Miss Carter, I did not hear you leave."

Elle smiled at him. "I left out the back door. I needed fresh air." She scrunched up her nose. "But I had to settle for London air instead."

The corners of Johnson's mouth quirked up. "The air here is not as fresh as you are likely used to breathing." He stepped to the side. "Hurry in, miss. This is not a warm summer rain."

Elle stepped into the entryway and pulled at the tips of her gloves.

"May I take your coat?" Johnson held out his arm.

Elle shook her head. "I shall take it with me to my room, Johnson. Thank you anyway."

He nodded. "You received a note earlier, miss." He moved over to the lone table in the entryway and retrieved the silver tray. Who would send her a note? Her heartbeat picked up when her mind thought of Philip. But surely Philip would not send her a missive. He likely did not even know she was in London.

"Who is it from?" Robert's voice echoed off the tall ceilings.

She jerked her eyes up to the second-floor landing. "I have

no notion." Turning it over in her hands, she ran her thumb over the wax impression. "It looks to be from the Duke of Larmont."

Her brother came down the last flight of stairs and stood at the bottom, blocking Elle from using them as an escape. "Why should he send you a note?"

Elle glared up at him. "We are engaged. There is nothing untoward in him sending me a missive."

"I simply have no notion what he could have to write to you about."

"I bumped into him when I visited the milliner's shop the other day. He said he would send around an invitation for tea so I might meet his son, Lord Ragsdale."

Robert reached for the letter, but Elle pulled it back. "My name is on the front, Robert. Not yours."

He raised a brow. "But I am your guardian, and the invitation should include us both. I am to be his brother, am I not?"

Elle broke the seal and unfolded the paper. A small card sat in the middle. She held it up. "It reads tomorrow at 3 o'clock. That is all. There is no mention of you."

Robert's jaw clenched. "That is a pity. I wish to become better acquainted with the duke."

I am certain you do. Elle knew of Robert's reasons for the acquaintance and had no intention of helping him to facilitate them. Granted, he had known the duke, just as Elle had, for many years. But she was very grateful the duke had not included Robert in the invitation.

Robert held out his hand. "May I see the card? Perhaps you missed something."

Elle fingered the card before placing it in his outstretched palm. "There is nothing to see." She glanced down at the paper still in her hand. What looked like a one-pound note, folded in half twice, sat where the card had rested.

266

Elle glanced up, relieved to see Robert looking at the card. He would surely take the money if he knew of its presence. Quietly, she folded the paper back as it had come and tucked it in the cuff of her sleeve. "Are you finished examining it, Robert? As I told you, there is nothing to discover."

Robert passed the card back to her. "Then I will not expect you for tea tomorrow." He turned on his heel and strode down the corridor.

It was not as if he had invited her to tea in the fortnight since she had arrived. Elle let out the breath she had been holding. She had nearly convinced herself he would demand to see the cover paper also.

She smiled one last time at Johnson, then hurried up the stairs to her room. Her ankle ached from the exercise, but she did not slow down until she slid the lock on her chamber door.

She threw her pelisse and bonnet on the bed before hurrying to the sofa in front of the fireplace. Pulling the paper from her sleeve, she opened it and the money fell out onto her lap. She picked it up and unfolded it with shaking hands.

Larmont had included two one-pound notes. It was no wonder he had used the outer paper. She looked down and noticed his tightly scrunched handwriting on the paper.

Elizabeth,

I have enclosed two pounds. Please try to find a suitable gown before your visit tomorrow. While I am accustomed to your serviceable dresses, I believe my son would find them rather appalling.

I also thought it best to inform you I have filed the charges of fraud against your brother, Lord Crammer. With my influence, action should be swift. I will send word when I hear more.

Until tomorrow.

L

Elle did not know what to think. She fingered the money. It

had been some time since she had such a fortune in her hands. While this would not buy a custom gown from even a lesser known modiste, it should be enough to buy one already made. Which was just what Elle needed. She did not have time for a custom-made gown. She tucked the money down the side of her stays. It was truly the only place she thought it safe from Robert.

With the money safely hidden, she looked back at the note. Larmont had filed charges against Robert? She looked from the paper to the door. What if Robert found the note? What would he do to her?

Elle ripped up the paper and threw the pieces into the fire. The flames flared as it engulfed the incriminating message.

She should feel a sense of relief, yet her shoulders ached from the tension. The courts would punish Robert for what he had done. And it was because of Larmont.

His actions surely did not come freely. He had done it to help Elle because she was to be his wife. Elle could not imagine he would have taken the same interest if she had declined his offer. If she'd had any thoughts of changing her mind, it was out of the question now. How could she cry off when he had taken a personal interest in her troubles?

Elle dropped her face into her hands. How was she to do this? How was she to marry a man when she could not stop thinking of another?

Her stomach roiled. She shifted on the couch, leaning heavily against the arm. Pulling her legs up underneath her, she laid her head down on the sofa arms. Two more weeks and she could put these thoughts behind her. Once she married, it would be the end. The little niggles of thought in the back of her mind which believed there might still be a way out would be put to rest for good.

As angry as she was at Robert for letting Blakely Hall, Elle was relieved she was not at their country estate. The banns had been read for the first time on Sunday last and she did not think she could have managed the visits and notes of well wishing, that would surely have arrived at the estate. Here in London, she was able to keep her presence quiet. And quiet was just what she needed.

———————— ⟨∽⟩ ————————

Elle walked to the front door of the Grosvenor Square townhouse and lifted the knocker several times. She looked down at her gown. It did not fit as well as if the seamstress had made it for her, but it was much better than anything else she had in her wardrobe. She felt pretty for the first time in years.

That was not completely true. She bit at her lip. She had felt beautiful when she was with Philip. Even when she was dripping wet and looking like a sodden pup, he had looked on her as though she could not be more handsome. And it had not taken fine gowns for him to think that of her.

She sighed. This was the first time she felt she would be pretty in the eyes of her old acquaintances. She had picked a white gown with deep green leaves. She thought, perhaps, the green would highlight the color of her eyes. She only wished Philip were here to see it. He would surely think her pretty. Or he would have.

Her lips pursed. She must stop thinking about such things. It was not Philip she should wish to impress with her eyes. Larmont would think the same, would he not?

The door opened, and the butler motioned her inside. Elle's stomach heaved like waves crashing dangerously upon a rocky shore. "Miss Carter? His Grace is waiting for you in the salon."

Elle followed the older man, but she could not help looking at the house as she walked almost without a limp down the corridor. Everything she saw, from the plasterwork to the papered walls, was of the finest quality.

She paused in front of a large vase of flowers; her brow creased. She had thought she would feel relief, or perhaps simply feel at home among all these fine things. She had thought it would remind her of the happier times of her childhood. But she felt none of that. Instead, she compared the splendor before her with the more modest decorations at Greystone. Indeed, she had felt more at home there than she did at her own house.

"In here, miss." Elle turned back and hurried to where the butler waited for her. She dipped her head. "Thank you."

He nodded once.

Elle moved into the room, and the duke stood up at once. "Ah, Elizabeth. You have come at last."

Elle glanced at the clock on the mantelpiece. It was only two minutes past the hour. Why had he said *at last*? Did it infer he had missed her, and he was glad she was there now?

"When I say three o'clock, I mean three o'clock. Not a minute past." He looked at her disapprovingly.

Then he had not missed her. Elle tilted her head to the side. "My apologies, Your Grace," she stammered out. Although why she was apologizing, she did not know. She had done nothing wrong.

He motioned to the gentleman standing beside him. "This is my son, Lord Ragsdale. Ragsdale, this is Miss Elizabeth Carter. I do not suppose you remember her from childhood. Her family stayed at Maple Grove on several occasions."

Lord Ragsdale looked Elle up and down, his nose crinkling the more he saw. "I cannot say I do, Your Grace."

Larmont nodded. "You were likely away at Eton and Oxford."

Ragsdale leaned over to his father and whispered loudly.

"This is the chit you are to marry?" His dismay was obvious. Whatever feelings of beauty Elle had felt earlier vanished. She felt every bit the poor pauper she had become.

"Are you certain she is not simply a fortune hunter, Father?"

Larmont shook his head. "While she needs my money, that is not why she pursued me. I am quite certain of it. We get on well, do we not, Miss Carter?"

Elle stepped back. He believed she had pursued him? How could that be? She swallowed, remembering the ambush in the gardens. She recalled her comments about him looking well atop Black Thunder, and her cheeks flamed. Lud, she could see how he might believe such things. But that had been the only time she had flirted in the least. And by that time, he had already invited her to dinner.

"Please, sit, Elizabeth."

Ragsdale took a step away. "Father, I shall not be joining you for tea. I am to meet Lords Berwick and Montcliff at White's."

Larmont sighed. "Very well." Irritation laced the duke's voice, but his son seemed not to notice.

"It was a pleasure meeting you, Miss Carter." He bowed to her and quickly left the room.

Elle sat down, clasping her hands in her lap. It was an odd way to begin tea, that was for certain.

"You received the blunt I sent along with the invitation, I see?"

Elle smiled and ran her hands down the front of her new gown. "Yes, thank you very much."

He gave a sort of shrug and nodded to the housekeeper standing nearby to pour out. Elle waited for a compliment on her new gown, but it never came. How could he not even mention it? Did he not think she looked handsome, or did he not care for the gown she had chosen? Surely he noticed the way it brightened the color of her eyes. Why did he not say anything?

"I suppose you saw my note as well?" Larmont asked as he picked up a biscuit and took a bite.

Elle nodded. "Yes. Thank you for seeing to it. While I expect nothing to come of the estate, they should hold my brother accountable for what he did."

Larmont shrugged. "Yes, well, I do not appreciate being denied what is rightfully mine."

Elle looked at him. What did he mean? Had he discovered Robert's intentions to forge Larmont's name? What else could he be speaking of? Had he been through this process before? Is that how he knew what action to take? "How did you learn Robert was planning to forge your signature, as well?"

"I did *not* learn of it." Larmont grunted. "I was acting on the notion that estate was to come to me once I become your husband. It was your dowry. It is I your brother stole from. But this new information is quite intriguing. I will investigate it further."

He had not known about the forging? Elle stared, open-mouthed, then blinked several times. Surely, she had misheard him. It sounded as if he was only pursuing the charges for his own benefit. She twisted her fingers. It had nothing to do with Elle or him taking an interest in her. He was not doing it to help her. Larmont was doing it to help himself.

Elle looked around. What was she doing? At every turn, the duke disappointed her. He treated her as if she were a servant indebted to him for raising her up. She was a nobleman's daughter. She was not some maid he could make to feel small and unimportant. She did not love him, and he did not love her. Elle doubted he even respected her. And she could not accept that. She did not belong here. She deserved to be where people loved her . . . cherished her. How had she thought this was her path? The only path she wished to follow ended at Greystone Manor and Philip.

She put her cup on the tray and ran her hands down her thighs. "I am sorry, Your Grace. But I cannot do this."

He looked at her teacup. "You cannot do what?"

She shook her head. "I cannot marry you. I know you think love is silly, but I do not. I love someone very much, so much that I thought I needed to sacrifice my happiness in order to secure his." She looked away.

He sat back and crossed one knee over the other. "And who is this someone?"

Elle looked at her hands. "The only thing that matters is that the someone is not you. It would be wrong for me to marry you when I can only think of him."

"You realize what this will do to your reputation." He was angry and she could understand why. He had offered for her in good faith, and she had accepted, only to reject him after it had been made public.

She nodded. "I do."

"And this man—" He leaned forward. "It is that Mr. Jenkins, is it not?"

Elle bit her lip but gave no indication he was right.

"Do you even know if he returns your feelings?"

Elle swallowed. "He did before I rejected him. I have no notion what he feels now."

The duke let out a wry laugh. "And you are willing to risk everything in the hopes that he still loves you? I am offering you more than Jenkins could ever dream of giving you."

Elle nodded. "Yes. I understand what I am giving up."

"What will you do if he will not have you? I hope you do not think to come back to me."

Elle shook her head. "No, Your Grace. I have no such

beliefs." What would she do if Philip would not have her? She had not considered that fully before making this rather rash decision. Lady Kirtley had said she was always welcome at Dovehaven.

"With your ruination, I cannot think anyone would hire you as a governess. You are risking everything on a man who is barely better than a servant himself. I had thought you an intelligent woman, Miss Carter. But I see now how wrong I was."

Elle looked around. How did she remove herself from this situation? The duke surely wished her gone almost as much as she wished herself to be. "He is a gentleman, Your Grace. He may have little, but he is respectable, and he loves me. That is more than enough." A lump formed in her throat, and she realized how true it was and how devastated she would be if Philip refused her.

But it was still better than the alternative, was it not? Returning to the life of a governess would be better than a life with this proud man. How had she not understood that sooner?

The duke waved his hands in front of him. "Then be gone."

Elle stood and hastened toward the door. Larmont's voice stopped her before she reached the corridor. "Miss Carter. Do not think you will keep that horse."

Elle closed her eyes. "Yes, Your Grace." She took another step then stopped. "Your Grace. I hope you will not hold this against Mr. Jenkins and his stables. None of this is his doing and I hope you will not punish him for my poor decisions."

Larmont scowled. "I am a fair man, Miss Carter. I will not disparage Mr. Jenkins." He lifted his teacup to his lips, but he did not drink immediately. "I believe you will do that all on your own."

Elle nodded as she turned toward the doorway and fled down the corridor to the front entry. She dipped her head to the butler as he opened the door for her. He could not possibly know what had happened, but he seemed to sense that she wished not to linger.

The door closed behind her, and Elle sagged against the railing. Now what was she to do? She looked down at her dress. Would the seamstress take the dress back so she could return the money to the duke? She would not put it past him to file charges against her for stealing the two pounds.

Not that she completely blamed him for his anger. He had likely never been denied anything in his life.

That thought brought a small smile to her lips. She would never have guessed she would be the one to do it.

Elle let out a deep breath and squared her shoulders. She would see to the dress first thing tomorrow. Lady Kirtley had sent the last of Elle's wages just this morning. Elle only hoped it was enough to pay for passage to Somerset on the mail coach.

CHAPTER THIRTY

Philip rode Adonis into the stable yard and dismounted. He ran a hand down the horse's side, murmuring softly. Leading him into the stable, Philip removed the saddle and placed it on the railing, then set to work brushing down the horse. This daily activity and the repairs on the tenant cottages were the only things that helped to calm his churning mind.

The quiet of the stable was a welcome reprieve. He did not have to endure the questions and suggestions of his mother and Grace. The horses were his focus here, not her.

Thankfully, with all the horses he had sold of late, those remaining now fit inside one stable. He need not even enter the one where he and Elle had kissed. He only prayed that once he needed that stable again, he would have pushed all thoughts of her away.

He grunted. So much for his careful plan to keep thoughts of her at bay. It vexed him how much time he spent thinking about her.

Adonis knickered and Philp reached into the nearby bag

and withdrew an apple. There were few apples left, but Adonis did not turn the shriveled thing away.

The barn door groaned open. Philip glanced up. The daylight at her back made it difficult to make out Gracie's features. "I have no time to escort you into the village, Gracie. And I just returned from my ride. If you wished to come, you should have readied yourself earlier. You must be content with the paddock."

"I did not come to ride, but I find the notion appealing, nonetheless."

Philip stopped brushing mid-stroke and stared at Adonis's side. His pulse hammered erratically at the side of his neck. That voice. He had only heard it in his imaginings this last month. She had come? But why?

He shook his head. Lawks, she would never leave his mind now.

"If you did not intend to ride, why did you come?" He barely pushed the words out of his parched throat. Where was a glass of water when he needed one?

"I wished to return to the place I felt most at home."

Philip swallowed. "This is not your home, Miss Carter. You rejected that opportunity."

She was silent for a moment, and Philip finally glanced up to see if she had left. But she still stood in the doorway.

"I made a mistake. I thought I was doing what was best. But it appears I simply made a muddle of things."

Philip laughed mirthlessly. "You thought only of yourself."

"You are right. I was scared. For so long I have longed to have my old life back—the life my brother stole from me. I thought I missed being a part of society. I thought I needed money to give me security. I tried to tell myself I was doing it for you, but I was lying to myself. And to you."

She stepped farther into the stable and her face emerged from the shadows. Philip's breath hitched.

"But I have discovered something this last month."

"Oh? And what is that." Sarcasm dripped from his lips. His stomach burned. He could not let her back into his heart. If he did, he would never survive when she broke it again. He continued brushing Adonis.

A slight rustle of fabric drew his attention back to the doorway.

She walked toward him.

Philip moved, putting Adonis between them, not trusting himself to keep a level head with her so near.

"Can you not understand?" There was pleading in her voice. "I had already been left with nothing by those who were supposed to protect me. When Larmont offered me a large jointure and pin money, I thought I was accepting security for my future. I was not, however, lying when I said I would bring you nothing but trouble. And I am afraid I have only made it worse with my dealing with Larmont. I have nothing to offer you, Philip and if you turn me away, I will understand why."

His breath hitched. Why must she use his Christian name?

"I have no dowry and little reputation. Even less now that I have jilted the Duke of Larmont." She sighed. "But I had hoped . . ." She shook her head. "I am being selfish again. Thinking you would offer for me again after all I have done. Instead let me simply say, thank you, Mr. Jenkins."

She turned to leave, but Philip lunged around Adonis and grabbed hold of her arm.

"What are you thanking me for?"

She looked down at his hand. "Thank you for showing me what I was truly missing. It was not the money or the status. It was the notion of belonging somewhere—that there was a place

I could feel safe and loved. I did not realize it was what I was missing, until I lost it again."

He wanted to be angry with her still for all the hurt she had caused him. But what good would that do? "How do I know you will not forget again and leave when you long for money and status? It is sure to happen when money becomes tight?"

Miss Carter looked thoughtful. "I don't know how you will know. I suppose you will just have to trust me."

"You have not given me much to trust thus far."

Miss Carter smiled. "I just jilted the Duke of Larmont for you, Philip. Does that not earn any amount of trust?"

He twitched his lips to the side, and she dropped her eyes.

He looked away so she did not distract him any more than she already was.

What was he to do? The hurt she had caused still burned inside him, but the joy at seeing her was nearly overwhelming. He could not deny he still loved her, which was likely the reason he could not put her from his mind. And why he could not let her leave now.

The urge to wrap her up in his arms was proving difficult to stave off. Was it wrong to forgive her so quickly?

Philip stared at her, his head shaking back and forth. *She* had broken her engagement to Larmont. The action had surely taken mettle. Who did such a thing? He looked back to Ellie. *She* did such a thing. And she did it because she loved him. She had not said it, but surely that is what it meant.

The niggle of doubt wormed inside his mind. He needed to hear her say it.

He gripped both her arms and pulled her a step closer to him.

She stared at his loosely tied cravat.

Releasing one of her arms, he lifted her chin with his finger until she looked him in the eye. "Why did you break your engagement to the duke?"

She lifted a shoulder. "I could not marry him when I thought only of you." Her gaze dropped to his chin. "Everything he said and did I compared to you. And in every way, he came out lacking."

A chuckle escaped Philip's lips. "I would wager Larmont did not appreciate hearing such an assessment."

Ellie smiled. "I only told him I loved another. I did not wish to anger him any more than I already had."

"I thought love was only for poets and silly, young girls?"

Ellie's brow furrowed. "Then I suppose I am a silly, young girl. Or perhaps a poet" She reached a hand up and traced her finger down the cleft in his chin. I love *you*, Philip. This is where I feel I belong. But I realize it is not for me alone to decide."

Philip's chest squeezed and his legs felt less sure. "I have very little to offer you. Marriage to me does not come with a title."

"And Larmont's offer does not come with respect." She shook her head. "I told you. You already have everything I need and want—a home filled with love and respect. Larmont and his title cannot give me that."

He tilted his head to the side. "I believe a title demands respect."

Ellie frowned in thought. "Yes, it only demands it, it does not *give* it. That is the difference."

Philip's hand tightened on her arm. "Did he disrespect you, Ellie?"

Her lips turned up only slightly. "In every word he said. But it is no matter. It is in the past, and I know it shall not happen again." She held his gaze. "At least not from you."

Philip sighed. "What are we to do now?"

Her gaze dropped to his lips again, and he grinned. One little kiss would not be harmful, would it? "Miss Carter, I do believe you think to compromise me."

She smiled and danced her fingers down his cheek. "Only if you do not compromise me first, Philip." She pulled back slightly. "But if it is to happen again, I am certain you shall have to marry me."

Philip ran his hands down her arms and wrapped them around her waist. "Only if you promise to accept this time."

"My eyes have been opened. I know now what is most important and my acceptance is assured. I can't imagine life without you."

Philip slowly lowered his head. If she had any reservations, he would give her time to retreat.

Ellie raised her hands to his cheeks and pulled him quickly —almost fiercely—to her, meeting his lips with determination. But that soon faded into soft, thoughtful kisses. Kisses that said they had a lifetime to discover everything about each other.

Philip pulled away, his lips warm and tingling. He dropped his forehead to hers. "Am I to believe we are engaged?"

Ellie nodded. "I had hoped this would end that way." She placed a finger to her lips.

Philip pulled back and looked around the stable. "Am I to assume Larmont did not send Black Thunder with you when you left?"

Ellie shook her head. "No, if you can imagine such gall. He said if there was to be no wedding, there was to be no wedding present. Black Thunder is still in his mews in London."

Philip held out his hand. "Then take your pick. You wished for a horse as a wedding present, and I intend to honor that wish."

Ellie shook her head. "No. I cannot take a horse you could

sell for a profit. I only asked for Black Thunder because it might lessen the sting of my rejection."

She did not want one of his horses? "Do not ladies of most fine houses have a horse of their own? I cannot offer you much, Ellie, but I can offer you this."

She turned in his arms and rested her head against his chest. "If it is what you wish, then I shall accept. But my knowledge is limited. Why do you not pick out the perfect horse for me? I am certain you already know which one will suit me best."

Philip smiled. He had known almost from her first visit to the stables that Adela would be perfect for Ellie. Adela was a mix of a hunter and a work horse, making her sturdy but with a swiftness usually found only in hunters. She had enough spunk to be interesting but would not be difficult or dangerous for Ellie to ride.

Adela stepped toward Ellie.

Ellie lifted her hand and rubbed along the horse's nose.

"Just as I predicted. The two of you will be fast friends." Philip's chest tightened. His two greatest loves were coming together.

"She is perfect, Philip."

Philip looked down at her. "I couldn't agree more."

Ellie shook her head. "I am far from perfect, as we have both witnessed."

He took her chin between his thumb and forefinger. "Then what if we simply say you are perfect for me?"

"I have a better notion. What if we say we are best when we are together?" She sighed in his arms, and he felt a peace he had never felt before. His life was complete and he felt nothing but utter happiness.

EPILOGUE

One year later.

Philip handed Elle out of the carriage and placed his hand on the small of her back. "Are you certain you wish to come? There will be many here you have an acquaintance with."

Elle nodded. "I should not like to be anywhere else. How could I watch your cricket match if I am at home?"

Philip bent and placed a lingering kiss on her cheek. "I am going to inform Ryecombe I am here. I will find you before the match starts." He whispered into her ear.

Elle shivered. How had she ever thought she could do without him?

She walked about the grounds of Briarwood—looking at the faces of those she knew and those she did not—when a familiar form caught her eye. Elle changed directions, intent on intercepting him, but not ambushing him. Their gazes met when she was not yet directly in front of him.

The Duke of Larmont released the hand of Miss Perdy and

gave her a little push away. "Please fetch us some lemonade, my dear."

Elle raised a brow. "I see you have renewed you acquaintance with Miss Perdy, Your Grace."

The duke raised his chin. "I have done more than renew my acquaintance. I have made her my wife."

Elle's eyes widened slightly. It seemed the lady's persistence had paid off. "Then I shall congratulate you. I hope it is a happy match."

"Indeed, it is." Larmont looked just over Elle's shoulder. "And what of you, Miss Carter?"

Elle smiled. "It is Mrs. Jenkins now, Your Grace. And I confess, I am very happily situated."

Larmont flicked up a brow. "I am pleased for you." He turned to leave, but Elle reached out to stop him. He looked down at her hand on his arm.

She pulled it back. "I was hoping to see you here today, Your Grace. I was looking for you, particularly."

"Oh?" Interest sparked in his gaze.

Elle nodded. "I wished to thank you. We have had several men come and purchase horses from Greystone stables, this month alone. Two of the men mentioned your name." She swallowed. "I wanted to thank you for not disparaging Philip's name, because of what I did."

Larmont sucked in a deep breath. "I am not a vengeful man—"

Elle tilted her head to the side and stared at him.

He smirked. "Except perhaps where your brother was concerned."

Elle's heart constricted slightly. Robert had received what he deserved, but still she pitied him. Larmont had ensured Robert was striped of his title and all property for what he had done to Elle. And Mr. Yates had been very cooperative in detailing Robert's plan regarding Larmont. Even now, Robert was serving his sentence in Newgate.

"But Mr. Jenkins did not wrong me. And after riding Black Thunder, I could see the skill and care your husband took with the animal. When people asked, I gave them my honest assessment."

Elle smiled up at him. "I thank you for that. Many would have done the opposite. And I cannot say as I would have blamed you if you had."

He stared at her. "And you truly are happy, Elizabeth?"

Elle bit her lip to staunch the overwhelming emotions that hit her. Every time she thought about what could have been, a lump formed in her throat. "I have not a single regret." She frowned. "I take that back. I have one regret. And that is that I led you to believe I would marry you. I treated you ill and I am sorry."

Larmont shrugged. "Then it seems everything has worked out as it should have." He looked at his wife coming toward them and his nose flared slightly. "She does not have your intelligence or conversation skills. But she is very handsome."

Elle nodded. "Indeed, she is."

Something slid around Elle's waist, and she looked up to see Philip smiling down at her. She sighed. Larmont was correct. Everything *had* worked out as it should.

Philip dipped his head to Larmont. "Your Grace. It is good to see you again."

Larmont nodded. "And you, Jenkins."

"I am glad to see you. I wished to thank you for your kind words concerning my stables."

Larmont held up his hand. "You need not say anything, Mr. Jenkins. I believe your wife has expressed enough gratitude for the both of you." He looked out over the pitch. "It looks as though the match is about to begin."

Philip looked back over his shoulder. "I should join my team." He dipped his head. "Your Grace."

"Jenkins." Larmont stopped Philip mid-stride.

"Yes?"

"I thought perhaps I could stop by your stable while I am visiting Briarwood and see what you have to offer."

Philip smiled. "Anytime, Your Grace."

Lamont nodded. "Capital. I shall send around a card."

Philip reached back and grabbed Elle's hand, pulling her even with him as they walked toward the far side of the pitch.

She looked back over her shoulder and smiled at Larmont, hoping he truly was as happy as she. Although she doubted such a thing was even possible.

KEEP READING THE NEXT IN THE
SERIES

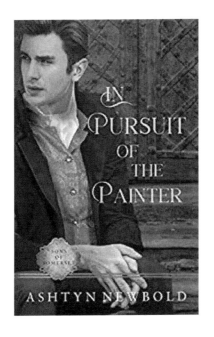

Available on Amazon

AFTERWORD

Dear Reader,

Thank you so much for reading *The Stable Master's Son*. I have loved working with the other four authors on this series. I rarely write about the working man, so this was a fun departure from my normal.

I have grown to love these characters as they have developed and come to life. I hope the same has been true for you as you read this story.

I had mixed emotions as Elle's story came together. I keep wanting her to make the decision from the beginning to chose Philip, but she just would not let me. She knew, like I didn't, that she needed to grow. One of my early readers called Elle shallow for choosing the Larmont. And I had a hard time with that description. I think many times we read historical fiction with modern lens and look at a lady choosing money and status over love as shallow. When in reality, in the Regency time period it was practical. Women had few options open to them. If they were not protected and taken care of by a man, in many cases they had nothing. So marrying for money was a very real possibility. It had nothing to do with shallowness, it had everything to do with survival.

In the end, Elle chose to marry for love, because for her, that was part her survival, but there were many who would not make the same decision as Elle. And I think it is important for me, as a 2021 woman, not to judge her for those decisions. After all, didn't Mr. Willoughby leave behind Marianne, whom he very likely loved, in favor of someone with a larger dowry? It is something to keep in mind when reading historical fiction to be sure.

Thanks again for reading!
Mindy

ALSO BY MINDY BURBIDGE STRUNK

Regency House Party Series

Mistaken Identity

Miss Marleigh's Pirate Lord

Scoundrels, Rakes and Rogues Series

Reforming the Gambler

Rake on the Run

The Secrets of a Scoundrel

Unlikely Match Series

An American in Dukes Clothing

The Baron's Rose

A Princess for the Gentleman

Bells of Christmas Series

Unmasking Lady Caroline

Thawing the Viscount's Heart

Top Flight Series

Bear: A Fighter Pilot Romance

Mustang: A Fighter Pilot Romance

Hidden Riches Series

The Mysteries of Hawthorn Hall

Want more? Sign up for Mindy's newsletter here to receive updates, deals, and new releases.

ACKNOWLEDGMENTS

To Jenny Proctor, my fabulous editor who helps me with my comma addiction and gives great insight when I have used all of mine up.

To my fabulous writers group, Esther Hatch and Anneka Walker. Thank you for all your help and suggestions!

To my proof-readers, Patti Knowlton, Rose Hutchison, and Heidi Troutman many thanks for all your help in catching typos on tight deadlines.

To my great ARC team. Thank you for all you do to help me be successful! I couldn't do it without you guys.

And last and most importantly, for all my boys who are my constant cheerleaders and support, and at times a great source of inspiration. I couldn't do this without you! LY

ABOUT THE AUTHOR

Mindy loves all things history and romance, which makes reading and writing romance right up her alley. Since she was a little girl, playing in her closet "elevator," she has always had stories running through her mind. But it wasn't until she was well into adulthood that she realized she could write those stories down.

Now they occupy her dreams and most every quiet moment she has—she often washes her hair two or three times because she wasn't paying attention when she did it the first time—which usually means really clean hair and hopefully a fixed plot hole.

Her kids are used to being called names they have never heard of before and know that look in her eye that says I'm thinking about a story and will not remember what you just asked me.

When she isn't living in her alternate realities, she is married to her real-life Mr. Darcy and trying to raise five proper boys. They live happily in the beautiful mountains of Utah.

You can connect with her on her website http://properlovestory.com/ or any of the links below.